FIC   Freadhoff, Chuck
FRE   Codename: Cipher

CODENAME: CIPHER

CODENAME: CIPHER

Chuck Freadhoff

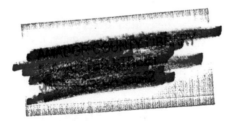

Walker and Company
New York

First published in the United States of America in 1991 by
Walker Publishing Company, Inc.

Published simultaneously in Canada by Thomas Allen & Son
Canada, Limited, Markham, Ontario.

Library of Congress Cataloging-in-Publication Data
Freadhoff, Chuck.
Codename: Cipher / Chuck Freadhoff.
p.   cm.
ISBN 0-8027-1150-2
I. Title.
PS3556.R365C641   1991
813'.54—dc20   90-24884
CIP

Printed in the United States of America

2 4 6 8 10 9 7 5 3 1

For my daughter, Nichole,
who shares the enthusiasm

ACKNOWLEDGMENTS

I wish to thank my friends Kathy Horak and Alexa Bell for the time they took to edit this book and for the advice they gave me.

I also want to extend a special thank you to Melba Newsome, my writing partner, for the many long hours she labored over this project with me and the encouragement she offered.

Last, I want to thank my good friend and technical adviser Lawrence Connell. Without his help and the inspiration offered by his kitchen this book might not have been possible.

ONE

The young lieutenant rushed past the busboy and moved quickly along the back of the elegantly set table, mumbling excuses to the German dignitaries and American officers as he went. He stopped when he reached the American army officer seated at the center. He leaned over and whispered, "Sir, we have a fire."

His message jerked Colonel Raymond Gill's attention from the polite meanderings of starched shirts to the immediacy of military action. It was a code to be used only in extreme emergencies. He turned away from Ochsenburg's Lord Mayor in midsentence.

"What is it?"

A moment after the Lieutenant's response, he and the colonel were moving toward the exit. From the corner of his eye, Gill saw Lieutenant Colonel Lawrence Anderson, the deputy community commander, coming through the crowd toward them.

They were almost at the door when Anderson reached them. Without breaking stride Gill said, "Make my apologies to the mayor, get Major Henry, and come to my office immediately."

Outside, the lieutenant made to open the colonel's car door but was stopped short. "Just drive, lieutenant."

As he hurried the sedan down the hill away from the officers' club the lieutenant's excitement mounted, but so did his fear of what lay ahead.

"What did they say when you called them back?" Gill asked.

[1]

"Pardon me, sir?"

"What did they say? You did try to call them back."

"No sir, I just came to get you."

The silence became an eternity. Eventually, Gill said, "Exactly what did they say?"

Lieutenant O'Connor repeated the message he had received while on watch in the commander's office.

"And that's all?"

"Yes, sir."

The sedan approached the intersection with the main highway, but O'Connor didn't bother to slow down. He could see it was traffic free and pushed the accelerator. The car shot through a stop sign, across the intersection, and moments later slid to an abrupt halt on the cobblestones in front of the headquarters building. The colonel was halfway up the cement steps before O'Connor passed in front of the car.

Three steps away from his office, Gill heard the soft buzzing sound of the phone that went directly to the engineers' ammunition dump. He marched through the open door, covered the distance to his desk in two strides, and picked up the receiver.

"This is Colonel Gill." His words were clipped and betrayed no emotion.

"I am Abul. I speak for the Pan Arab Revolutionary Council. We have control of the explosives. Do not attempt to retake them by force. We have armed them and we will explode them if our demands are not met. We will also explode them if any attempt is made to retake the compound." His English was excellent but seemed slighly out of sync, as if the speech patterns had been learned by rote.

"Why should I believe you?"

The question was met with a moment of silence. Then he heard the voice of Major Woodrow Wilson Henry.

"Sir, this is Major Henry. They threatened to shoot me if I didn't speak to you."

"Now do you believe us?" The man's voice seemed joyfully cruel.

"Yes. But I cannot negotiate with you. You must know that. I have no authority."

[2]

"But of course. We will speak to a representative of your State Department. I am sure one will arrive soon."

The connection was broken, and when Colonel Gill tried to reconnect, the signal told him the other end was still disconnected.

"Get me USAREUR on the secure line, lieutenant, and then find out what the hell happened to Major Henry. Get the MPs to his apartment to check on his family at once." As he spoke Lieutenant Colonel Anderson walked through the door.

"I couldn't find Major Henry. No one's seen him tonight."

"Andy, some terrorists calling themselves the Pan Arab Revolutionary Council or something have seized the engineers' ammo dump. They've got the major. Get the reaction team out there. Tell them not to let anyone in or out, and for God's sake under no circumstances are they to try and retake it. We've got enough problems."

"Sir, I have Heidelberg," O'Conner said as he handed Gill the phone.

Chain of command required the colonel call Heidelberg, headquarters of the U.S. Army, Europe, first. Within minutes, though, his call had been passed on to Stuttgart, home of the highest U.S. military authority in Europe.

As a young officer, Gill had been assigned to Stuttgart, and as he spoke, he could easily visualize the scene at the other end of the line.

In a windowless office in the center of the headquarters building behind eight-foot-thick concrete walls, a group of officers and enlisted men from all branches of the armed services would be monitoring the message traffic and watching the computers. A large illuminated map of Europe stretched across one wall; pinpoints of light representing the most recent positions of the allied forces and those of the Russian Army were scattered across the map. For some the Cold War had ended, but not for the men in Stuttgart. In the military, habits or precautions die hard.

"This is Colonel Gill, Ochsenburg community commander. We have a stage-one red alert."

"This is Captain Parker. What is your situation?" As the captain spoke, Colonel Gill could hear him punching keys on the computer console in front of him. He knew detailed information about Ochsenburg would begin appearing on the screen within seconds.

Colonel Gill quickly summarized his conversation with the man called Abul, related the orders he had given, and described, so there would be no question, which of the army's ammunition storage areas in Ochsenburg had been seized.

The other end of the line was silent, except for the clicking of computer keys as the captain retrieved more specific information from the depths of the computer's data banks. The silence stretched, and Gill knew the young captain's eyes had been caught by one word that seemed to glow more brightly than the others on the amber screen. "Sir, are there still—"

"Yes, captain," interrupted Gill. "There are still nuclear explosives there."

TWO

Jonathan Cane watched the leather, cloth, and plastic suitcases slide up one black conveyor belt and onto a second black band moving slowly in front of him and cursed himself again for checking his luggage.

The damned place might be blown up by the time he got his overnight bag. Finally, the oblong bag, just slightly too big to fit in the overhead compartment, moved onto the conveyor belt. Cane grabbed his backpack from the floor, snatched the bag from the conveyor belt, and rushed toward the exit. And, unlike so many times before, he got lucky. A customs line was clear.

The clerk looked at him indifferently and seemed to stiffle a yawn. "Do you have anything to declare?"

"No. Nothing."

With a slight wave, he passed Cane through. Cane pushed through the heavy, double glass doors to the inside of the Frankfurt International Airport terminal and confronted a wall of people held in check by a metal barricade. Waiting to meet friends and relatives, they peered past him into the baggage claim area. Some smiled enthusiastically and waved while others craned to get a better look.

Cane followed a young German woman, her suitcases piled high on an airport cart, through the crowd into the terminal then stopped for a moment to orient himself. Which way to the subway? It ran regularly from a station somewhere underneath the international terminal. But after so many years, he'd forgotten how to find it. He glanced at his watch. "Ah, the hell with it," he muttered and hurried outside to flag a cab.

"Hauptbahnhof, bitte."

The driver sighed deeply and jerked away from the curb to show his disgust with the short ride and small fare ahead. But Cane didn't notice. He stared out the window at the slate gray sky that always seemed to threaten rain and that melded perfectly into the polished cement buildings of Frankfurt. He smiled. Damn it was good to be back.

He had caught the flight to Frankfurt less than two hours after the AP moved the first notice. It wasn't a story the paper normally would cover, but Slovak, his editor at the *Los Angeles Journal*, suspected it could be the biggest story of the year. And, he knew, no newsman in America knew Ochsenburg better than Cane.

The cab pulled into the circular cobblestone driveway in front of Frankfurt's main train station. Cane paid the driver, tipping him generously, and hurried inside to a ticket counter.

"Ein mal nach Ochsenburg. Der schnell Zug, bitte," (One to Ochsenburg on the express train, please) he said, slipping money onto the metal tray that swiveled under the window separating the ticket sellers and railroad bureaucrats from the traveling public.

"Wohin?" The man seemed incredulous.

"Ochsenburg."

"Hin und zurück?"

"Nein, nur hin." (No, one way.).

The man blinked, shrugged, then took the money and slipped the small rectangular thick cardboard ticket back under the window. He mumbled the gate number and time and turned away abruptly.

Cane turned and looked at the huge clock with yellow neon lines to mark the hours that silently kept perfect time high above the tracks. He had hoped to get to Ochsenburg before night but knew now that was impossible. It would be dark within an hour, and the train wouldn't leave for nearly thirty minutes.

He weaved his way through the growing crowd of well-dressed business commuters and German workers in blue bib overalls and foreign laborers in worn-out wool pants and soiled sports coats. He climbed the stairs to the Post Office on the second floor, found a phone booth and pulled a small address

[6]

book from his backpack. He flipped it open and then dialed the American Consulate in Frankfurt.

It rang several times before the receptionist answered in perfect English.

"Simon North, please," Cane said. He waited and a moment later heard the click as the transfer went through.

"Communications, Sergeant Winters."

"Simon North please."

"He's not working today. Can I help you?"

"No, it's personal. But you can give him a message. Tell him Jonathan Cane called. Tell him that I just got in country and I'm heading for Ochsenburg."

"Ochsenburg. I wouldn't go near there if I were you. You know what's going on there?"

"Yeah, I'm a reporter. I'm here to cover it."

"Okay, I'll give him the message. What's the name again?"

"Jonathan Cane. We're old buddies."

He bought a copy of *Bild Zeitung* from the newsstand, tucked it under his arm, and wandered down the long narrow cement walkway that stretched between the tracks. Boarding the train, he found an empty compartment, dropped his bags on an unoccupied seat, and then flopped onto the seat across from it. For the first time the jet lag overcame the adrenaline, and a weariness settled over him.

He stretched his arms and legs then flipped open the newspaper and stared at the huge, dark headlines on the tabloid's front. His German was rusty, but he understood enough. Terrorists had seized nuclear weapons in Ochsenburg and were demanding the release of Hamid al Hamani. Nothing that he didn't already know. But if he understood correctly, the Ochsenburg *Tagesblatt* had broken the story. That was a twist. Cane remembered the paper as a sleepy, rural paper given more to school news than scandals.

Cane flipped the paper over and saw news of the seizure had bumped the story of another terrorist attack to the back page. The Red Army Faction had assassinated one of the nation's top policemen charged with hunting terrorists. A bomb had been placed beside the highway and detonated by remote control as his Mercedes passed.

Cane dropped the paper, leaned back in his seat, and again

asked himself the question that had bothered him from the moment he saw the first news bulletin. Why in God's name had they picked Ochsenburg?

O'burg, as the GIs called it, was a small, picturesque city "in the middle of Germany and at the end of the world," Cane used to write his friends in the States. Cane hadn't even heard of it when, a month after landing a reporting job for the *Stars and Stripes*, the editor had sent him there to run a one-man bureau.

Germany affected Cane, but Ochsenburg had changed his life. It was there, after all, that he had met Maria.

She was a teacher in the American elementary school, and he still remembered vividly the first time he saw her. He thought she was the most beautiful woman he had ever seen. Her hair was coal black. A few strands, prematurely silver, highlighted its darkness. She smiled at him, and her green eyes sparkled as if the two of them shared a secret, although they had just met.

And he remembered seeing the wedding ring she wore.

The memories were still fresh and the pain as real as yesterday. But what the hell, it didn't matter now. Maria was long gone. She and her husband were comfortably back in the States. In Georgia, the last he heard. And terrorists were in Ochsenburg.

The train jolted and then began to rock and clack on the tracks as it waddled out of the Frankfurt station.

It's sudden movement roused Cane from his thoughts. He dropped the paper on the seat and dug into his bag to retrieve the file on Hamid al Hamani that the paper's librarian had hurriedly copied for him.

Hamani was universally despised. Less an idealist than a madman, his name had become synonymous with random terror throughout the world. Eventually his band of zealots were disowned by even the most hard-line Middle Eastern states. Only Iraq had never publicly condemned him, but it was widely reported the Iraqis too shared an abhorance of the man.

The final straw had come the previous Christmas when his men used surface-to-air missiles to down Pan Am jets in Frankfurt and Rome and one El Al plane near Athens, within two weeks. Nearly a thousand people died. Six months later he was captured in Hamburg by German police, who burst into the apartment after receiving a tip they'd find members of the Red Army Faction hiding there. It was widely assumed Hamani had been set up and betrayed by his "brothers," who considered him a detriment to their world image. Now he languished in a German prison, serving a life term.

The train swayed gently as it rushed along the tracks away from Frankfurt. Cane looked around the empty compartment then let his gaze wander out the window at the countryside rushing past. It had started to rain, and water streaked the windows. But he saw none of it. His mind was on the ammunition dump the terrorists had seized.

He had seen it once at night when a hike in the woods with friends lasted longer than expected. Coming home they had stepped into a clearing and seen it—a compound of harsh white light in the cool forest evening.

Cane closed his eyes and carefully studied the picture his memory painted.

The ammo dump was brightly lit by incandescent lamps spaced around the perimeter. Two fences, topped with a razor-sharp barbed metal tape, surrounded the site. The two-man patrol that roamed the ten-yard space between the inside and outside fences gave the scene animation but not life. Most of all, though, Cane remembered the dirt-covered humps with the huge steel doors. Inside these burial mounds they kept the nuclear explosives.

The train raced across the flat farmland, slowing only to pass through villages. As it neared Ochsenburg, it cut through a small forest, the trees blending into a dark green blur, then burst into the open and swung parallel to the autobahn. Through the rain Cane could see the autos backed up on the highway like carts in a checkout line.

At first he didn't realize. He'd seen traffic jams before. They were notorious on the autobahn. Two- or three-hour delays were not uncommon. But this was different. He stared at the traffic in the last of the gray late-afternoon light for several minutes, then suddenly understood.

There was no traffic in the other direction.

For the first time he stared closely at the endless line of cars, trucks, and vans and saw what was happening. They were piled high with belongings. Suitcases, baby strollers, and boxes bound in plastic to protect them from the rain had been tied to the trunks and roofs.

The residents of Ochsenburg were fleeing. The refugees formed a slow-moving tide that filled the autobahn and flowed out of Ochsenburg. No one was driving toward the city.

Cane leaped from his seat, ran to the end of the long, swaying car, and pushed through the air-tight doors into the next car. It too was empty. He ran on. The dining car. Empty. Into tourist class. Empty. Empty. Empty. Car after car. And Cane understood. He was the only passenger on a train no one wanted to board.

He pushed on through the cars. He was almost at the end when he saw a conductor slumped in a seat. The man was startled by Cane's sudden appearance.

"Where the hell? . . ." Cane began and then stopped. Searching his mind for the German he tried again. "*Wo sind die Leute?*" (Where are the people?)

For a moment the conductor merely stared, his expression a mixture of disbelief and awe that anyone could be so ignorant of the world around them.

"*Der Zug,*" (The train) Cane said, gesturing widely. "*Die Leute. Wo sind die leute?*"

The conductor shrugged and merely said, "*Angst. Atom bomb.*"

Curling the tips of his finger together he suddenly flicked them in the air. "Poof," he said and again looked at the floor.

Cane should have known, should have been ready for the Ochsenburg station. But he wasn't. As the train pulled to a stop a tide of people swelled across the platform. The crowd pushed up the steps and through the doors, forcing Cane back into the train. The first ones in pulled others through the windows.

Cane pushed back and fought his way off, fiercely shoving people back down the steps. As he wedged his way down the last step, he saw a woman and boy knocked off the far side of the platform to the tracks below. No one stopped to help them. Everyone was pushing toward the train.

He was barely off when the conductors forced the doors closed and the train began moving again. Cane had to brace himself as the frustrated tide pushed again, struggling to gain a last foothold before the train picked up too much speed and disappeared.

He pushed, picked, and squeezed his way across the loading platform and up the steps to the terminal. At the top of the steps he turned and looked again at the loading platforms below. He doubted the people knew where the train was going. It probably didn't matter. It was leaving Ochsenburg. For the first time Cane wondered what the hell he was doing there.

He elbowed his way through the crowd that mobbed the lobby struggling to reach the ticket windows and finally fought his way outside. He stood for a moment to get his bearings and looked around the large cobblestone plaza that spread in front of the station. Beyond the plaza was a traffic circle encompassing a fountain; three narrow streets converged on the circle.

He crossed the plaza in front of the station to a bright yellow phone booth at the street's edge. He pulled the door closed and dialed a number from memory.

"Public affairs office, Sergeant Green." The voice sounded young.

Cane introduced himself and asked for an update.

"Well, Mr. Cane, the situation hasn't changed. There will be a press briefing in the theater at Boelke Kaserne at eight tonight. You're welcome to attend."

"Sure, I'll be there. Sergeant, what's this about nuclear bombs? I used to cover Ochsenburg for the *Stars and Stripes*, and I don't remember any nuclear bombs being here."

"Just a moment, Mr. Cane, I'll read you the statement." He read with a bored rythm, as though he had recited the statement a hundred times that day. "And there is no immediate danger to either the population of Ochsenburg or to property surrounding the ammunition site," he concluded.

"Thanks, sergeant, I appreciate it. But I have a few other questions. Can you tell me what the terrorists' demands are? Who's the officer they kidnapped? And have they really seized nuclear weapons?"

"Sorry, sir. I am not allowed to go beyond the statement."

"But that's absurd, the whole goddamned town is fleeing in stark terror and you're saying there's no danger." Cane could feel his anger rising. The military never learned, never changed.

"I'm sorry, sir, but I'm not allowed to go beyond the statement."

He knew further fighting was useless, but he tried anyway. "Okay, sergeant, I understand. But at least you can give me the name of the hostage. Hell, by now everyone in the community is going to know. It'll only take a couple of phone calls to get it, so what's the big deal."

"I'm sorry, I can only read you what's on the statement."

"Yeah. Well, I guess I'll see you at the briefing."

He hung up and pushed the door open in disgust. But then what the hell had he expected? He'd covered the military long enough for the *Stars and Stripes* to understand the army's idea of a free press was about the same as Beijing's.

He stood in the cool evening and looked up the empty streets running from the traffic circle. There were no buses in sight. The taxi stand was empty too. But across the street Cane saw a long, low, cement building. A small brightly lit office on the end caught Cane's eye. The sign written in English and German hung above the door. In English it read: CARS BOUGHT, SOLD, AND RENTED. Beyond the end of the building was a lot crammed with old cars.

He crossed the street and walked into the shabby room. There was one desk. Behind it sat a pale man, rumpled and weary. He was perhaps fifty, maybe older. It seemed impossible to know. He looked up as Cane walked in, appraising him in a instant.

"American, right? Yeah, I can always tell. Must be a reporter, right? Yeah. No other Americans coming in here right now."

With his first words, Cane knew the man himself was American. The man took a long drag on his cigarette and stubbed it out in an ashtray already overflowing with butts. His bloodshot eyes, oily hair, and stained underarms testified to a long stretch in the small, nicotine-soaked office.

"I'm surprised you're still open," Cane said.

"You kidding, Bud? Look at the crowd over there," he said

waving toward the train station. "Pretty soon people will start giving up hope they'll ever get on a train. Then you know what they'll do?" He paused to light another cigarette and lean back in his chair. He exhaled and smiled through nicotine teeth. "Pay." He smiled again.

"Fear's a great motivator. By tomorrow night they'll pay anything to get out of here. A thousand marks, two thousand, five thousand. They don't care, just get them out. I'm already doing a land office business. Cash, check, credit card." He beamed.

"And you still have cars left?" Cane nodded at the over-flowing lot next door visible through a side window. The skepticism was obvious in his voice.

"Hell, I'm running 'em in from anywhere I can get 'em. Buying anything. Make, model, condition, year, it doesn't matter. Just so it runs. Besides, with each one that leaves, the next one goes up in price. Simple economics. Supply and demand." He grinned.

"Well, I'm not leaving town. What do you have I can rent for a few days?"

"Well, since you're going to be here, how about that Ford Taunus sitting over there?"

Cane looked and saw a small rectangular red car with the engineering elegance of a brick. It's left front fender was deeply dented. Cane turned back to the nicotine smile.

"How much?"

"Three hundred a day."

"Three hundred marks a day? Are you crazy?"

"Okay. For a fellow American, two fifty."

"I'll walk."

"Suit yourself. There are hundreds of people over there. I'll get my price." The smile was gone.

Cane suddenly felt very tired. There were no taxis and he couldn't walk. He had to have a car.

"One hundred," he said.

Nicotine teeth smiled, happy again. They haggled, and in the end Cane gave him his credit card and rented the car for four days, at one hundred and fifty marks a day. God, almost a hundred dollars a day for a car that might not last four days.

Suddenly there seemed no balance left in the world.

THREE

They had learned of the incident almost instantly. But thanks to the mismatch between instantaneous communication and the plodding progress of time the news had arrived in the middle of a hectic Washington afternoon. It was early evening before the President could gather the small group of men he depended on for advice.

His first questions were direct.

"Who are these people and what options have they given us?" His flat midwestern voice was cool, as though discussing the price of winter wheat.

The director of the CIA, the nation's chief spy, answered, "We don't know. We're running every possible check through the computers and we've sent bulletins to every station chief. But so far we don't have much. The Pan Arab Revolutionary Council isn't in the computer, and it seeems no one has heard of them. We've got more than a dozen Abuls but we're pretty sure none of them are the guy in Ochsenburg. We're checking with the Mossad, and one of our men is helping debrief Maria Henry, Major Henry's wife. We're hoping to learn something from that. We've been monitoring almost all the message traffic throughout the Middle East and at all their embassies in Germany, and we've never had even the remotest indication that something like this was being planned. We're double checking all the past message traffic again in case something was overlooked. But frankly, we don't think there's much chance of that."

"You mean these people just appeared out of thin air? Is that what you're telling me?"

"It would seem so, sir."

"Jesus Christ." The words were whispered but heard throughout the room. He nodded to the secretary of defense. "What's the situation?"

The secretary of defense straightened the pile of papers in front of him, cleared his throat, and droned his report in the precise monotone of an accountant reading a phone book.

"The terrorists have seized a small storage area used by the Eighth Engineers Batallion to store explosives on the outskirts of Ochsenburg. The area now under their control is about two hundred and fifty yards long and about one hundred yards wide."

A vein in the President's temple began to throb, protruding from his skull with each heartbeat. But he made no attempt to rush the report.

"There are guard towers at all four corners and a main guard tower in the middle of the compound. There are four concrete bunker-style buildings, called igloos, inside the compound. That's where the munitions are stored. We believe only one has been seized. That one has a direct telephone link to the base commander's office. We know they're in that one. But all the igloos may contain nuclear devices.

"Each bunker is covered with dirt and grass and has a big sliding steel door in one end. The area has been sealed off by troops from Ochsenburg. No one has entered or left since the area was seized. We think there's little chance they know how to arm the explosives. That requires knowledge of the codes and special keys. Both are strictly guarded secrets. And the codes are changed monthly. If they try to pry open the weapons, a nonnuclear charge will explode and the nuclear device will be rendered useless. Furthermore, I have been assured that the weapons cannot be detonated by other explosives—by, say, tying a couple sticks of dynamite to the outside of it. Still, not knowing the exact state of the explosives puts us at a disadvantage.

"I had experts assess the likely damage if one of the devices were exploded. Of course the exact extent of the damage isn't known. We've never actually set one of these off in a situation like this. But our preliminary estimates indicate that if even just one is detonated, it would be pretty bad. It would wipe out the town. Depending on the winds, fallout could also be a problem. Of course, it depends on whether they set it off inside the building or not. We're not sure how that would affect the blast and the fallout."

He flipped the report closed and slipped off his glasses. Then, looking directly at the President, he added, "With that in mind, sir, I think we should be planning an attack on the storage area. With a quick strike we could end it. Maybe we could capture the terrorists alive. But either way, we'd have the explosives back."

"What do you have in mind?" the President asked.

"Sir, I've already ordered the Delta Force to Germany from Fort Bragg. They are a highly trained unit capable of swift, decisive action and have been given the very latest, most sophisticated hardware available. They should be in position within a few hours."

"Thank you." The President nodded to his secretary of state. "What do you think?"

"I think that would be a mistake. We're in a high-stakes game for world opinion. What we need is patience and wisdom here, not a gunfight at the OK Corral. There's a hell of a lot more at stake here than just one bomb, as cruel as that may sound.

"We're already having a hell of a time with the Germans on NATO. Now that they think the Russians are no longer a threat, there's a real anti-NATO sentiment growing. The chancellor and most of his Christian Democrats want to keep Germany in NATO. But even they admit there are not going to be many American troops left in Germany in a few years. The far-right Republicans aren't much better than the damned Greens on this. The Republicans want all foreigners, including us, out so Germany can once again claim its rightful place as the dominant European power.

"Look, we've already accepted the fact that there wasn't much hope of keeping our nuclear weapons in Germany for more than another year or two. Our priority all along has been keeping NATO together. This thing really puts us in a bind. We've got to look like we want peace as much as the Russians."

"We do want it as much as the Russians," the President interrupted.

"Yes, sir. But we're talking about perceptions here. What the Germans think. I don't want to sound melodramatic, but with the Berlin Wall down and the Russians pulling back everywhere, how we handle this may be the determining factor in whether NATO survives."

The President sat silently for a moment, weighing what he had heard. "Who do you have in Ochsenburg?" he asked finally.

"Mathew Burt's our chief negotiator. He's there now, and he's already started talking to the terrorists."

"Is there any chance we can convince them to surrender?"

"I don't know. Burt's probably the best we have. I talked with him just a couple of minutes ago. He told me these guys are different from others he's dealt with in the past. They seem cooler, more calm. Deliberate. They may be anxious to be martyrs, and his best guess at this point is that they'll blow it up if they have to and if they can. And these guys aren't sitting on a runway someplace stringing dynamite around a 747. They're sitting on an A bomb. I think we need to go slow. Besides we still don't know what the Germans are going to do. They may want to let al Hamani go."

The President nodded silently then looked again at the secretary of defense. "I need your best assessment on this. Can they set those things off? Is it possible they somehow got ahold of the codes and the keys?"

"It's possible, sir. But I don't know how. Those codes are top secret. I think they're bluffing."

The President stared at the limp American flag across the room for several seconds before speaking again to his secretary of defense. "Okay, get your men in position out there and get them ready. We've got a few hours yet, but we may not have much of a choice. As long as we're sure they can't set those things off we're going to have to take 'em back, even if it means getting that major killed. We can't give in to terrorists. In the meantime lets light a fire under the Germans. We need to know what they're willing to do. I want to cover all the bases."

The President remained seated while the others gathered their papers and closed their folders. It would be a long night.

He looked around his office, filled with his personal mementos and the abstract paintings he had chosen to lighten the Ethan Allen decor. Despite the touches, it seemed suddenly a cruel and distant place.

FOUR

Cane drove slowly through Ochsenburg, looking at the dark buildings, tightly shuttered against unknown assailants and well-known fear.

Without thinking, he navigated through the city's narrow, winding streets until he turned the final corner and came to the Zum Engel—The Angel. He had stumbled across the Engel the day he arrived in Ochsenburg for the *Stars and Stripes*. He had intended to stay a few days, a week at most, while searching for an apartment. Instead he occupied the corner room on the second floor for nearly two months. And in the following years he spent many nights at the Engel, drinking beer and practicing his German with Hildigard and Margaret, the two unmarried sisters who owned and ran the inn.

Cane came to treasure them. Hildigard, who kept the books and cooked, was more shy and conservative than her younger sister. She favored sensible shoes, kept her hair in a bun, and seldom, if ever, wore jewelery. She was dumpy and dowdy.

Margaret waited the tables, talked with the customers, and drew the draft beers. Her large breasts and shapley legs had drawn the fancy of a few young men before the war, but none had returned to finish the courting.

To them Cane became a combination younger brother, son, and simply the first person to pay genuine attention to them in thirty years.

It had not occurred to Cane that Hildigard and Margaret might have abandoned Ochsenburg with the others. Yet when he arrived, the gravel courtyard was empty and the single downstairs light was little more than a flicker in three stories of darkness. He pounded on the door and called three times before Hildigard finally cracked the door to look out.

"Ah, Herr Cane, Herr Cane, *bitte, bitte,* please come in. Margaret, come, come see it's Herr Cane."

Margaret hurried in from the kitchen and they all shook hands in the strangely formal way that often substitutes for a show of affection between friends of different generations in Germany.

The pension was empty, they said. The guests had fled, and the traveling salesmen, the backbone of their business, were avoiding Ochsenburg. They too were frightened but wouldn't leave, the sisters said. They had survived the war in that house, and if the town blew up, they would just as soon die together and at home.

"Well, you'll have at least one guest for as long as this lasts," Cane said with a smile.

While Margaret drew three beers from the tap, Cane carried his two bags to the corner room on the second floor and threw them on the bed. When he returned, Margaret and Hildigard had moved to the "regulars' " table in the cozy, wood-paneled corner. But as he drew near, he saw the sisters were arguing in whispers. They stopped suddenly when he sat down, but said nothing of their argument. Then Hildi lay a folded copy of the local newspaper, the *Tagesblatt,* on the table.

"We thought you knew. We thought that was why you came," she said. Her voice trailed away. Cane looked at the two sisters blankly, but they didn't return his eyes. Instead Hildi simply flipped opened the paper.

Two photos dominated the front page. One, a regulation army-issued publicity still, showed Major Woodrow Wilson Henry, staring, unsmiling, at the camera. The second, obviously shot with a telephoto lense, was of his wife being escorted to a waiting sedan by military police.

Cane stared at the picture of Maria for a long time.

"We're sorry, we thought you knew," Hildi said again.

Very few people had known about Cane and Maria, but Hildi and Margaret were exceptions. They had known the first time he brought her to the pension for lunch and sat under the huge oak tree in the patio. They saw the look in his eyes and the way she responded to him, laughing at his jokes and gently touching his fingers. They saw the flowers Cane thought he had so cleverly hidden and the small gifts he believed had escaped notice.

But the two sisters had been innkeepers for too long. They had perfected the art of seeing everything while appearing to notice nothing. They saw the romance blossom. They also saw the wedding band Maria wore.

The three sat around the oak table in silence. Cane stared at the picture, his eyes focused on Maria. She was supposed to be somewhere in Georgia, not back in Ochsenburg. But she was here, and the terrorists had done something to her. She looked shaken, vulnerable in the photo.

When he saw her picture, the pain of losing her, slowly banished over the years, filled him again. He knew instantly he still loved her, deeply and passionately.

He wanted to hold her and comfort her and reassure her that she would never again be hurt. And suddenly he was angry. He wanted to punish the men who had caused her pain. He knew it was a silly, romantic idea, bred by matinee cowboys and nick-of-time television heroes. He couldn't touch the terrorists any more than he could protect the woman in the grainy picture he stared at so ardently.

"Will you read it for me. My German isn't very good anymore."

"Of course," said Hildi, and she began.

When she finished, Cane picked up the paper and glanced again at the article. Only then did he notice the byline: Rolf Makler.

So Rolf was finally breaking the big story about the Americans, Cane thought. He almost laughed. He remembered Rolf well. In fact he had been one of the few Americans who genuinely liked Rolf. On more than one occasion he had passed an evening drinking and arguing politics with the young German journalist. He called Rolf "a Commie pinko" and Rolf called him a "a fascist flunky." It was an odd friendship, but real. Sometimes Cane thought they understood each other and at other times he wasn't sure.

Cane knew Rolf saw himself as a crusading journalist. "It's a shame to let the facts get in the way of a good story," Rolf once joked. Cane knew it was a joke, but it didn't seem funny when Rolf said it. And now, Cane found himself wondering how Rolf had managed to break such a big story.

"Thanks, Hildi," he said. "I think I'll try another phone call or two."

He had sworn he never wanted to see her again. But now, despite the painful memories, he had to try. It wouldn't be easy. It would be a long time before the military allowed her to talk with the press. But he had to try. And there was one person who might be able to help him.

"Hello." Cane recognized the husky voice.

"Hi, Barbara. It's Cane."

There was a pause. "Hi, Cane. I guess I'm not surprised to hear from you. She'll be okay, though. You don't need to worry. She's a tough lady, you know that."

"Yeah, I know. Look, Barbara, I'm here, in Ochsenburg. I've got to see her."

"Oh, Cane, I don't know." There was a pause and finally she said, "I'll see she gets the message."

"Look, I'm not going to try and start anything. I just want to see her."

"Okay, I'll tell her."

"Look, why don't you give me her phone number?"

"Only if you promise not to call her unless I tell you it's all right first."

"Sure."

Barbara recited the number and Cane wrote it on a small piece of paper, then stuck it in his wallet.

"Thanks, Barbara. By the way, I'm staying at the—"

"I know. You're at The Engel."

"You got it. Hey, Barbara, what the hell is she doing back here? I heard they were in Georgia."

"Beats me. Woody volunteered. Promised her it would mean great things for his career. They got here six months or so ago. He's supposed to be working on some big deal project or something. She didn't want to come back here, Cane. Believe me. And get this, they were scheduled to go to Hawaii, and instead he turned it down and volunteered to come back here."

"Did he ask her what she wanted to do?"

[24]

"Come on, Cane, you know the answer to that."
"Yeah, I guess I do."

Their affair would not have been possible without Barbara because the wife of a young officer couldn't be seen going to dinner with an unmarried man. Cane and Maria could be discrete, but Ochsenburg is a small community. It wouldn't take long before everyone knew.

Eventually, Maria had turned to the one true friend she had in Ochsenburg: Barbara Darling, who taught in the classroom next to hers.

During her years in Ochsenburg, Barbara had seen a multitude of military wives, but Maria was different. She had the tough exterior of an army wife whose husband's career comes first, but she wasn't just filling time by teaching. She genuinely cared about teaching and her students. They quickly became close friends.

When Maria finally asked for help, Barbara didn't hesitate. Soon everyone thought Barbara, the single teacher, and Cane, the young bachelor, were quite the item, and Maria was just Barbara's friend along for the ride.

Cane hung up and stared at the phone, forcing memories from his mind and trying to focus on the reason he was in Ochsenburg, a city he was supposed to know better than any other reporter. He picked up the receiver again and called the man he hoped could help him immediately with the story.

Rick Plummer was a close friend from Cane's earliest days in Ochsenburg. While others had drifted away from the city, Rick's work and a series of promotions had kept him there. He knew the base as well as anyone. And he was an engineer. If anyone could help him, it would be Rick. He had a quick wit and was one of the smartest men Cane had ever met.

They hadn't spoken in years, so Cane knew how to begin his conversation.

Rick answered on the third ring. "Yeah, hello."

"Is this Dial-a-Curse?"

There was no hesitation. "Yeah, Dial-a-Curse here."

"Well, I'm having a rough day. I need a good curse to help me make it through."

"May you have a daughter who wins the Broderick Crawford look-alike contest."

"Whoa. That's a heavy curse to lay on someone."

"Well, we aim to please here at Dial-a-Curse."

"You succeeded. How the hell are you, Rick?"

"Pretty good. How are you? You calling from the States? You sound like you're next door."

"I am, sort of. I'm here in Ochsenburg. At The Engel. The paper sent me here to cover this terrorist thing. I've got to go to a briefing at eight o'clock. I was hoping we could get together after that."

"Sounds great. You want to come by here?"

"Sure. Hey, Rick. You know anything about this?"

"Not much. The whole community is going ape, but you've probably figured that out by now."

"Yeah, I came in on the train. The station was a zoo. But, I mean do you know anything about the nukes. They haven't moved bombs in here since I left, have they?"

"They're not bombs, but they're nukes all right. I'll fill you in when you get here. But you don't know where you got the information, or it's my butt."

"No problem. If I told, you'd probably lay another curse on me anyway."

FIVE

The terrorists had drastically altered the military's daily rhythm. Cane saw it immediately as he turned the Taunus into Boelke Kaserne's narrow cobblestone entrance.

The guards all carried guns now. When he lived in Ochsenburg such security had been rare. Occasionally a line of cars had backed out of the entrance into the street as police with dogs checked each vehicle for drugs and explosives.

Normally, though, soldiers and their families would be waved through automatically, and only cars not bearing the special U.S. forces license plates were stopped. At other times a sleepy guard would lazily wave every car through without hesitation.

Not now. Soldiers with automatic rifles lined the short driveway. A row of oil drums stretched across the entrance, an additional barrier to intruders from the world outside the gates. A freshly starched second lieutenant, his gold bars glistening on his shoulders, approached, a hand gun on his side. He paused while Cane rolled down his window.

"Can I help you?" the lieutenant asked. His voice was stern but not unfriendly.

"Hi. My name's Cane. I'm here for the press briefing."

"Do you have some identification, sir?"

"Sure." He pulled his passport and press card from his pocket and handed them out the window. As the lieutenant studied the documents, Cane studied him.

His closely cropped brown hair and soft skin gave him a fine scrubbed look. When he glanced up from the passport to look at Cane and then down at the documents again, Cane was struck by his brown eyes. No bags, no lines, no age.

Cane remembered the first time he had entered Boelke Kaserne. To him the entire U.S. Army had seemed a sagging, aging dinosaur. Flush with youth and antiwar sentiments fired by the carnage in Vietnam, Cane looked at the military as something beneath him—to be tolerated, perhaps, but not deserving much respect and certainly not to be trusted. He had walked into Boelke Kaserne that day years ago humming, "one, two, three, what are we fighting for . . ." His own, private lyrical nose thumbing.

And now a young man who probably had never heard of Abbie Hoffman, or Tet, let alone Country Joe and the Fish, was inspecting his credentials. Cane had to smile.

The army didn't get younger or older, it just kept grinding along and watched the world change around it. Cane knew the same wasn't true of him.

"Okay, sir. You can park over there. The briefing will be held in the theater. To get to the theater, you want—"

"That's okay, lieutenant. I know where the theater is."

Boelke Kaserne was the military community's town square. Its red sandstone and brick buildings, spaced precisely around a center parade ground, held the PX, the post office, education center, bookstore, bank, and other offices.

And in one corner was the theater. Like the rest of the Kaserne, it had been built in the run up to World War II as Hitler was expanding the influence and strength of his army. With hundreds of reporters, cameramen, and photographers expected, it would be a perfect place for a press conference.

Cane walked up the worn stone stairway and into the lobby. He peeked inside the cavernous theater. It was as big as some of the ersatz Victorian movie houses erected in America during the 1930s and 1940s, with a high ceiling and hundreds of seats. But where the American theaters had been built with a sense of style and adorned with rococo splendor, this had been designed only for utility.

Inside, television technicians were working rapidly. Already they had crisscrossed the theater floor with their cables and wires, bound together and fastened to the carpet with duct tape. Halfway up the sloping floor from the stage, in the middle of the seats, they had planted a forest of tripods crowned with television cameras and lights.

On stage the podium was thick with microphones. Technicians were testing the equipment and laying even more cable along the floor. The camera's logos told Cane how big the story had become. Each of the three major American networks had sent a crew. And there were German, French, Italian, British, Dutch, Norwegian, Japanese, Spanish, and even Brazilian networks.

Cane returned to the lobby and was about to serve himself a cup of coffee from one of the large urns the army had provided when someone yelled, "Cane, you fascist flunky. I thought nothing could get you back to Germany."

He turned and saw Rolf smiling at him across the lobby.

"Rolf! Still fighting the imperialist dogs on behalf of the downtrodden of the world?" He walked over and stuck out his hand.

"Too good a story to miss? Or did you just have to see Ochsenburg one more time?" Rolf asked.

"Couldn't pass up something like this. Hey, I saw your piece. I have to admit, it was good work."

"Thanks, Cane. Just got a little lucky."

"Modesty, Rolf? That's something new for you, isn't it?" He had meant it as a dig, and Rolf's reaction surprised him. Instead of an angry retort, Rolf simply looked at him, as if weighing a decision.

"No, Cane, it is luck. I don't understand it myself, but someone who calls himself Jurgen told me terrorists had seized the Americans' nuclear bombs in Ochsenburg and were threatening to blow them up."

"Who is this guy?"

Rolf shook his head.

"From what I can see he's giving you good stuff."

"His information is always right. Still, I'm a little worried."

"Why?"

"What happens if he stops calling and writing?"

"Then you'll have to do your own work, just like the rest of us poor slobs, Rolf." Even as he said it, Cane knew it was wrong. He couldn't explain it, but there was a subtle change in

Rolf. Seconds before he had seemed almost warm. Now he shifted again to the cold, aloof German newsman Cane had always known.

"Yeah. Hey, don't mention this, okay? Look, we'd better get our seats before the crowd gets here or we'll be stuck in the back." Rolf turned and disappeared into the auditorium.

Other newsmen began arriving within minutes. The very polite but all-business Japanese were the first. A contingent of Americans followed, more than one looking bleary eyed from jet lag. Next came two fellows with BBC stickers on their Sony tape recorders. The French swept into the theater, and then five haughty chaps from Reuters (God, they cover the shit out of a story, Cane thought).

By eight o'clock the auditorium was half filled with reporters, television cameramen, sound men, technicians, gofers, and military men. More than two hundred people by Cane's count.

At five minutes after ten, a middle-aged man in a dark blue suit walked down the side aisle and up to the podium. A lieutenant colonel in a crisp, U.S. Army uniform accompanied him.

"Good evening, ladies and gentlemen. My name is Porter Caldwell. I am a public information officer from the embassy. This is Lieutenant Colonel Lawrence Anderson, the deputy community commander in Ochsenburg. Colonel Gill, the community commander, will not be here. He feels it would be inappropriate to leave his office until this problem is successfully resolved. Before I take questions I'd like to read a short statement."

Caldwell sketched the situation, accenting the potential for success and minimizing the risk. "Now, are there any questions?" he concluded.

There were dozens. Rolf was first.

"Do you really think the German government will refuse the terrorists' demands and take a chance on an atomic bomb being exploded on German territory?"

To Cane it was less a question than a statement.

"We are sure the German government fully appreciates the situation and understands the danger in giving in to terrorists," Caldwell responded coolly.

Other questions sought facts, not opinions: "Are the Americans considering a military move against the terrorists?"

"Absolutely not."

"What is the deadline set by the terrorists?"

"Midnight tomorrow."

"Did the German authorities know the Americans were storing nuclear explosives in Ochsenburg?"

"Of course."

"Did the terrorists know there would be nuclear weapons in the depot?"

"We believe so."

"How did they know they were there?"

"We don't know."

The questions continued for nearly an hour, until it was apparent little more could be learned.

During his years as a reporter, Cane had covered hundreds of press conferences, but none where the questions were as tough or as pointed as they were in the theater in Ochsenburg.

As the reporters sought Caldwell's attention to ask their questions, Cane had to fight to keep his mind focused on the story at all. The newspaper picture of Maria, being led away by military police, constantly forced its way into his mind. The press conference was almost over when Cane finally asked his only question.

"Mr. Caldwell, what about Major Henry's family. Were they hurt?"

"No. Mrs. Henry and their two children are fine. In fact, the children slept through the entire incident. Now, if there are no more questions, I'll be available throughout the night. You all have the number of the public affairs office. If there's any major change in the situation, we'll try to inform you. Thank you, ladies and gentlemen."

Cane moved quickly, pushing his way through the reporters crowding into the aisle, and scurried to the lobby. He knew that even pros could be ambushed, especially in the midst of a storm. The front, direct approach worked best in these situations. And as Caldwell and Lieutenant Colonel Anderson pushed through the doors to the lobby, trailing the hoard of reporters behind them, Cane advanced.

"Mr. Caldwell, where are Mrs. Henry and the children now?" The question verged on a challenge.

"They're safe."

"Are they still in Germany?"

"Yes."

"In Ochsenburg?"

"I, ahh, don't think we want to answer that question. As I said, they're safe." Caldwell pushed past Cane as the other reporters crowded around.

Cane relaxed. He would have a chance to see her after all. His fears were unjustified. The military had not sped her and the boys back to the United States on the first available flight. The army probably wanted to, but knowing Maria she wouldn't go. She wouldn't go until she knew what happened to her husband.

Those reporters who hadn't followed Caldwell and Anderson out of the building milled around, playing back tape recorded sections of the press conference and exchanging theories and gossip on the terrorists. The network newsmen exited quickly to beam home standup deliveries against a background oozing the ambience of prewar brick buildings.

Cane glanced at his watch, it was almost ten o'clock. He subtracted nine hours to figure the time on the Pacific coast. He had plenty of time before his first deadline, but he knew the city desk would be getting anxious. He walked across the lobby to the long table equipped with typewriters. A few years ago there would have been a crowd of reporters fighting for them. No more.

Today's reporters traveled with lap-top computers and modems. They wrote their stories in their hotel rooms, made a quick call, pressed a couple of buttons, and were done.

When they first replaced the manual typewriters with electrics, Cane had loved them. They made typing so easy, so much faster. Now typewriters of any kind seemed so hard, so unforgiving. Words sat there in black and white. There was no delete key on a Royal.

It went slowly at first. Ninety minutes later he was finished and on the phone dictating.

When he hung up he felt a sudden rush. It was thrilling, covering the most important story in the world, dictating a front-page story to someone halfway around the world. He clapped his hands together, slapped his notebook shut, and turned to smile at the others.

But he was alone. Caught up in the story he hadn't noticed anyone leaving. Only their trash was still there: a few sheets of paper and copies of press releases scattered on the floor and a Styrofoam cup lying in a pool of coffee near the door of the lobby.

He felt his shoulders sag, his euphoria dissipate. There was no one to share his excitement. He stuck his notebook in his hip pocket and walked slowly out of the theater. Turning his collar up against a heavy mist, he descended the steps and headed for his car.

How had the *New York Times* and the *Washington Post* handled the story? How were the pieces written? What would be their leads? he wondered. It didn't really matter. He knew he would think theirs better.

His red shoe-box car squatted on its springs at the far end of the parade ground, which years ago had been blacktopped into a parking lot. Reporting and writing could be exhilarating, but it was also exhausting. And in those moments of fatigue his worst self-doubts crept in.

He tugged at the door of the shoe box. It refused to open. He pulled again. In frustration he grabbed with both hands and jerked hard. The door swung open suddenly and violently, the edge smashing into his shin.

He steadied himself on the door as the first wave of pain swept past leaving him momentarily light-headed. He thought he would vomit, but the feeling passed. He slipped awkwardly behind the wheel and sat, eyes closed, waiting for the pain to subside.

He leaned back, turning his face to the roof. The seat leaned against an empty plastic beer case that had been wedged onto the floor behind the seat for support.

Suddenly it all seemed funny, ludicrous. What else could happen? He was sure he had fallen short again in his chosen profession. He had smashed his shin on the door, felt locked inside a rusted-out, used-up car that needed a beer case just to keep the seat from flopping over. It was great *Three Stooges* material.

[33]

But, Cane didn't feel like laughing. He was tired and denied himself the humor of it all.

"What the hell's the point?" he muttered to himself.

He left Ochsenburg confident of his abilities and certain he would take the journalism world by storm. And now here he was, after years of being a reporter, employed by a second-string newspaper, covering one of the biggest stories in the world and probably not measuring up.

He considered calling Rick, canceling his visit, and just going back to the Engel. At least there he could feel sorry for himself, and curse the world with a beer in his hand and a schnapps on the table.

But he hadn't seen Rick in years and he needed a little R and R. And if he went to see Rick, he was bound to laugh.

"To hell with 'em all" he said aloud and gunned the car to life.

SIX

The white, cement block duplex was quiet when Cane pulled into the driveway. The bottom floor was dark, and only one light burned in Rick's upstairs apartment. The glass door to the entryway swung open at Cane's nudge and he walked up the narrow steps without bothering to buzz.

He knocked lightly, and a moment later Rick swung the door wide and smiled. "Welcome home," he said and stuck out his hand.

Cane, stunned by the change in Rick, offered a limp handshake and stared at his old friend. When Cane left Germany, Rick was a round, rambunctious man with a full head of black hair. Now, his hair was thin and much of it was silver. And he wore glasses.

But just as remarkable, the round, pudgy body was gone, replaced by muscle. The once soft, fluffy tummy was flat and hard. His T-shirt pulled tightly across his chest and shoulders.

"Rick, you look great."

"Ah, bullshit. I look a hell of a lot older."

"No, seriously, you look great."

"Well, I've been working out, lifting weights. Funny, isn't it? Now that none of the women want to look at me because I'm such an old fart, I finally get in shape. What's that about knowing then what you know now? Anyway, come in, come in."

"Yeah, well, we're all getting older at the same rate: one day at a time," Cane said. As they walked to the living room Cane thought of his own sags and puckers. He had promised himself he would do something about it, maybe take up jogging

[35]

or swimming but so far had done nothing. In truth, he shared a common failing: a decades-old self-image that refused the updated evidence of mirrors and belt notches.

"True, true. But you know what pisses me off. I mean really pisses me off?"

"What?" Cane was bewildered.

Rick whipped his glasses off and squinting myopically, shook them indignantly an inch from Cane's nose.

"Bifocals! Damnit. Bifocals. And I'm still getting zits. It's not fair. There's no justice. Pizza faced, four eyed, and I'm only a step away from prunes for irregularity. It's a shitty deal."

Cane's laughter was instantaneous and full, wiping away the exhaustion, stress, and pain of feelings he thought long ago buried. He sank to the floor, his back pressed to the wall, laughing until he had trouble breathing. Rick waited silently until Cane finally wiped the tears from the corners of his eyes and struggled again to his feet.

"Hey, you want a beer?" Rick finally asked.

"Sure, I'd love one."

"There are a couple of cold Henningers in the fridge. Bring me one while you're out there, okay?" he said with a grin.

"Sure, glad to," said Cane.

Rick dropped a cassette in the deck. Jimmy Buffet had just started singing about changes in latitudes and attitudes when Cane reached the kitchen. The unrelenting fluorescent light flickered on and Cane took in the urban blight that was Rick's kitchen.

It would terrify a cockroach.

In a corner, a case of beer bottles propped up a sagging cardboard box of electronic components with wires dangling over the edge. Leaning against the wall below a window was the door to a Volkswagen beetle sporting an array of stickers, including a happy face with the words *Atom Kraft, nein danke.* Plastered next to it was an *Ochsenburg German-American Volksfest, Peace Through Friendship* sticker.

The door was a new addition, but Cane was unsure about the rest. Rick's table was lost under a Gordian knot of cassette tapes, candles, empty beer bottles, and a game of Trivial Pursuit apparently abandoned in the middle. On the counter was a stack of debatably clean dishes crowned by a carburetor and spark plug wires.

"Hey, Rick, you rebuilding an engine or going into competition with NASA?" Cane shouted to the living room.

"It's for the Moto Guzzi. Having a little trouble with it and I got a wild hair one night and thought I'd fix it."

Cane could only guess how long ago that had been. Inside the refrigerator he found a shelf full of beer bottles and three jars of pickles. Nothing else. Oh, well, all the essentials, he thought.

Cane used the opener dangling on a string from the refrigerator door to pop open two beers and wandered back to the living room. He sank onto Rick's futon couch and glanced around the room. Two huge Klipschorn speakers dominated one end of the small living room. Records, tapes, and books were stacked everywhere. And, on almost every flat surface, was a thriving plant. Rick couldn't keep house but he had one hell of a green thumb.

"You ever think of getting a cleaning lady?" Cane asked.

"I tried one once. We couldn't agree on terms," he said. "I wanted to pay her a flat rate by the hour, but after seeing the kitchen she insisted on bringing in subcontractors and getting paid by the square foot."

Cane chuckled and took a long sip of beer.

"I wasn't sure you'd remember how to get here," Rick said.

"Neither was I, but they haven't changed the roads any."

"No. Things are pretty much the way they've always been. They don't change very quickly around here," Rick said.

The conversation drifted in and out of the past, the present, and the future. They brushed into music and politics and their jobs and the general state of the world. There was no rush to get to business. They had time. Eventually, though, the subject drifted to Ochsenburg and then to the terrorists.

"Have you talked with Simon yet? Maybe he's picked up something at the consulate that could help," Rick asked.

"I tried calling from the Frankfurt train station but he wasn't there. I'll probably give him a call tomorrow. In the meantime, what can you tell me about these explosives."

"Well, like I said on the phone, they're nukes. But they're low yield, designed to blow bridges, rail lines, river fords,

[37]

anything like that where denying the enemy access is considered important. But that's low yield by today's standards. I mean, they're not the really big monsters you're going to find on a B-1 or a B-52, but they'll do enough damage. If they set even one of those off, Ochsenburg will be a memory. Fallout could be a pretty big problem, depending on the weather, of course. Still, all together they won't cause near the trouble one Pershing missile would. Oh, yeah, and they're portable. You can put them in a big harness-type backpack and carry them to wherever you want to put them."

"You mean they could take them with them?"

"Sure. The whole point of those things is to move 'em in quickly and touch 'em off. Here let me show you."

Rick fetched a piece of paper and pencil from another room and began sketching. "They're called Special Atomic Demolition Munition or SADMs for short," Rick explained while he sketched. "The thing's contained in a cylinder-shaped metal box probably about the size of two jerry cans, you know, those five-gallon fuel cans. There are handles to make it easier to carry.

"From the outside it looks sort of like a rounded, olive drab suitcase. But open it up and it gets interesting. When you pop the top there's this dome made of titanium. Real shiny. Just under the dome are a bunch of wires and fuses and batteries. Exactly what you'd expect a bomb to look like. Under that is the atomic core."

"How easy are these things to set off?"

"Not very. No, that's not true. Actually, they're really easy to touch off. Just like blowing up a stick of dynamite. But before you can set it off, you have to have special codes and keys that are kept in a safe over at the engineers' headquarters."

"Suppose you have all that stuff, how do you set 'em off?"

"Once you arm them, you can use a timer or a remote, it doesn't really matter." Rick dropped his pencil and smiled at Cane. "So, there, now you know more about those damned weapons than you probably ever cared to know."

"Thanks, this has been really helpful. But you know, Rick, one thing keeps bugging me. I've been asking myself this since I saw the first news flash. Why Ochsenburg? Why the hell did they pick on this out-of-the-way spot? Why not someplace closer to a big city? We must have stuff stored near Frankfurt or Munich or someplace a hell of a lot bigger than Ochsenburg that would make a better target. You know, increase the threat."

"Yeah, I know. And I sure as hell don't have an answer. But to tell you the truth, I think you're asking the wrong question."

"Oh? And what should I be asking?"

"Why are they still in that bunker?"

"What do you mean?"

"Why didn't they just take one or two of those things and split?"

"It was probably a hell of a lot easier to get inside and make the threats from there. I mean wouldn't they have had a pretty hard time walking out with them?"

"No. That's my point. A few years ago we started getting really worried that terrorists would try something like this. So the base commander asked a Green Beret outfit out of Bad Tölz to make a mock run at the depot and find out how secure it was. Well, they came down and went through the drill, and when they were done, they said it would be pitifully easy to take.

"First, they'd wait until a comm check was completed then cut the land line. You know, the telephone back to the base. Then blow the guard towers and guard shack with rockets. Those guards at the site could easily be handled by a few pros, believe me. So, then they'd stick a bangalore torpedo under the wire fence. Blow themselves a big old hole in there, then run in and stick a satchel charge on the doors to the bunkers and blow' em. Hell, they could be in and out with the goodies before anybody had a chance to stop them."

"What about the quick reaction team?"

"Well, like I said, they could cut the telephone lines. But even if they did get the word there was trouble at the site, it probably wouldn't do much good. I mean, those guys are always on alert, right? Their weapons are always ready and they have ammo in the back of the guarded truck that's parked right in front of their barracks. They're ready to go. Sounds great. But they're in the barracks, in town, and the ammo dump's out in the woods. They're not going out there in BMWs. They're riding in the back of deuce-and-a-halfs. By the time they get there they'd find nothing but dead bodies and empty igloos."

"God damn. So why the hell didn't they beef up security?"

"Oh, they did. Some high-ranking senator or congressman was over here on an inspection trip, and when he heard about the Green Berets' report, he went ape. That led to this thing called the Long Range Security Program. We spent a bundle to upgrade places like this one all around Germany. New lights, new hardened guard buildings with gun ports to shoot out of, and new guard towers. Hell, they even put in some really fancy shit, like infrared lights and motion detectors inside the bunkers. They put vibration detectors on the outside fences and in the area between the two fences. All this stuff was wired to a central alarm console in the guard building. Boy, it was fancy. It was great. And it was just about useless.

"When the whole thing was done, the commander asked the Green Berets to come back again. All the fancy shit was noted and they were duly impressed. Impressed to the point that they said the first notification the site was under attack would come when they took the towers out with rockets, then blasted a hole in the fence. They weren't too worried about the hardened guard huts. They'd lay a machine gun on the exits and kill the first few folks who stuck their brave little heads out. They could avoid the guards still in the huts because vision from the gun ports was so poor. Then they'd blast the doors off the igloos with satchel charges, steal the explosives, and be gone. They figured the elapsed time from when the first rocket went off until they were driving away at fifteen minutes, tops."

"What happened to the Green Berets' second report?"

"What do you think? It got buried, of course. The army wasn't about to admit it had spent all that money and not gained much."

"So as far as just about everyone on the outside knows, it would make sense for them to stay in the bunker."

"Sure. But anyone with a little bit of military sense could take a look at the place and see it wouldn't be that tough to take."

"Which brings us back to your original question. If these

terrorists are as smart and well trained as I think they are, why didn't they just steal the weapons?"

"Exactly. Why the hell would they lock themselves up in the bunker with the explosives. What they've done is stupid. They've made themselves sitting ducks. I mean, hell, if you didn't care about saving any lives, you could just ring the whole damned place with tanks, allocate maybe five per bunker, and simultaneously blast a few rounds through the doors and the show's over."

"But you've got to make damned sure you get the guy inside that has his finger on the button, right?"

"You'd have to take the risk that they're bluffing. But I think its a safe bet they don't have the keys and codes."

"I see what you mean. It doesn't really make a lot of sense, does it?"

"Nope. I sure can't figure out what the hell they're doing in there."

SEVEN

Lieutenant Colonel Jerry Rizzo carefully studied the compound bordered by the two twelve-foot-high barbed wire fences again. The harsh perimeter lights carved the area into patches of stark white and looming black shadows. A spotlight focused on the front door of each igloo.

It was such an easy target to assault.

His men could literally stroll in through the two front gates, set a charge on the igloo doors, and within seconds be spraying the inside of the hut with automatic weapons fire.

Rizzo, a short fiercely competitive man whose highly polished jump boots always glistened, smiled as he looked at the target. It would be a piece of cake.

The terrorists had locked themselves inside a box with no windows to see what was happening around them and only the threat of the explosives to prevent a strike. And no one believed they had armed the nukes. No one believed they could. That required keys and codes they could never get. Still, he admired their bluff. It had scared a hell of a lot of people. But it hadn't worked, and in a few minutes they would all die because of their miscalculation.

From the mist-filled darkness of the forest, he scanned the area a last time. There was no change. His Delta Force team was ready. Their faces darkened, they huddled in the trees nearby, less than fifty yards from the first gate. Rizzo knew they wanted to go. The trip from Fort Bragg had taken only nine hours, but jet lag had begun to settle over them as they waited in the cold and wet outside the ammo dump. And the adrenaline high of an approaching operation had waned as they awaited final approval from the White House.

Finally, it had come, and now it was his mission.

Eight of them would go, divided into two groups. One would attack the hut nearest the edge of the compound. It was the one with the phone. They were sure the terrorists were there. One man would plant the charges on both doors. The others would rush in with the smoke and noise. Rizzo would lead the team into the igloos himself.

When he gave the last-minute instructions, his mouth was dry and he felt a bead of sweat run from his armpit to his waist. He had been through similar operations before, but it didn't seem to matter how many times he went through it. His stomach still tightened and he wanted to pee.

It was then the door to the Quonset hut banged open.

In the trees, the soldiers, thinking it was the exploding charge, didn't understand at first. Then, wiping the mist from their eyes they stared at the door. The snipers adjusted their focus yet again and tightened their ungloved fingers around the triggers. Rizzo whirled his binoculars at the igloo door. It hung open but nothing happened.

The Delta Force soldiers stared at the door and waited. No one was prepared for the possibility the terrorists might try to leave.

And then he was in the doorway. They hadn't seen him move, even those with scopes and binoculars, hadn't seen him. He simply appeared. Short and slender, he wore a dark blue sports coat with the collar turned up against the mist and a ski mask but no hat.

The order to hold fire passed quickly through the troops. But none of the soldiers dared relax. The threat of nuclear death was now visible. They stared at the doorway and realized anew that unseen men in the dark interior of the hut could kill them instantly. They would see a flash, and then die.

The man stepped from the door, and in an apparent gesture of nonbelligerance, raised his hands, as if under arrest, and then slowly lowered them again. Looking neither left nor right he advanced slowly, almost ponderously, across the mud toward the inside gate. His breath came in white puffs as he walked.

A young sniper was the first to see it. From his perch atop a small knoll to the right of the gate, he called softly to the lieutenant below him. "Sir, he's carrying something in his hand. It looks like a small package."

The man stopped in front of the gate and waited. None of the soldiers moved. The man continued to stand silently in front of the gate, a solitary black figure in the white glow of the ammunition site.

Rizzo was unsure what to do. He wasn't there to negotiate, he was there to retake the dump and kill all the sons-of-bitches inside.

The man continued to wait, as though expecting a bus to rumble out of the dark woods and disappear into the night. Finally, Rizzo stepped into the whispy edges of the ammo dump's light and walked slowly toward the gate to meet the terrorist. His steps were cautious lest he slip in the mud and accidently set off a chain reaction as the soldiers fired and the terrorists detonated the explosives.

"Stop," the man called when Rizzo was within ten feet of the gate.

"A message," he shouted and slowly drew his arm back and with a powerful throw lofted his package over the two fences. It landed with a splat in the mud at Rizzo's feet. Without another word, the man turned and just as slowly as he had approached, retreated into the hut. Rizzo watched, the heavy mist condensing in his hair and trickling into his eyes. Still, he did not move to pick up the package until the man had disappeared and the igloo door slammed shut again.

The men in Colonel Gill's office, some of whom had seen massacres and butchery firsthand in little wars the world ignored, looked at the photos and saw death. They looked at the pictures the way a victim stares down the barrel of a gun and knows there is little hope and little mercy in the world.

The photos were Polaroid snapshots slightly washed out from too much flash and from being shot just a bit too close, and they were obviously done by an amateur. But spaced neatly across the desk they cried "checkmate."

The pictures showed keys being inserted into locks, and codes being punched onto numbered buttons. They showed the arming of the nuclear explosives. And, lest anyone miss the point, there was a closeup of Major Henry, blindfolded, with a pistol at his temple.

Mathew Burt, the United States's chief negotiator, was staring so intently at the pictures he didn't hear the phone ring.

"Burt, the phone," prompted one of the men from the State Department.

Abul's voice on the other end was clear, cold, and seemed to hold a hint of amusement. And in that moment Burt hated him. It was an emotion he knew he couldn't afford. He had to maintain his sense of balance, to remain calm. But the man who called himself Abul was no longer a disembodied voice, a professional challenge. He was a man with a nuclear bomb and no moral compunction about using it.

"Did you get the package?"

"Yes."

"Our demands are real. If they are not met, we will explode the bombs. Do you understand?"

"Yes."

Silence. The connection wasn't severed. But only by not speaking could Mathew Burt control his anger. He waited. And finally, Abul spoke.

"What does your President say?"

"He is doing everything he can. It's not easy. The Germans must be convinced to let Hamid al Hamani go. We hope to have an answer soon."

"The time approaches."

"Yes, I know. We're doing . . ." but it was useless, the line was broken.

[46]

EIGHT

Cane had legwork to do. And if he did it right, he could get a scoop.

He had managed only about five hours sleep on Rick's futon, but despite the short night, he was enthusiastic. The morning briefing was still more than an hour away and that would give him the time he needed.

Two miles outside Ochsenburg he turned off the main highway onto a narrow, hard-packed dirt road that cut across a field toward the woods. It ended abruptly in front of a long, low wooden building: the German-American shooting club. It was shuttered tight.

He knew the club and the nearby camping sites well from his days in Ochsenburg. It was part of Ochsenburg's Outdoor Recreation Area, or ORA in army lingo; facilities used mostly by GI families cruising the autobahns across Germany from one safely familiar American campsite to another.

While living in Ochsenburg, Cane had hiked extensively in these woods, and he remembered a particular clearing just off one specific trail. From there he could get an unobstructed view of the ammo dump. He would refresh his memory with a quick walk and be back in time for the briefing. He could combine a description of the area and the activity around it with what Rick had told him to write a story full of details and a sense of authority other reporters lacked. Eat your hearts out, he crowed silently.

It took a few minutes to orient himself, but as he walked into the forest the sights of the woods began triggering memories.

He ignored the warning signs written in English and German, ducked under a single sagging strand of barbed wire and pushed on, already thinking of how he could use his eyewitness account. If he remembered correctly he was only a few yards from the trail that led to the clearing. Yes, there was the path just ahead.

"Halt."

Cane froze, his heartbeat accelerated and his muscles tightened. At first no one was visible. Then, a German Army officer stepped carefully onto the path about ten yards in front of him.

The officer was a tall, lean man, clean shaven and bareheaded. His dark brown hair was closely cropped. His eyes didn't move from Cane as he slowly advanced along the path. Cane returned the stare but was aware of movement in the woods. There were probably a dozen or more soldiers just waiting for him to do something stupid.

The German stopped less than three feet away and stared, unsmiling. "You are American," he said in heavily accented English. It was not a question.

Cane knew he had done nothing wrong. He knew that he was just a journalist, not a terrorist, that he was perfectly innocent, that he could prove who he was and that he could easily explain why he was there. But it didn't matter. He looked into the stone face of the officer and was frightened.

"I'm, ah, a journalist. I'm here covering the incident." Cane deliberately spoke English. The officer continued to stare at him and said nothing.

The words came with a rush. He felt stupid, but as the German officer remained silent Cane felt a need to fill the void and couldn't control his mouth.

"My name's Jonathan Cane, you can check with the public affairs office. I covered the briefing last night. I'm staying at the Engel, you can check that too. Call Sergeant Green at the public affairs office at Boelke Kaserne, he knows me. I talked with him yesterday. Just check."

"You have identification?" The voice was cold and formal.

"My passport. It's in my pocket." The German nodded, and Cane carefully pulled the thin, square, blue book from his breast pocket and handed it over. The man studied it, looking closely at the picture and then at Cane and back at the picture again. He turned it over, examining the stitching and rubbing the pages between his fingers to test the paper's quality. He turned and called to a young soldier, who scurried up to him. The officer handed him the passport and delivered orders in German that was too rapid for Cane's unpracticed ear.

The aide disappeared into the woods with the passport and the officer turned again to Cane.

"Why are you here in the *Wald*" he asked, using the German word for forest. His manner was demanding but no longer threatening, and Cane began to relax. Besides, he reassured himself, he had done nothing wrong, he need not be frightened.

"I came to get a look at the ammo dump. I knew I could see it from here. I used to work for the American newspaper the *Stars and Stripes*, and I lived in Ochsenburg. I know the area because I used to hike out here. I thought it would help me write a better story. You know, to get a look at the ammunition depot. Hey, I'm not a spy or anything, I'm just trying to do my job."

"This is a restricted area. Why did you enter?"

"This has always been a restricted area, and everyone always hikes through here. Look, I probably should have figured that there would be soldiers around here, but it just didn't occur to me. I'm sorry. It was probably a stupid idea. But I didn't really do anything wrong. I'm just trying to do my job."

The officer stared at him as if weighing his next move, and Cane, feeling a measure of control, returned the stare. This time he didn't feel the need to fill the silence with conversation. It angered him that he had done so earlier. It was a good device, one he used all the time. Just keep quiet, let the person being interviewed do the talking. They'll just keep talking until finally they blurt out that nugget of gold; the quote that makes the story. Now the longer he remained quiet, the better he felt.

The aide returned, scurrying to the officer's side and handed him Cane's the passport. Again the rapid-fire German. Cane caught the occasional "okay" and "ya" but was lost beyond that. Still, the officer kept the passport, and that was a good sign. He looked at it again, as if weighing it, and then handed it back to Cane.

"You may go. This is a restricted area, do not return."

Cane took the passport and for the first time looked around him. He knew there were soldiers hidden in the brush watching him, but he could pick out only two who had abandoned their efforts at camouflage to watch.

He forced himself to walk to his car without running. He opened the door as if it were trip wired, and when he sat behind the wheel he realized he had been holding his breath, and exhaled deeply.

He drove slowly away from the shooting club still thinking of all the things he should have said and the way he should have acted, feeling vaguely guilty for having trespassed. But it didn't really matter, he told himself. They had let him go and nothing had come of it.

Only later would he realize how incredibly wrong he had been.

NINE

Almost every seat in the auditorium was taken. As the terrorists' deadline approached more television crews had arrived. More photographers and more reporters swirled through the lobby and into the high-ceiling theater. The place was beginning to take on the zoo atmosphere of big media events: hundreds of reporters, jumbles of languages, multitudes of translators, and no one quite sure who was in charge.

Just after the official starting time, Porter Caldwell, the embassy's public relations man, again led the military procession to the stage.

"Ladies and gentlemen, I wish I had some news for you this morning, but the situation remains unchanged from last night. The terrorists continue to demand the release of Hamid al Hamani. The United States government is continuing its negotiations with the terrorists and remains in constant contact with the government in Bonn. There are no new developments to report. Now, are there any questions?"

A reporter from *Stern* was the first to his feet. "Is it true units from the German border patrol have been deployed around the ammunition site. And if so, why?"

Lieutenant Colonel Anderson fielded the question. "We don't comment on our military decisions involving the deployment of either our forces or the forces of Federal Republic of Germany."

"However," Caldwell added, "you can be sure that German authorities, both civilian and military, have been involved in every phase of the situation here."

The reporters pressed on.

"Will Hamid al Hamani be released?" That was a decision for the Germans.

"What will happen if Germany refuses to release him?" That was a decision for the terrorists.

"Is the United States considering using force to retake the ammunition dump?" Absolutely not.

And so the dance went for almost an hour. Finally, it wound to an end, and reporters began heading for the phones to dictate, to their hotels to write, or to the streets in search of interviews with "average residents."

Cane waited until the crush of reporters had thinned before moving up the aisle toward the lobby. As he approached the door he spotted Rolf sitting alone in the back row.

He plopped down in the seat next to him. The poorly upholstered plastic cover creaked under his weight. Neither man offered a greeting and they sat in silence until the last of the reporters disappeared through the door.

"They're lying, you know." Rolf finally broke the ice.

"Yeah, I know. I had a run-in with some of Germany's finest before coming here. I went out there figuring I could get a look at the ammo dump. You know the woods out by the Outdoor Rec Area? They run right to where they keep those explosives. I figured I'd get a good look and maybe pick up a little color for my story. Only I didn't make it. I got stopped by some German officer. Told me to go away and never darken his woods again."

"Not about the border patrol. About their plans to storm the place."

Even without looking at him, Cane knew Rolf was smiling. And he knew it was the cat's aw-shucks-I-didn't-see-no-canary grin.

"Oh? You been hearing from Jurgen again? By the way, Rolf, just how do you say 'Deep Throat' in German?"

He meant the remark as a jab even though he was sure Rolf had no idea who Deep Throat was. But Rolf's superior German attitude rankled him, particularly in light of his own failed attempt at getting an edge on the competition. And, although he wouldn't admit it, Cane was jealous. Rolf was the one breaking probably the hottest story Cane would ever work. Rolf ignored the remark.

"I was late, but I heard the question about using force to end the seige. What lies. I was late because I was writing a story saying the American Army wanted to shoot its way into the storage area. The only reason they didn't was because the terrorists showed them pictures of themselves arming the bombs."

Rolf glanced at his watch before continuing. "The paper will be out in less than an hour. Then they'll have to eat their lies."

"Jesus, Rolf, are you sure?"

"Yes."

"Well listen, Rolf, I've got to file a story. I'll catch you later. Hey, maybe we can get together later for a beer."

He took the theater's steps two at a time and trotted across the parade ground toward the community headquarters building. It was a square, brick box housing the people whose job it was to make the military base a community: officers and NCOs who worked diligently promoting youth programs and movie theaters and libraries and recreation centers in the vague hope the Americans would believe they were really only three heel clicks away from Kansas instead of plunked down in the middle of Europe.

Cane began to fade as he climbed the final steps to the third floor. He rested to catch his breath before walking into the long attic room that served as the public affairs office. Porter Caldwell sat on the edge of a desk talking with a major Cane recognized from the press conference.

Caldwell rose and stuck out his hand as Cane walked in. "Cane, isn't it? You caught me after the first conference and asked about the family, right?"

"Yeah. By the way how are Mar . . . Mrs. Henry and the kids? How are they doing?"

"Fine, just fine."

"How about an interview with them? It could make a great story. You know, strong wife and family refuse to leave until the loved one is freed. A lot of people are just as concerned about Mrs. Henry as they are about the major." It was a crazy idea, and he figured they wouldn't go for it, but what the hell. Nothing ventured . . .

"No, that's not really possible yet. But I'll put your request in later."

Caldwell's answer was smooth. He was good, Cane thought. Very good. Right down to remembering his name.

"Say, I just had one follow-up question about something that came up in the conference."

"Oh, what's that?"

"You said there have been no attempts to retake the storage site by force and no such efforts were being planned."

"That's right."

"Well, I was wondering why the Ochsenburg *Tagesblatt* is reporting that a raid was set to begin and was only called off because the terrorists showed you pictures of themselves arming the nuclear explosives? I mean, the *Tagesblatt* has had everything else right so far. It just makes me wonder."

From the corner of his eye, Cane saw the major stiffen, and he knew the question had startled Caldwell, but the PR pro didn't miss a beat.

"Of course I can't comment on the story you're talking about because I haven't seen it. When was it in the paper?"

"It's on the street now. First afternoon edition."

"Well, I can assure you no force has been used in an effort to retake the storage site. I can guarantee you that." Caldwell's answer came easily and sincerely. But, Cane noticed, he hadn't responded to the question.

"Well, does that mean you're denying the story?"

"I can't respond to something I haven't seen."

Cane looked at the nattily dressed man with the light switch smile and thought again of being turned away by the German officer in the woods. Suddenly he didn't feel like dancing anymore.

"Was a raid planned?"

"We don't comment on military matters." It was the major who answered.

Cane ignored him and kept his eyes on Caldwell. "Did the terrorists give the army pictures of the nuclear weapons being armed?"

"I am afraid I'm not authorized to make any statements about the negotiations process and what information passes between the negotiators and the people who seized the site."

Cane smiled then. "Okay. But, I'll tell you something. You're going to hear these questions again, and it would be a good idea to get some answers ready because I'm only the first one in here. You're going to be hearing from every reporter that's here. And the answers you just gave me will tell everyone that a reporter for the *Tagesblatt* knows more about what's going on here than you do. That's not going to do your credibility much good now, is it?

"Look," Cane softened his tone as he went on. "You know you're going to have a hard time with the German press and some of the other people that are here. I know it's tough. Hell, I used to work at the *Stars and Stripes*, I know your job isn't easy. But you're probably going to get fairer treatment from me than just about anybody else around here. So, why not just tell me what the hell is going on."

"Thank you for coming by, Mr. Cane, and letting us know about the story. We'll keep you posted." Caldwell's cold statement was meant as a dismissal.

"You can at least confirm or deny the *Tagesblatt* story, can't you?"

"We can't comment on the story until after we've seen it. We'll keep you posted along with the rest of the media."

"Okay, have it your way."

Cane descended the stairs slowly. He'd given it his best shot, he knew. They hadn't bought it, but at least he'd tried. And the funny thing about it was, he was serious. He probably would have given those assholes on the third floor better treatment than they would get elsewhere.

"Fuck 'em," he said as he walked through the heavy door to the outside. "I can get this stuff myself."

About fifty yards away, another brick building, this one long and rectangular, stretched along the edge of the post. Among the other offices it held was a German post office where the Americans could send letters through the international mail, pay their phone bills, and make overseas calls all with the assurance that the person behind the counter spoke English.

When Cane entered, the office was empty, except for the

young man behind the counter reading a novel. In the years he had lived in Ochsenburg, Cane had never seen the office empty.

"Things look a little slow today," he offered.

"Not a lot of Americans left in Ochsenburg. Maybe those that are still here don't make long-distance calls."

"I need to call Frankfurt."

The young man handed him a form and Cane quickly wrote the number and handed it back.

"Booth number one," the man said.

He turned and saw a row of three solid-walled, well-worn booths. In each a gray phone hung on the wall above a small shelf. There was no place to deposit money and there were no phone books.

Inside the booth he leaned against the wall made of rough particle board and waited. A moment later the phone rang, and as he picked it up he heard the click at the other end as his call was answered.

"American Consulate."

"Simon North, in the communications room please."

"Just a moment."

He was on hold for nearly a minute before a familiar voice answered.

"Hello, communications room."

"Hi, I'm trying to reach Simon North."

"Simon's not here at the moment. I expect him back in about an hour. Can I take a message?"

"Yes, would you tell him that Jonathan Cane called again. And ask him to call me. I'm staying at the Engel."

"Ah, Mr. Cane. This is Sergeant Winters. We spoke yesterday, I believe. How are things going over there. You learn anything interesting?"

"Oh, I've picked up a few tidbits. Look, I've got to go. Just tell Simon I called, okay?"

"Sure, no problem. Do you have the number at the Engel?"

"No, not with me. But I'm sure information has it."

As Cane paid his bill, he thought of his conversation with Sergeant Winters. With his first couple sentences, Cane had detected a very slight German accent. Yet he spoke as if English were his native language.

In all his years in Germany, Cane had met only one or two

Germans who had erased all traces of an accent. No matter how hard they worked at it, the accent, like a faded stain on linen, was always there. It made him wonder about Sergeant Winters. Was he American or German? It probably didn't matter, but Cane was curious and he made a mental note. Ask Simon about the sergeant in the communications room.

TEN

Cane sat on the edge of his bed, looked at his notes jumbled across the blanket in front of him, and considered again the story he had just dictated.

On the other end of the line, his editor, Eddie Slovak, was saying, "Hey, that description of the bomb, about it being portable and all that, is great. Good work, Cane. But now listen, goddamn it, be careful. If anyone is going to get blown up over there, let it be the AP man. That's what we pay them for."

"Don't worry, Slovak. I'll be careful."

"And Cane . . . "

"What?"

"See if you can get us some more stuff like this. Something everybody and their sister doesn't have. Find a different angle. The wires are full of stories about this place and it's all shit. Get some more good stuff for us. Okay?"

It was Slovak at his best, Cane thought as he hung up the phone. An arm around your shoulder to comfort you and a knife at your back to keep you moving.

And Cane knew he was right. The story was too good for average reporting. But, damn. He'd used everything Rick had given him, except the stuff about how easy a target the ammo dump was. As much as he believed Rick on that, he needed to confirm it, somehow. Still, after his run-in with Caldwell he was determined to try even harder, to find something that would make them wish Jonathan Cane hadn't left LA.

He picked up the phone again from the bedside table and dialed.

"Simon North."

"Hello, Simon, it's Cane."

"Hi, Cane. How are you? Hey, I got your messages. What the hell are you doing in Ochsenburg? I thought you were in love with LA."

"I am, but this is too big a story to pass up. But, hell, I didn't call to talk business."

"Bullshit."

"Yeah, well, maybe a little. But we can talk later. How about getting together for dinner?"

"I'd love it."

"Do you dare to venture into Ochsenburg, or should I come to Frankfurt?"

"You're at the Engel. The old sisters still running the place?"

"Yup."

"What the hell, I'll come there. I always liked living dangerously. I used to hang out with you and Rick, didn't I?"

It was true. Simon had been a charter member of the Fast Track Patrol, the group of expatriate teachers, stereo salesmen, ex-GIs, and journalists who had clustered together in Ochsenburg and made their own fun as they made their way in the world.

Simon had come to Ochsenburg as a draftee back in the days when young men's lives were still being decided by a someone they had never met pulling little numbered balls out of a bowl on the other side of the country.

He had been trained as an 11 Bravo, a rifle-toting grunt. The GIs called them eleven bullet stoppers. But within days of arriving, his commander discovered he could type. He was transferred to company headquarters and spent the next two years filling out forms.

When he decided to stay in Germany for a year or two following his hitch, his secretarial skills gave him the edge he needed. He landed a job in the American consulate in Frankfurt processing forms in the visa section. He had been promoted once or twice and gave no indication he planned to leave.

Cane grabbed his watch, wallet, and key from the nightstand, flicked off the light, and headed downstairs for an early evening beer. The dining room at the foot of the stairs was as silent, cold, and dim as a cave, the square tables and heavy, carved chairs little more than outlines in the darkness.

The adjoining bar, though, was living room warm. Hildigard stood on a stool dusting the tankards on a shelf that ringed the room high above the age-darkened wainscoting. Margaret was polishing the ornate brass spigots. Cane stood at the edge of the light for a moment and watched his friends lovingly preserve the orderly ambience of their home.

"Ah, Herr Cane," Margaret said as she paused for a moment. "A friend of yours called a few minutes ago. Your phone was busy, so I took a message. A Miss Darling. She said she would call back later."

"Thanks, I'll go give her a call. Will you draw me the beer, please?"

Margaret simply smiled as her hand moved to the tap.

Cane hustled up the stairs to his room, dialed quickly, and then cursed silently as the phone rang several times. Finally, though, she answered.

"Hi, Barbara, it's Cane. I got a message you called. What's up?"

"I saw her this afternoon," Barbara said. "It wasn't easy. They're keeping her under pretty tight wraps. But she's fine. I told you she's a tough lady. She's still shaken up some and she's really worried about Woody."

"Probably afraid they'll let him go."

"Cane!"

"Okay, okay. I know. He is her husband and all, but . . . well, did you tell her I was here?"

"Yes. She was pretty surprised. But she doesn't want to see you. No, actually that's not true. She wants to see you, but I don't think she can handle it, not on top of everything else that's happened."

"Is that what she said?"

"No. She just said to wait until it's over. Maybe she can see you then. But Cane, are you sure this is wise?"

"No, I'm not sure about much of anything. I mean what am I supposed to feel? Am I supposed to hope a bunch of terrorists blow up a nuclear bomb because they'll take that son-of-a-bitch husband of hers with them? Or do I hope he'll get out all right and become some kind of national hero. 'Interview with Major Woodrow Henry, film at eleven.' I can see it now. Tell me, just how the hell am I supposed to look at this?"

"The same way you did the last time you saw her."

"Yeah, well that sucks."

"You're right it does. But if you still care about her, you won't see her until this thing is over."

"Okay. As soon as this is over I'm planning to take a few days vacation anyway and I'd just as soon stay here if there's a chance I can see her."

"I'll let her know you're going to stay."

"Thanks, Barbara. Hey, Barb, why the hell are you still here?"

"The military insists there's no danger, so if there's no danger, the families should stay here. And if the families are still here, then the kids need to be in school. And if the kids are going to go to school, there have to be teachers, right?"

"Sounds like military logic all right. Tell me, you have any students?"

"Three. Everyone who could leave has. It's a joke."

"So why don't they just close the school and let you all get the hell out of here too?"

"You're a big boy now, use your head, man. If they close the school, they're saying the families shouldn't stay, and they'll be admitting there's a danger."

"But that's absurd."

"Cane, you've been in the States too long."

His conversation with Barbara depressed him. He walked slowly back down the steps to the bar, where he gulped his beer and ordered another. He had come as close to admitting his real feelings to Barbara as he had to himself. He knew rationally there was no chance his relationship with Maria could ever be the way it was. And he didn't really want them to kill her husband, the father of her children. But more than once since Margarget and Hildi had first shown him the newspaper he had wondered what would happen if . . . what would she do if . . . what if . . . well, they killed him?

Would she turn to him? Would she need him? Could they resume their relationship? They were ridiculous, even ghoulish thoughts, but Cane didn't mind thinking them because he couldn't help feeling part of the blame for Maria's pain belonged to Woody.

If he hadn't returned to Ochsenburg it would have been some other major locked away in the Quonset hut with his ass strapped to a nuclear bomb. And they—she—would have been in Hawaii.

Cane was swirling the last sips of beer in the glass, watching the trail the foam left on the sides, when he heard the heavy front door open.

"Hey, Simon. God it's good to see you," he said enthusiastically, rising to embrace him. Simon's timing was perfect. At that moment Cane needed to see an old and trusted friend.

"Sorry I'm late, I had a little trouble remembering exactly which way to turn a couple of times. But sure didn't have any trouble with traffic. I've never seen this city so empty. I didn't even see any taxis."

"I know. The whole town is just about deserted. Don't apologize for the time, it's no problem. I'm just glad to see you again. How are you?"

"Fine, fine. How long has it been, Cane?"

"Jesus, I don't know. Three years, maybe four."

Cane looked at his friend. He was tall and thin, with thick glasses and long black hair that curled around his ears and over his collar. As always, he was dressed in a dark suit, white shirt, conservative tie, and wore black loafers, giving him the look of a Mormon missionary gone to seed.

"When did you get to Germany?" Simon asked as they sat again at the table. "I got both messages from Winters, but he didn't put the time or date on them."

"Yesterday. As soon as the AP moved the first story I was on my way. For once I didn't have to fight to get something approved. Slovak, my editor, said he'd take care of all the details later. Anyway, I tried to call you from the Frankfurt train station on my way here but the guy I talked with said you were gone."

"Yeah, I had yesterday off. Ute and I went hiking in the Taunus. The consulate's a madhouse. There's message traffic flowing in and out like it's the second coming. They were really pissed I was gone. Damn, it was the first day I'd had off in two weeks. Hell, if I'd known what the hell was going on, I'd have gone in."

"Well, you're not alone in feeling ill used. My editor keeps pushing me for more and more, I'm still trying to figure this mess out, and I've already been here a day."

"Well, I don't think I can help you out much on that front."

"Let's talk business later. First I want to know about Ute. Are you ever going to marry her?"

Simon had met Ute, a beautiful German woman, when he first went to work at the consulate, where she was a filing clerk in the personnel division. They had been living together for years, but they never seemed to talk marriage.

"Oh, I don't know. No sense rushing into things, you know," he said with a laugh, realizing how silly his answer was. "I don't know, sometimes I think I should just go home and find a nice American girl. Sometimes she's just so German I can't stand it. I mean, take the mixer for example."

"The mixer?"

"Yeah, the mixer. You know, the electric mixer. Bought it a couple of years ago at the PX. It's still in the original box. Every time she uses it she gets it down, takes it out of the box, uses it, and then washes it, dries it, puts it back, every piece in its place and then puts the box back in the cupboard. I mean is that German or what?"

"Hey, Simon, I'm no expert on marriage or living with anyone, but frankly if that's the worst thing you can think of to complain about, you'll get no sympathy from me."

Before Simon could respond, Margaret approached, bearing two beers. She set the glasses down and retreated quickly, leaving the two old friends alone.

"So, what's it like covering a big story in your old stamping ground?" Simon asked.

"Well, frankly I thought it would be a lot more fun. So far just knowing the layout of the place hasn't really helped me much. I tried to get a look at the ammo site from the woods in back of the ORA, but got stopped by some German officer. I was kind of hoping you might be able to help me out a bit. Anything happening at the consulate you can tell me about?"

[64]

"Like I said, it's a madhouse."

"I'll bet. But what's the feeling there? They know anything about these terrorists?"

"Cane, do you know what I do at the consulate?"

The question came as a surprise. "Well, I know you have something to do with communications, but I'm not really sure what."

"I'm in charge of the communications room. It's staffed by specialists the service sends over from Washington. I'm just supposed to make sure it runs smoothly, make sure they have enough paper and pens and there's always someone on duty. And I help out whenever they're shorthanded, which is most of the time.

"Anyway, every bit of information that comes into or goes out of the consulate is channeled through that room. You know it's ridiculous, I'm in charge of that office and I know more about running all that sophisticated technology they have than anyone and I'm making about nine bucks an hour and I get to shop in the PX. Millions of dollars' worth of equipment and a motherlode of information that some people would give anything to have, and they're not willing to pay more than nine bucks an hour for someone to keep the place running. Nine bucks, an ID card, and a load of shit if you take a day off at the wrong time. You know it's just plain crazy." He fell silent for a moment, as if weighing whether to continue.

Cane, unsure what to say, remained silent. It was obvious Simon was about to tell him something, and it made Cane uneasy. He desperately wanted to break a story or do a better job than the boys from the really big papers. But at the same time he didn't want to use his friendship to do it. He suddenly wondered exactly what price he was willing to pay to get a good story.

He was harder than he used to be, Cane knew. There had been a time he would have felt strange about interviewing a family whose house had just been destroyed by a fire or talking to the friends of a young murder victim. He would have felt like an intruder. No more. He had learned to be tough. But this was different. Simon was a friend. Maybe, Cane thought, the price was going up, or he just wasn't as willing to pay it anymore. There would be other stories, but old friends like Simon were hard to find.

"Hey, look man, if this is going to cause you any grief, don't worry about it," Cane said. "The way I see it, there's not really much subtlety to this anyway. A bunch of terrorists grab some nuclear weapons and blackmail the world. It's your basic good guys and bad guys. I don't know what it says about the military that it takes a bunch of terrorists to make them the good guys, but what the hell, don't worry about it."

He meant his comment to lighten the mood and give his old friend a graceful way out. But when Simon remained silent, Cane sipped his beer and waited. His friend stared at the table for several moments. Then he looked up.

"I think somebody knew in advance there was a possibility that terrorists were going to do something."

"What do you mean? They knew and they didn't do anything? How could that be?"

"You know, even with all the computers we have and all the electronics gear and all that shit, they still manage to screw up sometimes."

"Who is 'they'? Simon, what the hell are you talking about?"

"I don't know. Sometimes we get messages into the consulate that aren't supposed to be coming to us. You know, maybe somebody typed in the wrong access code or something. Usually it's pretty mundane stuff, like some embassy someplace ordering in supplies or something, or a message for the ambassador that ends up in Frankfurt instead of Bonn. Some of the stuff is in code, most of it isn't, and we'll just let the sender know he messed up and then put the telex or fax or whatever into the shredder.

"Well, not long ago, I was working late at night, filling in for someone. I was putting the finishing touches on a few things and we got a message for somebody—you know everybody that's in the loop has a code, like an ID number. Well, this thing was from someplace or somebody with a code number I'd never heard of and it was going to someplace I'd never heard of either. So, I tried sending back a message saying that it ended up in the wrong place, but it didn't go through. So I figure someone just screwed up and I take it and drop it in the shredder. But just before it disappears I could swear I saw the word *Ochsenburg*. You know how you'll glance at a newspaper or something and a word just hits you, but if you want to find that word again, you've got to read the whole page. Well that's the way it was with this. Only by then the whole damned thing had disappeared into the shredder. But somebody was talking about O'burg.

"So now I'm curious, I don't know, probably because I used to live here. I didn't really think much about it at first. I thought it was probably a drill or something. But, I know, or at least I thought I knew, all the destination codes for Ochsenburg. And this message wasn't going to Ochsenburg. So, I really don't know why, but I wrote down the code, or at least what I thought was the code for where the message was supposed to be going and I tried to find it in the files. I couldn't find it. It was like this message was coming out of nowhere and going nowhere. I figured it was probably from some branch of army intelligence or the CIA that I had never heard of. Hell, I don't know. But I knew they were talking about Ochsenburg.

"Then a month or two later the big shredder upstairs was broken and all the routine shredding was sent down to the comm room to be put through our little one. And I'm standing there sticking this shit into the shredder and I see a message with the same codes on it. It's on paper from a computer printer, the type you hook up to a PC. So the original message *was* meant for someone at the consulate, but I don't know who. And it looks like sometime after I saw the first message they decided to set up their own communications network. The message was in code, but I understood one thing, Major Henry's ID number."

"What?" Cane was struggling to understand what he was hearing. "How the hell do you know his ID number?" he asked.

"I was a clerk-typist for Major Henry for a while. I probably typed that damned number a thousand times. The same people were talking about him that were talking about Ochsenburg. It's probably nothing at all, you know. But I wonder, Why the hell would they be sending messages about him to the consulate? And who the hell are 'they,' they got no code numbers I've ever seen."

"So, you think someone knew in advance and decided not to do anything about it? But why the hell would they do that?"

"Jesus, Cane, I don't know. Interdepartmental jealousies, or they didn't believe their sources, or maybe they just didn't want to give away the fact they had someone that deep under cover. Hell, maybe Hamid al Hamani's an American spy. Or maybe they just ignored it, and now they're afraid to admit they knew. I don't know. You know I could be wrong, this whole damned thing could just be coincidence. I might have even gotten the destination codes wrong."

"But, you don't really think so, do you?"

"I don't know, Cane, I just don't know."

The two old friends stared at the table in silence, the weight of Simon's disclosure between them.

"Well, what are you going to do now?" Simon finally asked.

"I don't know. Try to get some more information, I guess. Get some confirmation somehow. I won't mention you, that's for sure. You don't have to worry about that."

"You don't reveal your sources, right?" Simon asked in an amused tone.

"Don't worry, Simon. No one's going to know I talked to you. Besides, who gives a shit about another nosy reporter? There must be at least a couple of hundred here already trying to find out whatever they can. And with all that's going on, how much attention do you think they're going to pay to me?"

ELEVEN

The President of the United States lay the report on his lap and let his half glasses, held by a brown cord around his neck, fall to his chest. He peered at the man sitting in the high-backed chair across the room.

"Do you know what you're saying here?" the President asked.

"Yes, sir, I do."

"There are no alternatives?"

"Mr. President, I don't know that it matters," the national security advisor answered from across the thickly carpeted room. Less than an hour before, the President had left the Oval Office for a rest. It had been brief. Now the President sat in a rocking chair, dressed in blue jeans, a sweater, and loafers without socks, looking once again at the papers in front of him.

"We've talked to the base commander in Ochsenburg, experts on the SADMs, and we even talked with the engineers that built the damned ammo dump in the first place. They all agree that now that they know how to arm those explosives, we have few options: the most extreme of which is to blow up the whole damned place and hope we kill them all. We've been assured the explosion itself won't set 'em off."

"And what happens if we don't kill them? What happens if they're all dead except the guy with his finger on the trigger, or if they've got the damned thing set on a timer and it's suddenly buried under a couple of tons of concrete and steel? And do we just kill the major too? What the hell kind of signal does that send to our men in uniform?"

"I'll admit there are problems with the plan. The only alternative seems to be to bargain with them."

"Shit, I hate this," the President said as he pounded his fist on the rocker's edge. "What do the Germans say?"

"We really haven't discussed it with them."

"Have they said anything about freeing al Hamani?"

"No, sir."

"Well, hell, we know what their position is going to be anyway. They've caved in before and I can tell you they're not about to hang too tough this time, not when the bomb's in their own backyard. It's only a matter of time until they tell us they've decided to let the bastard go and ask us to agree. But Jesus, I hate to knuckle under to terrorists."

The two men sat silently, knowing they could plan, scheme, and argue, but the terrorists' photos had already written an end to the game. Finally, the President's security advisor broke the silence.

"We'll have clear shots at them when they leave the building. Should we try to stop them then?"

"No. They may have the damned things on remote. But if it looks like they're trying to take those bombs with them, we'll have no choice. We'll have to stop them. Otherwise, we keep our part of the bargain."

"Yes, sir," the advisor said and rose to leave. He stopped as an Air Force officer in a crisp uniform walked into the room and handed the President a message.

"Thank you," the President said. He waited until the messenger had closed the door before opening it. "The Germans have agreed to free al Hamani," he said. He was silent for a moment, then in a low, slow voice edged with sadness he said, "Okay, tell Burt to tell the terrorists that we've agreed to meet their demands, but it'll take a while to make the arrangements."

TWELVE

It ended as quickly as it had began. Minutes after Germany agreed to set Hamid al Hamani free, the President of the United States made his decision. There would be no further attempt to retake the ammo dump.

The decision was quickly relayed to Ochsenburg, where the chief American negotiator picked up the telephone for the last time and told the terrorists they would get what they wanted.

Abul's instructions were immediate and direct.

"You will free Hamid al Hamani from prison and bring him here. He will enter the ammunition storage area alone. If anyone tries to accompany him, we will set off the explosives. After he is inside, you will lower the flag in front of Boelke Kaserne to half staff. Then a car will come. It will blink its lights three times before it turns off Ochsenburgerstrasse. You will not stop it. Once it is here we will drive away. If you try to stop us or follow us we will set off the nuclear explosives with remote detonators. The major will remain our hostage until we are safe."

Then the line went dead.

The Germans were ready to move. The moment the President told the chancellor of Germany of his decision, word was flashed to the prison. Hamid al Hamani, who had been held in solitary confinement since the crisis began, was hustled out of the prison under heavy guard and put aboard a waiting helicopter that had set down just outside the front gate. The clouds closed in and the first drops of rain fell as the helicopter lifted off.

Forty-five minutes later the chopper circled the Ochsen-burg military headquarters once and then descended through the growing clouds and gently set down on the base comman-der's helipad.

Mathew Burt stepped to the window of the headquarters building and watched as al Hamani, his hands manacled behind him, stepped uncertainly to the ground. He was a young man, perhaps thirty, thin, and still wearing his lightweight prison uniform. He appeared disoriented, and Burt thought he saw him shiver as he moved to the waiting U.S. military sedan.

The sedan followed a jeep filled with Special Forces sol-diers slowly out of the base onto the street, which led to the highway that led to the edge of Ochsenburg, where the woods began.

Hamani's handcuffs were removed at the ammunition storage area and he walked hesitantly through the gates into the compound; a man alone with infinite time. He was less than ten feet from the igloo when the door opened slightly, and a second later he disappeared into the hut's dark interior. The door shut quietly behind him.

Then the final wait began. For three hours there was nothing. No movement, no sign of a car on the highway. Then, as the day wore toward evening, a maroon Peugeot 604 turned onto Ochsenburgerstrasse in the heart of the city and headed for the city's outskirts.

As it reached the turnoff for the dirt road leading into the woods, the car slowed and stopped. The driver flashed the headlights three times, drove down the dirt road, and disap-peared into the woods.

In the forest, the barriers were swept from the car's path as it neared the ammunition depot. The once-solid curtain of soldiers melted into the woods at the sound of the approaching automobile, just as they had hours before when the procession bearing Hamid al Hamani had arrived.

The Peugeot moved slowly along the hard-packed road, steadily advancing to its rendezvous. But even before it ap-peared, the soldiers heard it. The growl of its low gears carried clearly through the damp afternoon, a whining signal that it was all about to end. And then it was there. The car slowed to a crawl as it reached the front gates and made a wide 360-

degree turn. Then, three quick blasts of the horn and the door of the hut banged open.

Five men all dressed in dark pants with dark hooded windbreakers walked out. None wore bulky sweaters or overcoats that could conceal a portable atomic bomb. The hoods of their sweatshirts were pulled tightly around their heads, which were bowed, making it impossible to see their faces.

The soldiers studied them as they walked, searching for a clue: which one of the five was the U.S. Army major? Which one was Hamid al Hamani? If they could just pick out the major, it would be easy to drop the other four. But they all knew they could do nothing. The orders had been clear. The terrorists were to leave unharmed.

The five advanced in a tight group to the Peugeot and climbed in. The last man pulled the door shut even as the car began moving. It turned at a bend in the woods and was gone.

High in the air, military helicopters tried to track the car, but it became increasingly difficult as the cloud cover thickened and hovered ever closer to the ground. The car was lost altogether when it turned off the main highway and disappeared into the woods less than five miles from Ochsenburg.

President Kandell made the announcement himself. While hundreds of the world's journalists crowded the base movie theater in Ochsenburg, Germany, a handful of newsmen were quickly assembling in the White House press room.

Television technicians were still adjusting their equipment when the President walked into the room, stood at the podium, and read from a prepared statement.

"Ladies and gentlemen, the seige in Ochsenburg, Germany, has ended. The nuclear explosives are again under the control of U.S. military forces. The terrorists have left the ammunition storage site under a guarantee of safe passage. Hamid al Hamani was released from prison as part of the agreement.

"I wish to thank the German government for all the help and support it has given us during this ordeal. I know that the world joins me in condemning terrorist acts such as those we have witnessed in the last forty-eight hours. I also want to thank German Chancellor Kohl for the strong support he and German military forces provided during this trying time.

"Let this awful incident remind us of the horrors of nuclear war and firm our resolve to take all possible steps to lessen the likelihood of such a war starting by accident or by design of a few fanatics.

"Thank you, ladies and gentlemen. Now if there are questions, the secretary of state will take them."

And with that the President turned and walked from the room.

For forty-five minutes the secretary ducked and sidestepped questions about the incident. No, the terrorists had not been captured. Yes, the U.S. Army major was safe. He had been released in a nearby village. He had been blindfolded the entire time, but no, he said he had not been mistreated. No, they were still not sure how the terrorists had gained access to the secure ammunition storage site. They hoped to know that after U.S. representatives had a chance to talk more with Major Henry. Details of the entire operation were still sketchy. More information would be provided as soon as it was available, the secretary assured the reporters.

In Ochsenburg, Porter Caldwell faced members of the world's media corps a last time and said almost nothing.

"I am not authorized to go beyond the announcement made by the President of the United States and the information provided by the secretary of state. I have been told to direct all further inquiries to the White House press office. All requests for interviews with officials, including Major Henry, will be handled by that office."

As the reporters shouted questions, Caldwell, eyes straight ahead, left the theater stage, walked up the aisle, and out the front door. The reporters were outraged but powerless. Washington was now in control.

The press center was dismantled. The tables and added phone lines were removed, the coffee urn taken away, and the theater's popcorn wagon once again pulled into the lobby.

A few reporters planned to stay, filing stories on the city's return to "normalcy," but their dispatches probably would receive little play. The world had been reminded by Ochsenburg how vulnerable it really is, and now simply wanted to forget.

[74]

THIRTEEN

Cane moved his copy of the *International Herald Tribune* aside, took a sip of his coffee, and asked himself the same questions again. There were too many "why"s. Why had the terrorists chosen Ochsenburg? If Simon was right and the government knew, why did it do nothing to stop them? And above all, there was Rick's question: why had they stayed in the igloo?

He grabbed the last *brötchen* from the bread basket, tore it open, and spread it with jelly. Perhaps, Cane thought, he should call Porter Caldwell at the embassy and put the questions to him directly. But he knew he'd get nothing but hedged nonanswers on a background-only basis.

He picked up the paper and started reading. The top front-page story was a piece about the arrest of two members of the Red Army Faction in a rural area of what once had been East Germany. Three formerly high-ranking members of the old East German secret police, the Stasi, had also been arrested and were being questioned about their support of the terrorists. All of them were linked to the assassination of a top German policeman charged with hunting terrorists. Cane remembered the story from a few days earlier. The cop had been killed when a bomb exploded beside his car on the autobahn.

The story on the terrorist attack in Ochsenburg was still on the front page, but barely. Below the fold, the *Tribune* carried a *New York Times* story quoting anonymous intelligence sources who said the terrorists who attacked the O'burg ammunition dump were backed by Iraq and had been trained at a secret base outside Baghdad. Beyond that, there was little new.

It had been three days since Ochsenburg's terrorists drove boldly away, and still there was no trace of them. Their car, stolen from Frankfurt, had been discovered abandoned deep on a seldom-used forest road. But the terrorists themselves had evaporated like ghosts in a fog.

Cane drank the last of his coffee and thought of the *Times* story. How the hell did they get that stuff, he wondered. He felt a pang of jealousy. Here he was in the city the terrorists hit, and the *Times* was scooping him from Washington. There had to be a way to dig up something in Germany, to find an angle that no one else had thought to explore.

His thoughts drifted to Hamid al Hamani and suddenly he had an idea. Wolfgang Otto Von Stueben. Who better to ask? Cane remembered Von Stueben as a distinguished man in his midsixties. But that had been years ago. He also remembered his reputation as one of the best attorneys in Germany. It was Von Stueben who had defended Hamid al Hamani.

On the surface, Von Stueben's defending a murderous Middle Eastern terrorist made no sense. He was already a highly successful lawyer with some of the world's biggest corporations as clients. Why take on the defense of such a man when the outcome was a foregone conclusion? Hamid al Hamani would never be a free man.

The answer, *Der Spiegel* had speculated at the time, lay in Von Stueben's client list, which included some of the Middle East's biggest oil companies and richest men. Von Stueben, the magazine claimed, often served as a back channel between Bonn and Middle Eastern organizations and leaders not officially recognized by the Germans. Defending al Hamani merely cemented his ties in the region.

Now Cane faced only two problems. Finding Von Stueben and getting him to agree to an interview.

He left the newspaper on the table and climbed the stairs to his room. Sitting on the edge of his bed, he dialed information in Frankfurt and got the phone number almost immediately. But when he called, the receptionist didn't speak English and put him on hold for several minutes. Finally a man, young by the sound of his voice, picked up.

"I speak English. May I help you?"

Cane explained he was a reporter writing a story about Hamid al Hamani and hoped to arrange an interview with Herr Von Stueben. He was put on hold again. Unlike the United States, however, there was no mortuary mood music piped into his ear, just a silence that stretched for more than five minutes. Finally the young man was back. He was sorry, he said, but Herr Von Stueben was not giving interviews about Hamid al Hamani. Cane thanked him and hung up.

Cane fell backward across the bed and wondered what to do next. Von Stueben's refusal did not surprise him, but he was determined not to be brushed off so easily. He found the number of the *Tagesblatt* in the thin phone book on the bottom of the nightstand and dialed. The switchboard put him directly through to Rolf.

"Rolf, it's Cane. I'm hoping you can do me a favor. That is if you're not too busy getting messages from your friend."

"You're a funny man, Cane. I'm pretty busy now, but I guess for a poor *Ami* I can find some time."

"Thanks. I need to get a home address for Wolfgang Otto Von Stueben. Can you help me?"

"Von Stueben. Why?"

"I want to go out to his place and see if I can interview him about al Hamani. I tried his office but they said he wasn't giving interviews, so I figured I'd try his house."

"Von Stueben, that's a pretty good idea. It may take a few phone calls. He's a very private man. I'll call you back as soon as I can."

It took less than an hour. Rolf didn't explain how he got the address and Cane didn't ask. Instead he merely thanked him and offered to return the favor if he ever got the chance.

Von Stueben lived in a village in the Taunus Mountains, which rise from the Rhine River plain and run north and east from Frankfurt. It took Cane almost two hours to make the journey from Ochsenburg past the city into the mountains to Von Stueben's home. It was a small village, and he found the house easily. It sat alone at the end of a road that wound its way up a hillside from the village.

It was a new, two-story home built into the side of the hill. In the bright afternoon sun, the brilliant white of the freshly stuccoed walls contrasted sharply with the black tile roof that seemed to rise like huge airplane wings from the hill. Across the front were windows and a large balcony overlooking a green lawn and the fields and village below. Ornate, wrought iron lamps the size of streetlights rose from the front corners of the balcony. And below were sliding glass doors that appeared opaque or fogged over.

Cane turned his car and drove back down the isolated street into the village to wait. He stopped in front of a small grocery store, parking the car half on the sidewalk. He left just enough room on one side for a car and on the other for a baby carriage, as is the custom in Germany.

Inside he bought rolls, cold cuts, and a Coke, and knowing his presence wouldn't go unnoticed, mentioned he was waiting to meet a friend. Back in the car he settled down for a long wait.

It was nearly eight o'clock when the large black Mercedes rushed down the narrow street and turned up the road toward the house on the hill. Cane watched the taillights wind into the distance, pull into driveway, and then blink out. Wolfgang Otto Von Stueben was home.

Cane waited about ten minutes and then followed. Stopping just below the house, he walked the last fifty yards and followed the cement walk to the front door. Within seconds of ringing the bell, the door swung open and an elderly man looked at Cane.

"Guten Abend. Sprechen sie English?"

"Yes, I do."

"My name is Jonathan Cane. I'm a reporter for a newspaper in Los Angeles. I would like to speak for a moment with Herr Von Stueben. I don't need much of his time."

The man looked at Cane intensely for a moment, as if trying to understand exactly what he had said. Finally, though, he nodded and said, "Just a moment please." Then, to Cane's astonishment, he gently closed the door, leaving Cane to wait outside.

He returned quickly. Opening the door he smiled gently. "I'm sorry, Mr. Cane, but Herr Von Stueben is too busy to see you this evening," he said. And the door closed again before Cane could respond.

Leaning against the hood of his car, Cane stared at the large house and wondered if Von Stueben was really too busy, or if he was hiding something. Either way, he wasn't yet ready to quit. He walked back toward the house, crossed the lawn in front, and stood under the balcony by the opaque glass doors he had seen earlier.

Cane was considering his next move when he heard a large splash. He stepped back and looked more closely at the steamy glass doors in front of him. Then he understood. Herr Von Stueben had that ultimate luxury in a country that imports all its oil: an indoor swimming pool. The door was slightly ajar, and Cane pushed it back just enough to walk in.

As he entered the small fully tiled room and stood at one end of the small pool, he saw Von Stueben climbing slowly out of the water at the other end, his back toward Cane. He was slightly overweight, and a small roll spilled over his tight-fitting trunks. But he had powerful shoulders, and as he turned to pick up a towel, Cane saw that he was remarkably fit for a man Cane judged to be in his early seventies. Von Stueben still had not seen him and was beginning to towel dry.

"Herr Von Stueben, please excuse my sudden appearance but—"

"*Wer ist da?*" He turned quickly and, for a big man, very gracefully to look in Cane's direction. As he did, he grabbed a pair of glasses from a small pool-side table.

"Excuse me Herr Von Stueben, but my name is Jonathan Cane. I'm a reporter and need to ask you a few questions."

And for the second time within a few minutes something happened that almost stunned him. After Von Stueben's servant had so quickly and surprisingly closed the door in his face, Cane had anticipated anger or even outrage. Instead, Von Stueben grunted a half laugh. "Mr. Cane, you are a persistent man."

"I've found it often helps in my profession."

"Yes, I imagine it does. I turned down your request for an interview because I know nothing about the incident in Ochsenburg. But, you are here, so would you like a drink." He motioned to a chair opposite the small table. It was then that Cane noticed the bottle of Johnnie Walker Red and several glasses on the table.

As Cane walked carefully around the edge of the pool, Von Stueben pulled on a thick, white terry cloth robe and lowered himself into a chair.

"It must be pretty important if you wanted to speak to me this badly. I could have you arrested, you know."

"Yes, I thought of that," Cane said as he sat down. Von Stueben poured stiff shots of Johnnie Walker and offered Cane one. "Thank you." He took a sip. "Let me ask you first, do you have any idea where Hamid al Hamani is now?"

"None. I represented him at his trial. But I haven't spoken to him since. He could be anywhere. He certainly didn't consult with me about his plans." He chuckled.

"Herr Von Stueben, is there any reason to think Hamid al Hamani has been cooperating with the German authorities or with any Western intelligence agencies?"

"Hamid cooperate?" Von Stueben almost laughed. "He wouldn't help with his own defense. All he would ever say was that he was justified. That in a holy war, everthing is okay. No, Mr. Cane, if you think Hamid could be bribed or intimidated, you are very ignorant of the Middle East in general and of Hamid al Hamani in particular."

"I know it sounds stupid, but a source told me there's evidence that the Americans knew there might be an attack on Ochsenburg but didn't do anything to stop it. The only reason I can think they might do that is it would be a convenient way to let him go free."

"Ah, yes, I forgot for a moment you're an American and Americans love conspiracy theories. Nothing is ever as it seems, is that it?"

"Why else would they ignore a warning like that."

"Perhaps they're incompetent. Don't forget, it was America's intelligence agencies that failed to foresee the downfall of the Shah, something you are still paying for dearly. And all your intelligence agencies, with their supersophisticated equipment, were still worried about the Russians, even as the wall was coming down." His tone had become pedantic. "No, I think incompetence is a much greater possibility, if they knew at all."

"Herr Von Stueben, just one more question. What will he

do now that he is free? Will he plan more terrorists attacks, more bombings and killing?"

Von Stueben didn't answer for a second. His gaze seemed to settle on the pool surface. "I don't know," he finally said. "But I'm afraid that's entirely possible."

He paused, and Cane sipped the last of his Johnnie Walker, preparing to leave when the lawyer suddenly turned and looked directly at him. "Now I have a question for you. It is a question that no one has asked. It is, perhaps, too obvious. But you're a reporter, a lover of conspiracy theories, so I offer you a question. Why Hamid al Hamani?"

"Pardon me. I'm not sure I understand."

"This took planning and money. It wasn't done by amateurs. I can think of a dozen people that could be freed more quickly and easily. Jian Hakimpur is in jail in France. He's a brilliant tactician, fearless. His loss was a tremendous blow to Abu Nidal. And France is even quicker to appease than we Germans are. Or there is Abdul Hakbany in Sweden. There are many. But Hamid al Hamani? Whose purpose does it serve for him to be free? Don't forget he was betrayed by his own people. That is why he was in prison. I have friends in all parts of the Arab world, Mr. Cane, and I can assure you that the idea that Hamid al Hamani is again free does not please them. Someone, someplace wants him free, but I don't know who that could be. Even those who hate the Great Satan more than most have no love of that man."

Before Cane could answer Von Stueben rose. "Now, if you will excuse me, I have much work to do yet tonight."

"Yes, of course. Thank you very much for your time."

"You may go out the way you came in," Von Stueben said and waved toward the open door.

Cane returned slowly to the car, thinking of what Von Stueben had said. The car door creaked loudly as he pulled it open and climbed behind the wheel. He started the car but didn't put it into gear for a moment. His visit hadn't turned out the way it was supposed to. He had come looking for answers and instead found more questions. Not the least of which was whether he could believe Von Stueben. He had seemed open and sincere. But Cane knew it was in the attorney's own interest to make it appear that none of his Middle Eastern clients wanted Hamid al Hamani free.

Cane shook his head slowly side to side then slipped the car into gear and began the long drive back to Ochsenburg.

FOURTEEN

The drive down the twisting, two-lane road from the Taunus Mountains to the autobahn and back to Ochsenburg took almost two hours. As Cane pushed his underpowered car against its limits, he returned again and again to Von Stueben's question. Why Hamid al Hamani?

He was no closer to answering the question when he parked in front of the Engel than when he talked to Von Stueben. But as he climbed the stairs to his room his concentration began slipping. Von Stueben and Hamid al Hamani receded, replaced by Maria.

He was to see her tomorrow and suddenly anticipation flooded him, banishing any thoughts of terrorists or scoops. He looked at his watch and quickly calculated how many hours it would be until Barbara Darling took her to lunch and left them alone. How would she look? What would she wear?

They could talk innocuously about the weather and books and movies or stick with safe topics such as Maria's children and their own middle age. It wouldn't matter because just by looking at her Cane would answer the question that for the past several years he had examined so many times in his mind, worrying it as smooth as a prayer bead: did she still love him?

He hadn't always wondered.

Cane met Maria because a drunk assistant principal sauntered over and sat down next to him one evening at the officers' club bar. The man was talking about a map, and initially Cane only half listened. It was a great geography lesson, the man insisted. Finally Cane understood. A teacher had taken her class to the playground where the students painted a map of the United States on the blacktop. Well, what the hell, Cane figured. It might make a good photo. *Stripes* was, after all, basically a hometown newspaper.

Two days later he went to the school, ready to grab a quick picture and leave.

He walked into her room near the end of the day, long after her students had abandoned their desks in erratic rows across the room. The sun, low on the horizon, flooded the classroom with warm light. The blackboard was a mass of swirls where erasers had obliterated earlier lessons. Students' art projects were taped to windows and walls. Cane immediately felt the constructive chaos of learning in Maria's room.

As he walked in, she looked up from the partially corrected papers on her cluttered desk. She brushed back an errant strand of coal black hair and smiled. Her skin was a smooth white and her green eyes sparkled in the sun. She needed no makeup and wore none: a pretty lady.

"Hi. I'm Jonathan Cane. I've come to make you famous," he flirted.

"You must be the man from the *Stars and Stripes*." She spoke softly, almost shyly, but her eyes looked at him as if he were an old and dear friend.

"What was your first clue?"

"The camera, Mr. Cane." She laughed lightly as she pointed to the Nikon slung around his neck.

"Oh, yeah. So, are you Mrs. Henry?"

"Yes. But, please call me Maria."

"Okay, all my friends, or at least the one that still speaks to me, just call me Cane." It was inane and he knew it but didn't care. "Well, I hear you have one giant map around here somewhere," he said as he lifted the top of the nearest desk and peeked inside. She smiled.

By the time they walked to the playground to survey the map he had almost lost interest in it. He was far more interested in her. He sensed a silent magnetism, as though she were flirting without smiling or speaking. She was, he thought, the most beautiful woman he had ever met. He wanted to stare at her.

He took a few perfunctory pictures of the map with her

standing in the middle, her arms stretched out at her sides, and they returned to the classroom. Cane pulled a chair to her desk and asked a few quick questions about the map then allowed the conversation to drift.

They talked easily. She appeared unconcerned about the stack of work at her elbow, and he wasn't anxious to leave. Eventually, though, as it grew dark outside and the fluorescent lights took over for the fading sun, Cane knew it was time to go.

He thought about her all evening and repeatedly told himself it was stupid to be interested in her. She was married, to an officer no less. But he couldn't shake the feeling that she was interested in him too. And, damn, she put him in a joyous mood.

The photo ran a few days later. It was the excuse he needed. He stopped at the school to give her the original print. But as he walked into her classroom again his spirits sank. She wasn't alone. She was talking with another woman.

"Hi, Mrs. Henry." Jesus that sounded ridiculous. Why was he acting so formal, as if they were merely acquaintances? Hell, he'd called her Maria the other day. He was friends with a lot of people he interviewed, he could call her Maria. "Listen, I just got the photo of the map back from the main office and thought you might like to have it. But I can come back later."

"Oh, no, please come in. This is my friend Barbara Darling. She teaches with me. Join us."

"Okay." Cane dragged a chair across the room and sat next to Barbara. They became friends almost immediately. That afternoon, Cane was funny, charming, and suitably outrageous. He was openly insulting toward the military, several times stopping just short of angering Maria. Barbara loved it and egged him on. Maria argued, but Cane could tell she was enthralled.

He left feeling giddy, almost foolishly in a good mood. For more than a week he tried to be where she would be. He spent Saturday loitering outside the commissary hoping she would come shopping. He spent another day on the main base hoping he would see her going to the PX or library. But accidently bumping into someone takes both patience and luck. Cane was patient but not lucky. Eventually he gave up and dropped by the school on a made-up errand. There was a holiday the following week, and he asked her to lunch.

"Hey, why not let *Stars and Stripes* buy us lunch? You deserve that much for helping us get a good photo."

Immediately he sensed her hesitation. "Hey, if you don't want to, that's okay," he said raising his hands, as if surrendering. "In fact, why don't you ask Barbara to join us? The more the better."

She hesitated, but agreed.

Cane spent the days before their lunch trying to understand what was happening. There was no question in his mind that when he was with her, she was telling him without words of her attraction to him. But when he asked her to lunch she seemed genuinely surprised. He couldn't tell if his invitation pleased or affronted her. But above all else he knew one important thing: he was falling in love with her. He would find out how she felt about him at the lunch.

Maria had insisted lunch be at the officers' club. It made him smile. It was a such a safe place. If you were having an affair you didn't meet at the O club, where other husbands and wives could see you.

He arrived about five minutes late. Cane considered himself skilled at flirting and knew enough about seduction games to be a little late. Still, he arrived before she did. He waited in his car, ready to pretend he had pulled in an instant before her. God, he couldn't believe he was actually playing these games; he was a grown man, not a gangly seventh grader who was dying to know if some girl "liked" him too. Finally, when he was ready to give up and wait inside, she arrived.

He waved and walked slowly toward her and glanced quickly into the car. She was alone.

"Where's Barbara?"

"She couldn't come."

"I'm sorry she couldn't make it," he lied. "Maybe next time." And immediately he wondered if it was really a coincidence that Barbara couldn't come for lunch. Maybe Maria wanted to be alone with him too.

They found a small table near the window with a view of the lawn and trees outside. Despite the view, the ambience wasn't what Cane had hoped for: more army efficient than romantic. Overhead, flags bearing the crests of the different outfits stationed in Ochsenburg hung from the ceiling. The tables were Formica formalized with worn, white tablecloths and red plastic flowers. It seemed a luncheonette overdressed on the cheap.

But none of it really mattered. Maria seemed relaxed and even pleased to be with him. They ordered, but when it came, Cane could barely eat. Finally he had to say something.

"You know, Maria, you're really a neat lady. I've never met anyone quite like you." A wariness leapt into her eyes and she stiffened, as though insulted.

"Well, thank you. That's very nice of you to say," she said, her tone suddenly formal.

"I'd like to get to know you better." He said it calmly, trying to erase any overtones of desire, or flirtation from his voice. He feared then that he had misread her and overstepped the boundaries she had staked out around her. He was ready to double back on his words and recast them into another, different, safer meaning, pretending she had misunderstood.

"Look, Cane, you're very nice." He knew he was in trouble. "But this isn't the first time this has happened to me. Men . . . I don't know, they seem to think I'm coming on to them or sending them signals or something. I honestly don't understand it. Why do men think that?"

And Cane began to talk, to reweave the meaning of his words, to lessen her fear of him and what he wanted of her. He spoke quickly, deftly, trying not to frighten her away.

"Hey, wait a minute here. I think you're a great person, but I'm not stupid. I'm not asking you to run off with me, I'm asking you to be my friend. I don't know a lot of people here yet. Hell, I just met Barbara, and I think she's a great person too. I mean, I thought she was going to join us today. Look Maria, I didn't ask you to have lunch with me because I thought I could get you in bed, for Christ's sake. If I gave you that impression I apologize. I just think you're a neat lady."

"Okay, Cane. I'm sorry. It's just that, well, like I said, this has happened to me before."

It wasn't turning into the romance he had hoped for. Maria had set the relationship quickly and firmly. And when they said good-bye it was as friends, not lovers.

He tried to be rational. He repeated the obvious to himself again and again. It had been ridiculous from the beginning. He had misread her. She was just being friendly. She was a married woman, *a married woman*. It would never work.

He didn't see her again for almost three weeks. Then one afternoon, while checking out a book from the base library, he looked up and saw her. She smiled and approached.

"Hi, Jonathan, how are you?"

He looked at her and was instantly in love again. He felt alert and clever.

"Okay. They passed me over for a Pulitzer again this year, but hell, maybe next year I'll find out about a supply sergeant who's selling light bulbs on the black market and blow the lid off this joint."

She laughed. "You know, I don't think I ever thanked you for lunch."

He looked at her for a long moment staring into her eyes. Dammit, there was something there. She seemed genuinely glad to see him. No, even more than that. Affection radiated from her.

"Well, as one friend to another, how about lunch again sometime?" he asked.

"I'd like that. But we don't get out of school until two."

"We'll make it a late one."

They had lunch and then another and another. They met at the Engel and at different restaurants in different villages near Ochsenburg. To hell with her husband, he thought, and set about capturing her heart.

He asked her if she like classical music. She didn't dislike it, she just didn't know much about it, she said. He made her cassette tapes of Mozart, Beethoven, Debussey. Without telling her, he put her name on the waiting list for *The Magus* and *The Great Gatsby* at the library.

They were just "friends" she continued to insist. And Cane agreed. He was scrupulous not to touch her. Over the weeks, the intense, painful excitement that Cane had felt so strongly in the beginning faded. Their conversations drifted toward the mundane details of their lives instead of skirting along the edges of safe neutral first-meeting chatter. A sense of ease began to pull them together, replacing the tension of early attraction.

And one afternoon as they walked through a park, Cane momentarily forgot his caution and put his arm around her. His move came from reflex not planning, and he almost pulled back, alarmed as he realized what he'd done. But Maria moved close, put her arm around him, and pulled him tight.

He didn't kiss her until she was ready to leave. He hesitated at the last moment, but she returned his kiss with equal tenderness and longing.

"I have loved you for a very long time," he told her.

"Yes, I know. I love you too."

They agreed to meet again the next day and she left. It was only as Cane watched her drive away that he truly began to feel the excitement of the day. She was in love with him. God dammit, she was in love with him!

FIFTEEN

Cane leaned against the Taunus in the small parking lot of the Zur Sonne and stared down the road for sign of Barbara's car.

Despite a clear sky and bright sun Cane had to shuffle his feet and rub his hands to fight off the cold locked in the still-frozen ground. But he refused to go inside. He wanted to see her the moment she arrived.

Then, just after noon, the yellow Volvo rounded a distant corner and a few moments later pulled to the curb. Maria got out and Barbara drove away.

Cane smiled broadly as he looked at her. She wore brown wool slacks and a white cashmere sweater. She looked thinner. Her once-black hair was now a deep brown. There were lines near the corners of her eyes, but she was still a very pretty lady.

He walked to her quickly and embraced her so tightly he was suddenly afraid he would crush her. He pulled away and held her at arms' length.

"You look great."

"Thanks, Jonathan. You look pretty good yourself."

"You've lost a little weight."

"Yes, but it looks like you've found it."

He laughed and put his arm around her shoulder and they walked slowly into the Zur Sonne. Neither one looked back to see the green sedan that coasted to a stop a half block away.

The restaurant was empty except for an elderly couple sipping coffee at a table near the window. Sunlight filled the room, and the blond wood furniture, linen tablecloths, and freshly cut flowers gave it a simple country elegance. Without asking, Cane led Maria to a table in a far corner.

"It's good to see you. To see that you're really okay. I just had to know how you are. You know, to make sure you are all right."

"I'm okay, Jonathan. I really am. But I was really surprised to find out you were here. Barbara said you got here right after it all started."

"Yeah. I saw the story on the wire and my editor agreed almost immediately to let me come. I didn't know about what happened to you until after I got here."

He felt the anger and resentment rising again. And he felt more helpless than he had before. Now she was sitting with him, and he could touch her and hold her, but he could neither ease her pain nor promise to protect her.

"Maria, I wish I could help. I wish I didn't feel so helpless. When I heard they'd broken into your house with guns . . . well, I don't know. It just made me mad, I guess. "

"Oh, Jonathan, I'm okay, I really am. They scared me, but they didn't hurt me."

"I know. But still . . . it makes me reexamine some of my liberal principles. I mean, I think about them harming you and I swear to God, it makes me want to kill every Iraqi in the world."

And then Maria shocked him. She laughed.

"You are such a romantic," she said. "You used to call me provincial, but you're as bad in the other direction. You see the world the way it should be, not the way it is, so when something like this comes along, you feel personally affronted."

"I *am* affronted. You were involved. They did this to you, not some stranger. You know, most of the time you see these terrible things on television and the people might as well be mannequins. It doesn't really matter if it's Northern Ireland or the Middle East, the people just don't seem real. You lose your sensitivity. But not this time. This time it was someone I care about."

She held up her hand to stop him. "I know. But there's nothing you can do. When we first met, you used to tell me that I had led a very protected life, and you were right. But you see, even though I was protected, I was taught to be tough. You don't grow up in a house full of brothers who want to be soldiers without learning a little something about taking what's dished out. Jonathan, those men scared me, but they didn't hurt me. They barely even touched me. I can handle the fear. Besides, killing Iraqis wouldn't do any good. I don't believe those guys were Arabs."

"No? They must have been. This morning the *New York Times* had a piece that said the government had proof the thing was planned in Baghdad. They had to be Iraqis."

"Really, Cane. You of all people should know enough not to believe everything you read in the newspaper." Her tone was light, joking.

"I guess, but . . . well, I don't know. What makes you think they weren't Arabs?"

"When I was growing up my dad was stationed briefly in Jordan as a military attaché in the embassy. I learned a few words in Arabic, like 'where's the toilet?' and stuff like that.

"After the three took Woody away that night, the others held me for about twenty minutes so I wouldn't call the MPs. While they were still there, I asked them in Arabic if I could go to the bathroom. You know, I don't think they understood. They just looked at one another like they didn't know what I was talking about, and one of them finally pointed his gun at me and just said 'sit.' So I figured they weren't Arabs."

"Yeah, but why would anyone other than a bunch of fanatical Arabs want Hamid al Hamani free?"

"Oh, Cane, I don't know," she said, trying to dismiss the subject.

"Maria, I have to ask you something."

"Is this Jonathan Cane, the journalist, asking?" Her tone was lightly mocking."

"Well, yes, I'm afraid it is. But really, I only want to ask one question. Did your husband say anything about them not being Arabs, or about why they stayed in the igloo instead of stealing the bomb and leaving?"

"Look, I really don't want to talk about this now."

"Okay, okay. I understand."

"But, to answer your question. No. We haven't even talked about it. Woody said we'd talk later, when we have our privacy back."

[93]

"Well, I guess lacking any concrete information on who to punish, I'll just have to bomb Iraq, Libya, and Lebanon. And, by the way, what's the capital of Pakistan, while I'm at it?"

"Jonathan, you're hopeless." She laughed, and the subject of Woody and the terrorists was gone.

Cane felt the old ease returning. A tightness in his chest, which he hadn't even noticed before, began to dissolve. The waiter arrived and Cane quickly ordered fresh trout for both of them and turned to Maria again.

"How are your boys?" he asked.

As they talked he stared at her, trying to commit her face to memory. And then he noticed, she had been very careful with her makeup. Her eyes were subtly, but very carefully, done. She had wanted to look good when she saw him again. And from her laughter and her mood he could tell that she still cared.

"What will happen now?" he asked.

"Happen with what?"

"With you. With your family. Will you stay in Ochsenburg?"

"No, Woody's requesting a transfer. It'll take them a little while, a week or two maybe, to find a place to send us. But the boys and I are leaving the day after tomorrow. We're going to my folks' place for a few weeks. Who knows, maybe when everything is said and done, we'll actually get to Hawaii."

"Day after tomorrow. God, you must be busy. How did you get away today?"

She laughed. "It wasn't easy. Actually, it wasn't that hard. I just told Woody that I needed to get away for a while, that Barbara and I were going out to lunch and he could stay home and spend time with his sons. And then I reminded him of all the evenings he's spent playing in his band and told him I deserved to get at least a couple of hours today."

"No. Not the same band that he played with before? The one in Heimstadt?"

"The same one. The same old geezers. He said they were overjoyed when he showed up again."

Once a week a small group of men who probably had never left their village gathered to play old German songs and drink beer. And Woody, despite his almost total lack of German, had faithfully showed up and played with them since shortly after he and Maria arrived in Ochsenburg. Cane smiled, remembering Woody's band nights. When he and Maria had been lovers, those nights often had been a blessing.

Suddenly Barbara Darling walked in, smiled at them, and left. It seemed they had just begun talking but their hour was gone.

Cane paid and assured the waiter that the food was fine although they had hardly touched it. As they walked to the car, he put his arm around her and pulled her close, as comfortably as if they had been married for twenty years. He turned to face her and hugged her tightly, and as she turned her face toward him he kissed her, slowly at first and then hard and passionately. Finally, she pulled away.

"I love you Maria. If you ever need someone, just call me."

"I love you too, Jonathan. You know that. I have to go."

And then she was in the car and the Volvo was driving away. It rounded a corner and was gone.

SIXTEEN

Cane spent the afternoon driving aimlessly through the nearby hills, passing from one village to another with no destination. The wandering didn't help. He still had to face the old reality: yes, Maria loved him. But that was totally irrelevant.

It was early evening when he finally returned to the Engel. He guided the Taunus to the end of the parking lot and parked perfectly parallel to a green Mercedes sedan, as if neatness and order were now a priority in his life. He sat for a moment and looked outside at the gathering darkness. His disappointment was his creation, not hers. If the reality hadn't matched his dreams, whose fault was that? After all, what the hell had he expected?

He climbed out wearily and shuffled toward the restaurant. Inside he plopped down at the familiar round table and in a soft voice ordered a beer. He glanced around the *Gasthaus* without interest. Customers were beginning to return, a few old and a few new. Traveling salesmen, who had stayed with the sisters for years, were enjoying beers in the adjacent dining room before ordering their dinner. A young couple was already eating, and a lone man sat in the far corner casually reading a German news magazine, a half-empty beer glass at his elbow.

Margaret, who had seen Cane leave in such high spirits only a few hours before, brought him his beer and an unordered shot of clear, cold pear schnapps. She set it in front of him and smiled motherly as he picked it up.

Cane tilted it toward her and said, "*danke*, Margaret. *Prost.*" The schnapps disappeared in a gulp and Cane shivered as the liquor's cold fire hit home. He chased it with a long swallow of beer and leaned back in his seat.

"Oh, Herr Cane, I almost forgot. Herr Plumber called for you."

"Great. Thanks, Margaret, I could use some company tonight."

As Margaret moved back to the bar, Cane downed the last of his beer in two swallows and headed for the stairs. As he walked through the dining room he glanced at the lone man. For a fraction of a moment he appeared to be watching Cane, but lowered his eyes immediately as Cane's gaze swept past. Yet in that portion of a second Cane caught a glimpse of the man's blue eyes and they startled him, piercing his stupor. They were alert and very cold. Cane looked again but the man was lost in his reading.

By the time he reached his room, though, Cane was again lost in his thoughts of Maria and had forgotten the man. Dropping to his bed, he picked up the phone and called Rick's office.

"Rick Plummer."

"Hey, Rick, it's Cane."

"Hi, how you doing?"

"Shitty, but I'll live."

"Sound like you could use some company. We could have some beers, grab a bite to eat, and hit a couple of the high spots in Ochsenburg. What daya say?"

"High spots in Ochsenburg? I didn't know Ochsenburg had any high spots."

"Oh, hell yes. I know one place with enough cheap sauerkraut to give New Jersey gas for a month."

"Great, the sooner the better."

An hour later there was a loud pounding on the door. Cane leaped off the bed and jerked the door open. There was Rick, grinning broadly. Slowly, he opened his mouth and stuck out his tongue. A neatly rolled joint nestled in the crease. He plucked it from his mouth and held it out to Cane.

"God dammit Rick, not here. The sisters . . . they'll—"

But it was too late. Rick had already lit it and was inhaling greedily. Teeth clenched, his diaphragm tight to hold in the smoke, he again held the joint out to Cane and spoke in the strained, squeaky voice of Flipper on amphetamines. "Here, put this in your lungs. It's a little soggy, but what the hell, it'll still smoke. It may not make you feel any better, but then again it won't make you feel any worse, either."

Cane shrugged, pushed the door shut, and took a drag on the joint as he walked across the worn carpet to the long windows. He unlatched them, pushed them outward, and blew the smoke into the night.

"Hey, this stuff isn't half bad."

"Thanks, I grew it on my balcony. Had a good summer last year." He took the joint back, looked at it, and smiled again, taking pride in his craftsmanship. "You've heard of Panama Red and Maui Wowee. Well, meet Bavarian Balcony Weed." He grinned.

"It gets the Cane stamp of approval. Okay. So what do you have in mind for dinner?" Cane asked.

"You know the place down by the brewery called the Weisses Ross? They lay out a mean wurst plate. More food than you can imagine. Pretty cheap too. My kind of place. And by the time we finish this we'll be hungry."

A few tokes later, Rick stubbed out the joint and they left. At the bottom of the stairs, though, Rick grabbed Cane's shoulders and steered him away from the dining room toward the back door used by hotel guests returning after hours.

"Come on," he said. "I'm not in the lot, I parked out on the street."

Rick's old, red Fiat sports car was half a block away facing down a slight incline. As Cane opened the passenger door a beer can, papers, magazines, and one ski mitten fell onto the street.

"Hey, does the EPA know about this?"

"Just throw that shit in the back," Rick said as he climbed in.

Bent over, half in the car with the door pressing against his leg, Cane tried to shovel the assorted leftovers of Rick's last several months from between the bucket seats onto the small rear seat, which was already overflowing. After a moment he gave up and shoved part of the pile onto the floor and sat on the rest.

"Is there any particular reason you parked here?" asked

Cane, rising on one cheek to extricate the pop top of a beer can imbedded in his leg.

"Had to. Starter's shot. Most of the time it works, but sometimes it doesn't. I figured this would be better than having you push."

"You got that right."

With that Rick released the hand brake and the Fiat slowly picked up speed. He popped the clutch and the engine jumped to life.

"Ahhh, Fiats. Designed by Kafka and fine tuned by a committee of midlevel Italian bureaucrats," Rick shouted above the roar of a rusted-out muffler.

The noise prevented conversation, so Cane stared out the window, searching for recognizable landmarks in a changed city. About ten minutes later, Rick suddenly turned a corner and pulled to the curb in front of the Weisses Ross.

It was a neighborhood restaurant and gathering place where the beer and schnapps, not dinners, paid the bills. Its floors were designed to be mopped, not vacuumed. The light fixtures were there to provide illumination, not atmosphere. And the proprietor, a taciturn woman in a white apron, was there for function, not idle chatter. She pulled the draft beers, took the dinner orders, kept strict track of the tabs, and occasionally called taxis for customers who lost their ambulatory abilities.

Rick ordered two beers and a large platter of mixed cheeses and wurst. The cool of the outside began to fade and Cane felt the warmth of the restaurant slowly flush his cheeks. The pot made him feel lazy and hungry.

"You know, that Bavarian Balcony Weed's pretty good stuff," he said.

"Thanks. It took me a few tries to get it right. You should have seen the first year I tried to grow reefer. It was a German summer, cold and rainy for three months. I don't think we had more than a week of sunshine. I ended up with two bonsai marijuana plants. I couldn't have gotten a pygmy stoned. Now I've got so much left from last year I don't even know if I'll plant any this summer."

"Great harvest?"

"Yeah, that and, to tell you the truth, I don't smoke as much as I used to."

"You slowing down?"

"Aren't we all? It just seems to take longer to get over the night before these days. If I've been smoking and drinking I kind of drag through the next day, coffee cup glued to my hand, you know what I mean?"

"Yeah, I know exactly what you mean. Hey, what ever happened to the hippies? I thought our generation was going to change the world and never grow old."

"The hippies all grew up, got thirty-year mortgages, moved to the suburbs, and had kids who turned out to be punkers. There's a perverted justice in that, I suspect."

The woman in the white apron brought their dinner on a large platter. Without a word, she set the platter on the table, turned, and marched away. One side of the large plate was covered with an array of sliced wursts: pale pink, blood red, and dark brown . On the other side were the cheeses: yellow, white, one with globs of blue, and another that oozed its way along the platter's edge. A moment later she was back with a basket of bread and more beer.

They ate without conversation. Finally, when the platter was almost bare, Rick said, "Let's pay up and hit another spot or two. I know a place near the barracks. Right across the street from where they park the tanks."

"Gee, imagine my excitement."

"Hey, it might be fun. You never know what the hell's going to happen in that place. The tankers like to drink there, and every once in a while a couple of the young yahoos get to believing their own bullshit and get into it. Could get interesting."

It was a bar only a Bolshevik could love: utilitarian with no pretentions. It was housed in a gray cement building with a brewery sign above the door, the only indication there was a bar inside. It had sturdy, solid wood tables with Formica tops, worn linoleum floors, and heavy wooden chairs. And on that night there was only one customer.

A young, drunk soldier, his olive drab uniform well wrinkled and his black army jump boots scuffed, was putting money in a rectangular, electronic slot machine that hung on the wall. He clutched the machine tightly with one hand to keep his balance as he fed coins in it.

Cane and Rick slid onto two wooden stools at the bar, ordered beers, and for lack of a better diversion, briefly watched the young soldier.

"Shit!" he yelled and pounded the slot machine. Giving up, he shuffled to the bar and sat down next to Rick. Then, with a slow, exaggerated movement, he turned to looked at them.

"You guys Americans?"

"Yes," answered Cane, looking past Rick.

Up close he could see the soldier was probably no more than eighteen, perhaps twenty.

"So, soldier, come here often?" asked Rick.

"Yeah. Used to be the only bar in the whole town you could come into without running into assholes."

"Oh, yeah, I know what you mean. You got to really watch out for the assholes," Rick said deadpan.

The young man looked sharply at Rick, suddenly cautious that he was being mocking. Then, apparently satisfied, he glanced down at his beer and continued.

"It's better now, though. David Lee Roth came in here and ran all the assholes out of the bars."

"David Lee Roth? The singer?" Cane asked, incredulous.

The soldier's face was scrunched into a scowl, his bloodshot eyes narrowed, and he leaned forward on the bar to look defiantly past Rick at Cane.

"Yeah. He had a concert in Frankfurt and came to O'burg afterward. He went from bar to bar and ran all the assholes out."

"Well, I haven't been to many bars lately. I guess I'll have to get back to them now," Rick said. His tone had changed to the anything-you-say-mister attitude of a bored cab driver listening to the life story of a five-dollar fare.

"I'm a painter," the soldier said suddenly, as if that were naturally the next topic of conversation. "I painted the barracks next to the commissary last month. Took us almost a whole month. But hell, we painted that ammo dump in one day. No windows, just spray it on. Easy."

"What ammo dump?" Cane asked, suddenly interested. "The one where all the trouble was?"

"Yeah, the one in the woods. Shit, we was there just a day before them terrorists. Man, that job was easy. Just one day. Nothing to it. Just go in and spray the walls. But shit, man, they don't have no windows in there. I hated that. Breathing that shit all day. I don't know how those assholes put up with it locked in there all that time. It must have really stunk. No air. It's got to be bad for your lungs, you know? Maybe I'll get a medical discharge. You think?"

"What about the stuff inside?" Cane asked.

"What stuff?"

"You know, the explosives and stuff?"

"I don't know. Shit, there were only a couple of things, covered with sheets and stuff. I just went in and sprayed it."

Rick slid off his stool and turned to leave. "Well, take care, maybe we'll see you in one of the other bars sometime."

"What?" The soldier didn't understand.

"The other bars. Now that David Lee Roth ran the assholes out, remember?"

"Who?"

In the car Rick paused before turning the ignition. "Ah, the forces of freedom. Gives you a warm feeling all over, doesn't it?"

"I guess. By the way, you have any idea what the hell he was talking about?"

"Absolutely none. I learned long ago it's futile to attempt to reason with a man whose idea of a good time is sniffing the tools of his trade. Never mix business and pleasure, I always say."

"Yeah, but what did you think about what he said about the ammo dump? They really just leave that stuff lying around while last year's hemp poster boy spray paints the walls?"

"No, no way, not with Woody Henry in charge. He'd never be that careless. But then, I'd be surprised if that guy gets much of anything past yesterday right."

"I don't know. There are a whole lot of things about this that suddenly don't make much sense."

"Maybe not, but I wouldn't put too much faith in what that guy said. If his brain was dynamite, it couldn't blow a turd out of a toilet."

The engine fired and the conversation was over.

SEVENTEEN

Jonathan Cane lay fully clothed on his bed, staring at the ceiling. The fluffy down comforter puffed up at his sides, almost folding him into a cocoon. He should forget it, he told himself. He could be back in LA tomorrow. Back in "the world," as the GIs called it.

Still he had too many questions: why didn't terrorists from Iraq speak Arabic? Why had they demanded freedom for a pariah like Hamid al Hamani? Who organized and paid for the operation? Could he believe Von Stueben? If the government knew terrorists were planning an attack in O'burg, why didn't it stop them? What did he make of what the igloo painter said? Why Ochsenburg when there were better targets elsewhere? And why the hell had they locked themselves away in the igloo when they could have just stolen the damed thing? To each question the answer was the same—he didn't know.

Cane debated staying a few extra days to run down some of the answers. But that led to another question. Was he really pursuing a story, or was he was chasing useless leads because the terrorists' seige was now the only connection he had with Maria?

Maybe that was part of it, he admitted. But there was something else too. It might be the only shot he ever got at a story like this. Everyone outside the profession thinks reporters are all like Woodward and Bernstein. But it isn't that way. At least not at the *Los Angeles Journal*, where Cane was permanently a general assignment reporter. School board meetings, homicides, and flooded streets—none of it too hard, and, frankly, by now none of it too interesting.

This time, though, all his instincts told him there was more. This one time he should follow the story all the way to the end. This one was different.

Too often in his career he had been a hit-and-run reporter, interviewing a science fiction writer today, writing a murder story the next day and a budget story the day after that. His stories were accurate and well written but almost always lacked depth. Through the years he had come to prefer it that way. To get depth required involvement. He liked being a hit-and-run reporter. Being good required only a deft touch with words—not passion.

This time, he decided, it would be different.

Cane swung his feet to the floor, picked up the phone, and started to dial. But even as he did, he could feel his resolve slipping. All he had were a bunch of details that didn't add up to anything. Probably just coincidence. Probably nothing.

Weariness settled over him, and suddenly the task seemed unreasonable, even impossible. He put the receiver down. To give it up and simply leave seemed better than trying and failing. No. That was not true, he knew. It wasn't better. It was easier.

He picked up the phone again and dialed the number for the international operator. She asked him to hold, and a few moments later he heard the ringing.

"Newsroom."

"I have a collect call from Jonathan Cane. Will you accept?"

Cane could hear Ralph Granger's loud nasal voice as he called to Slovak.

"Hey, it's Cane again. Do you want to take another collect call from him?"

The question was quintessential Granger. It simply didn't occur to him that Cane could hear his words. And it would never cross his mind to just accept the call without comment. He was a man without finesse. Cane wondered what Granger would do if he ever had to cover a story or actually be subtle sometime. But Cane knew he never would. And, against all reason, it bothered him. It was more than Granger being promoted to assistant city editor after only six months on the job. It was a question of dues, he thought. Having rich parents and going to Stanford wasn't the same as working the night police beat. It wasn't even close. Granger hadn't paid his dues.

"Yes, we'll accept," Granger said.

"Go ahead, please."

"Hey, Cane. Nice to hear from you again. How goes your vacation?"

"Shitty. Is Slovak there?"

"Sure, just a minute."

There was a pause and Slovak was on the line.

"Don't tell me. They kidnapped the U.S. ambassador and you're off to cover it."

"No, not even close. It's the queen of England. She's been implicated in the plot. It has something to do with international arms and drug smuggling."

"Sounds good. You ready to dictate?"

"Not yet, I need a little more time. Actually, I really do need a little more time. That's why I called."

"Why, what's up?"

"I want to check this terrorist thing out a little better. There are a few things that don't add up."

"What do you have?"

Cane could hear the skepticism in Slovak's voice. Still, he knew his reputation was good. He didn't ask for something unless it was legitimate. Slovak was a cautious man, just the same.

"Probably not much. Just some unanswered questions. A couple of things that don't go together. I'm here, I might as well run them down."

He couldn't tell Slovak about his affair with Maria or that he'd seen her. That he had lunch with her. No, it was best to leave that unsaid. And if he told him about Simon's suspicions, Slovak would push for more—something he wasn't sure Simon could, or would be willing, to deliver. He considered telling him about his visit with Von Stueben, but what could he say? That Hamid al Hamani's former lawyer thought it was strange that someone would break him out of prison? No. That wouldn't convince Slovak of anything. He could say it didn't make sense for the terrorists to lock themselves up, but he had nothing but Rick's opinion on that. All he really had was the comments of a painter who appeared to enjoy the fumes more than the work and a couple of questions that didn't really make much sense. No, it was best to leave it vague.

"Jesus, Cane, you're not really giving me much here. Besides I've already given you a few extra vacation days. We're short handed as it is. How long do you think this is going to take?"

"I don't know. Tomorrow I'll go down to Heidelberg and talk to the folks at the European Army headquarters and see what they have to say. If I don't get something, I'll drop it and head home."

"Okay. Take the time you need. I'll count it as vacation. If you come up with something, you'll get comp time to make up for it."

"Thanks."

"Good hunting."

Cane hung up and fell backward across the bed. He lay motionless for almost ten minutes, thinking of the abundance of questions and the dearth of answers. Sitting up, he grabbed his notebook from the nightstand and made a shorthand list of all his questions.

He leaned over and grabbed several copies of the *Herald Tribune* off the chair next to the nightstand and flipped back through the issues until he found the article he was looking for and quickly reread it. Sure enough, the *New York Times* reported they were Iraqis. He closed the paper, folding it neatly in two. Where the hell was he going to go next?

And he saw it.

There, on the top of the page, was the story of the arrest of two Red Army Faction terrorists in eastern Germany. Suddenly the pieces began falling into place. The more he thought about it, the more outrageous it seemed. And the more logical.

He knew his theory would be difficult, perhaps impossible, to prove. Still, there was one man who would know and might help. Cane stood up and began undressing. He would need to get an early start tomorrow. Before going to Heidelberg he wanted to stop at the *Stars and Stripes*.

It was still early. There were few people on the streets of Ochsenburg. The drab green Chevrolet sedan, parked on the street across from the elementary school, drew no notice. The

U.S. Army captain sitting in the car sipped cold coffee from a paper cup and watched the teachers' parking lot. He had been there for more than an hour but didn't mind. He was a patient man. He glanced again at the photo on the seat beside him. There would be no mistake. He would recognize her.

The janitor was the first to pull in. Soon others began arriving. The man watched passively until Barbara Darling pulled her Volvo into the parking lot. As she got out of the car he glanced at the photo again and watched her walk into the school.

A few moments later the school secretary directed an army officer with a captain's parallel bars on his dress uniform to Miss Darling's room. She was sitting at her desk, sorting papers when he stopped at her open door and looked in.

"Miss Darling?"

Barbara looked up to see a thin, dark-faced man with blue eyes and thick black hair. She knew the parents of all her students and didn't recognize this captain.

"Yes."

"I'm Captain Montgomery. I'm with army intelligence. Can we talk for a moment?"

"Certainly. Come in. Have a seat."

The man walked in but didn't sit. Instead he remained standing, looking down at her. "I'd like to be able to speak privately."

"I'll make sure no students bother us," she said. But she made no effort to close the door. She didn't like the man. The way he stood, peering at her, made her want to shiver.

"I've been assigned to the task force that is investigating the terrorist incident here. I understand you're friends with Major Henry and his wife."

"Yes. What's this about?"

He ignored her question. "You and Mrs. Henry went out for lunch yesterday?"

"Yes, so? Maria needed a chance to get away. She's been under a lot of pressure lately. I'm sure you can understand that. I thought it would be a good idea for her to get away from all this madness for a couple of hours." Her tone was slightly defiant.

"Well, I think you're probably right. I'm sure it was good

[109]

for her." He spoke reassuringly, but it reminded Barbara of her father talking to his insurance clients on the phone. It was good salesmanship but not sincere. She became more wary.

"My concern is in making sure she stays safe," the captain said. "We're really quite worried by the fact that none of the terrorists has been caught yet."

"You don't really think they're trying to kidnap Maria or do something like that do you?"

"Well, frankly, we don't know. But as we've learned in all too clear a fashion over the past few days, we must be extremely cautious. Tell me, did anybody else go with you or did you meet anyone yesterday?"

Barbara didn't hesitate.

"No. Just the two of us."

He tried a new tact.

"We're trying to figure out how the terrorists learned of Major Henry's position and that he would be home that evening. You've known the family for several years. When they returned to Ochsenburg this time, did they tell you about anything unusual or different about their routine? Any old friends that looked them up out of the blue?"

Barbara turned away from the captain to tell two students at the door they would have to wait outside until her conference was over. She looked back up at the man.

"No. Nothing. I'm sorry I can't help you. Now, if you'll excuse me, class is about to start."

He thanked her and started to go but stopped in the middle of the doorway, as if suddenly remembering something.

"Do you know a man named Jonathan Cane?"

"Yes. Why?"

"I understand he's in Ochsenburg. Have you seen him?"

"I've talked to him on the phone."

"When did you meet him?"

"Years ago, when he worked for the *Stars and Stripes* as a reporter here."

"Is that when Mrs. Henry met him?"

"Yes, I guess so. We all hung out together, Jonathan, me, Maria, Rick, Roger, and Jane, a whole group of people. But I don't understand what this has to do with the terrorists."

"Were Cane and Mrs. Henry particularly close?"

"You'll have to ask her."

The bell rang and children started assembling at the door, but the captain blocked the entrance, keeping them out. He stood there silently, looking intently across the room at Barbara. She rose slowly from her chair and returned his stare. Finally he nodded and left.

Back in the car, he thought about the conversation. She had been tougher and less cooperative than he had expected. Sometimes it was all so easy. Not this time. Still, he had a clearer picture now. She had been hiding something, he was sure.

Maybe Jonathan Cane had only wanted an interview. But the captain doubted it. Maria Henry wouldn't have lied about having lunch with Barbara Darling just to give an old friend a chance for an interview. And Miss Darling wouldn't have insisted they met no one during their outing just for an interview. No, Maria Henry had gone to lunch to see a former, and perhaps present, lover.

He understood the motive for their meeting but the critical question remained unanswered. Had Maria Henry told Jonathan Cane anything that would hurt them? Barbara Darling couldn't tell him. She hadn't been there. He couldn't question Maria Henry, there were still too many U.S. agents and military people hovering around.

No. There was only one person who would know. There was only one man he could ask.

EIGHTEEN

The Taunus was not there. All the other cars were still parked in the lot, dew thick on their windows, giving evidence of a night's inactivity and a lazy morning's start. But the Taunus was gone. The blue-eyed man looked around the small parking lot again and swore under his breath. He slammed a fist on the steering wheel then glanced at his watch.

Not yet eight-thirty and the reporter was already gone. Perhaps he'd left for the base. Maybe he'd even left for the States, quit and gone home. Could it really be that easy? The man parked his car and walked into the hotel.

The two old sisters were rushing from the kitchen to the dining room, serving soft boiled eggs, refilling their guests' coffee cups, and bringing more rolls.

"Pardon me," he said in English as Margaret hurried past. "I'm looking for Herr Cane. Has he come down yet?"

"He's not here. He already left." She disappeared into the kitchen. A moment later she was back, carrying a tall silver coffee pot.

The man held up his hand to stop her. "Do you know where he went?"

Margaret stopped and looked closely at him. "You were here last night."

"Yes."

"But he was here last night."

"Oh. I'm sorry I missed him. I thought I would recognize him, but I didn't. It's not really important."

"Why do you want to see him?" Something about the man

[113]

bothered her. Perhaps it was the way he asked his questions. No, he didn't ask, he demanded.

"I'm Captain Montgomery with the public information office here in Ochsenburg. Mr. Cane asked for an interview with the Henry family and I wanted to talk with him about it. I dropped by last night on my way home, but I missed him. I thought I'd come by on my way to the office this morning. It's nothing."

The man's tone was light, easy. But Margaret knew it was a lie. Cane had seen Maria Henry the day before. Why would he ask for an interview? She wanted the man to go. "Herr Cane is gone."

She turned to walk away but he put his hand on her arm to stop her. She stared defiantly back at him. "Did he check out? Has he gone back to the States?"

"No." She pulled away.

"Do you know when he might be back?"

She ignored him and began clearing the dishes from an empty table.

"Here, this is my number. I'll be in Frankfurt today, he can reach me there. Tell him to call me, please."

The man took a small notepad from his breast pocket and scribbled a number on it. Margaret glanced at it then stuffed it in her pocket. He was at the door when she called to him. "You did not sign the paper. What is your name?"

"Captain Montgomery. Ward Montgomery." He pulled the door closed behind him.

He drove slowly through the main base, doubling back to cover each road and then along the road that ringed the *Kaserne*, searching for the old, beat-up red car. Convinced it was not there, he coasted through the large parking lot in the middle of the *Kaserne* a last time then drove to the front gate.

He slowed as he approached it. A young guard snapped a salute and waved him through. The captain, deep in concentration, merely nodded as he drove out of the *Kaserne* and into the street. He drummed his fingers on the steering wheel and thought of the only question that mattered now. "What do you know, Mr. Cane, what do you know?"

The headquarters of the *Stars and Stripes* lie at the end of a two-lane street that runs past high-rise apartment buildings and a huge supermarket. The pavement turns to cobblestones, trees replace buildings, and suddenly the street ends and there is a small guard shack, a gate, and a complex of buildings.

The gate was open and the guard shack empty as Cane approached. He drove slowly into the compound looking at the gray stone buildings on his left. Nothing had changed in the years he'd been gone, and probably nothing ever would change, unless with the coming troop reductions the paper simply went out of business.

Cane parked in the small lot across from the front entrance and stood for a minute, looking at the building. Going out of business was a distinct possibility now, he knew. Most people, including many soldiers, figured the paper was a government rag, bought and paid for with tax dollars and dictated to by the generals. But the *Stars and Stripes* didn't get any taxpayer money to support itself, and most of the editors and reporters were civilians, as were all the printers, truck drivers, telephone operators, and just about everyone else working there. And for many of the reporters and editors, tweeking the nose of a pompous general was the greatest thrill around.

The paper carried some classified ads now—a big change from when Cane worked there—and some ads from the PX, but that was it. *Stripes* earned its keep through contract printing—almost every U.S. military base in Germany has a paper that *Stripes* prints for a tidy fee—and profits on the bookstores it operates on hundreds of bases around Europe. If the U.S. troops go home, will there still be base newspapers and people to shop at *Stripes'* bookstores? Cane wondered.

Some of the reporters and editors had worked at the paper for decades. But none had the contacts Joe Rivers did. Cane had come to see Rivers. He had a theory, and Joe would be the perfect listener. He hadn't bothered to contact him earlier; Joe and Cane were competitors after all, and Joe never gave much away while covering a story. But now that it was over, Cane knew Rivers would listen.

Rivers was a tall, black, Santa Claus–like man of easy charm and good humor. His large, protruding stomach testified to his love of good food and fine wines. He'd come to Germany as a young draftee in the late 1950s and fallen in love with the country. He spoke fluent German and knew German politics better than the American ambassador. Over the years Rivers had made friends and had come to be trusted at every level of the German government and in every corner of the German military. His contacts with the intelligence agencies, both German and American, were so good that more than once he'd been accused of being a spy himself.

Cane found him in the long, narrow canteen frequented by the drivers, mechanics, pressmen, and others who kept *Stripes* running. He sat at a long table in the middle of the room, a huge black buoy in a sea of fluorescent light, blond Formica furniture, and yellow linoleum. He was drinking coffee and reading a German paper. That morning's *Stripes* lay at his elbow.

He looked up and smiled broadly as Cane approached. "Ah, Jonathan, my old friend. I heard you were back in Germany." He rose halfway from his chair and held out a huge hand that engulfed Cane's with a firm grip.

"Yeah, I've been in Ochsenburg. In fact, I was kind of surprised I didn't see you there." Cane pulled a chair from the utilitarian table and sat down. Near them, German workmen were finishing their breakfast of eggs, rolls, and coffee and drifting back to work.

"Oh, they thought it would be better if I stayed here and did some checking by phone." Rivers said it without even a hint of a smile, but Cane caught a sparkle in his eyes.

"I'll bet," Cane said. "Find anything interesting?"

"No, not really. The people I've talked to don't really have much on this. Well planned, that's for sure. Somebody sure knew the system."

"Well, I've heard a couple of interesting things and I've sort of wrestled them into the only pattern I can think of that makes any sense."

Rivers let the silence hang between them as he sipped his coffee slowly before saying, "Well, go on."

"For example, I've got it on pretty good authority that the terrorists didn't speak Arabic. And I've been told that whoever planned this could just as easily have shot their way in and stolen the damned explosives, rather than staying in there like sitting ducks."

"Well, nothing you've said so far is terribly surprising. It could be they were Iranians and only spoke Persian. But, I'm getting ahead of you. What's your theory?"

"I think the old East German secret police, the Stasi, was in on it."

"The Stasi?" Rivers seemed stunned. "Why the hell would they do something like that? These guys are so busy putting on false mustaches, practicing new names, and trying to blend in or booking a flight to South America they haven't got time to bust old Hamid out of jail."

"Listen, here's my theory. We know that members of the Red Army Faction had been hiding out in East Germany. They would train in the Middle East, come over here, blow the shit out of some politician, and then get asylum in the old German Democratic Republic. The Stasi would take care of everything for them over there. New names, new jobs, everything. Well, now the old secret police is on the run. These guys can't find jobs and they're disgruntled. They know they can't hide forever and that they might end up in jail for what they've done. Besides, the West Germans are rounding up the Red Army Faction. So, what if al Hamani knew too much about the whole thing. What if they were afraid he'd talk, you know, give 'em up. So some of the old Red Army types that haven't been found yet get together with a few old Stasi buddies and plan the whole thing. I mean they're still planting bombs over here aren't they?"

"Sure, but do you really think al Hamani would talk? Are you serious?"

"Well, what if they needed him as their entry into a safe haven in the Middle East. It would sure be one hell of a calling card. That explains why they didn't steal the bombs. The places they'd want to go to probably already have nukes or are going to get them soon, so there's no point in stealing them. It was al Hamani they wanted. It would certainly curry some favor." Rivers was silent. "Well, what do you think? It's the only thing that makes any sense to me," Cane said.

"I think you've been seeing too many spy movies," Rivers said, joking.

"Well, have you heard any rumblings along those lines?" Cane pressed.

"Cane, I haven't heard anything even remotely like that. Hell, the last political rumblings I heard were about six months ago, and they were from the other side of the spectrum. The Germans were looking pretty hard for Fritz Dietenbacher, the right-wing fanatic who calls himself the minister of war for the Republican Party. They keep pretty tight watch on these neo-Nazi types, and he dropped out of sight. They were afraid he'd show up in the East raising all kinds of hell about reclaiming lost Polish territory just as Chancellor Kohl was putting that fiasco behind him and trying to patch this country back together. Come to think of it, Dietenbacher never did show up. But he's not involved in this. The last thing he'd do is go out of his way to free someone like al Hamani. And I don't think he's looking for a calling card to Baghdad or Tripoli."

"Yeah, but what about the RAF or the Stasi? There's no reason to think they're not involved."

"Look, Cane"—his voice dropped and he spoke earnestly, as though explaining the facts of life—"I'll admit the RAF are crazy bastards and they might have had a hand in this. But if you're right about someone being able to bust in and steal one of those explosives, they sure as hell wouldn't have just sat around inside that place, now would they? I mean a nuclear explosive they could throw in the trunk and go cruising on the autobahn? Think of what they could demand with that. If they had something like that, I don't think they'd use it just to free one crazy Middle Eastern terrorist, especially Hamid al Hamani. There are people in jail who could do them more good than he can, believe me. No, they'd do something bigger than that. The Stasi? Hell, I don't know, I just don't see it. And I sure as hell haven't heard anything from anyplace to indicate that they're involved in this."

"Well, maybe you're right. Listen, one more thing. You hear anything about the government knowing in advance about the attack?"

"Are you kidding? No way. I mean if they did, they're keeping it damned well covered up. Why, what have you heard?"

"Nothing. Just a rumor I picked up in O'burg. Heard dozens

of them while I was there. Look, I've got to go. I'm on my way down to Heidelberg, to see if I can shake anything loose down there."

Cane stood and held out his hand. Joe shook it lazily. "Happy hunting. And if you pick up anything interesting, you might consider giving your old friend a call."

"You bet. Thanks for the help, Joe."

Cane was nearly at the door when Joe looked up from the table again and shouted, "Hey, greet old Biff for me, okay.?"

"Sure," Cane called back and waved without turning around. By the time he was outside he'd already forgotten Joe's request. He was thinking of something else. He was thinking that Joe was right. His well-constructed theory about the Stasi and the Red Army Faction just didn't hold together. And now he was right back where he had started: lots of questions, no answers.

NINETEEN

The U.S. Army, Europe headquarters, had not changed. Its massive, red stone front stretched almost a city block, giving it the appearance of an ancient fortress. Only a large archway in its middle broke the solid facade. Oil drums barricaded the entrance, and the military policemen directed all pedestrians to a small gray plywood building just outside the arch.

Cane parked in the housing area across from the entrance. He hadn't bothered to phone ahead. It was always easier for the bureaucrats to say "no" on the phone than in person. You show up, someone, someplace, will see you, he knew.

Inside the plywood building he lay his passport and press credentials on the counter. The young MP behind the counter ignored them and just looked at him.

"Hi, my name's Jonathan Cane, I'm a reporter. I'd like to see Biff Fribble in the public affairs office." The soldier then picked up the passport and credentials and looked at them carefully.

"Do you have an appointment?"

"No, but it's really quite important that I speak with him. It's about Ochsenburg. If you'll call him, I think he'll sign me in."

The MP shrugged, looked up the number in the thin base directory, and dialed. "This is Pfc Anderson at the main gate. There's a newspaper reporter here named Jonathan Cane. He says he needs to speak with Mr. Fribble." He listened for a minute and went on. "No, he said he didn't have an appointment, just that it's about Ochsenburg." He paused again and then said, "Okay, I'll tell him."

He hung up the phone and looked up at Cane. "Someone from his office will be down in a minute to sign you in."

Ten minutes later a petite blond sergeant arrived to escort him. Cane followed her out the door and under the arch and into the base. He looked around him as they walked, remembering his visits years before. The grassy areas, trees, and shrubs were neatly trimmed. The large, rectangular stone buildings showed a sense of care and maintenance and durability.

At other bases across Germany the buildings often were dowdy; paint peeled and stone structures, layered with decades of exhaust fumes, were gray. Not Heidelberg. Not where the army's generals were. The buildings were all fresh paint and sandblast: robust.

Cane remembered Biff Fribble as a rumpled man with disheveled black hair streaked with gray. He probably had the shortest job description in the history of the army: stonewall. And Fribble was a master at it. With an easy-going, bumbling manner he deflected criticism and rarely gave an answer that was useful or helpful.

He was an avid skier and took long vacations in the Alps. Little work was accomplished in his office while he was gone. It all seemed to suit the generals of Heidelberg, not known for wanting publicity, just fine.

Fribble was at his government-issue gray metal desk, leaning back in his chair, talking on the phone. He looked older, but otherwise unchanged. His clothes were still rumpled and his hair disheveled. His half glasses had slid down almost to the end of his nose. And, judging from his end of the conversation, he was making arrangements for a ski trip. Biff looked up and motioned Cane to the wooden chair next to his desk. Covering the mouthpiece with his hand he whispered, "Be with you in a second." He spoke for a moment longer, hung up, leaned over, and held out his hand.

"Good to see you."

"Nice to see you, Biff. I'm Jonathan Cane. I don't know if you remember me. I used to work for the *Stars and Stripes*. Sounds like you're still a ski bum."

Biff laughed. "Yeah. But with all this stuff happening in Ochsenburg, I had to cancel my vacation in Austria last week.

Not much skiing time left this year, either. But we're all set now," he said, patting the telephone. "Anyway, it's good to see you again. What brings you back to Heidelberg? "

"I was in Ochsenburg covering the deal up there and I'm still working on it."

"Okay, so what can I do for you?"

"Well, I came across some pretty interesting information and I need an official response."

"Sure. What do you need?"

It was time to run his bluff. Time to look the man in the eye and lie. "I'm filing a story tonight for tomorrow's paper that says the United States knew in advance that terrorists planned to hit the nuclear weapons depot in Ochsenburg and ignored the warning. I also know that the terrorists were not Iraqis despite what the government said."

That would do for starters. Although he had known the outline of what he would say before he began, he surprised himself with the conviction and seriousness he managed to put into his concocted story.

He waited for Fribble's reaction. Biff simply stared. Slowly a smile formed at the corners of his mouth and his eyes twinkled. He was about to laugh, but as he watched Cane's face he realized the reporter wasn't joking.

"That's preposterous," he said, still wanting to believe it was a joke. "That's the most craziest thing I've ever heard of," he said, tripping over his own syntax. "You can't write something like that."

Cane smiled. "Come on, Biff, I'm not making this up. My sources are excellent and they assure me the information is correct."

Fribble was now convinced it wasn't a joke. "I shouldn't even bother to respond to that kind of crap," he sniffed.

"Okay. If the official reaction is simply to say it's preposterous, that's fine, I'll quote you as saying that. But I thought you might want me to talk to someone else. Maybe one of the spooks around here."

"You don't need to talk to anyone else. I can tell you right now, there's nothing to it. You got bad information. The U.S. Army completely denies it knew anything about this in advance."

Cane pressed harder. "That may be, but this place will be crawling with reporters after my story runs." By now he was actually enjoying the exaggeration. "I can't wait to see what that guy Rolf Makler at the *Tagesblatt* will do with the sources he has. You know Rolf. He's the guy that broke the story in the first place and then followed up with the piece about how the army was ready to storm the storage area. You remember him, don't you, Biff?"

Fribble simply stared.

"Hey, Biff, I'm just trying to get both sides of the story." Cane shifted to his let's-reason-together tone. "If you think all my sources are off-base, let someone tell me. Otherwise you're going to have to make the same denial hundreds of times over the next week after my story runs."

Cane hoped his last statement, with the implied promise of another ski vacation canceled, would prod Biff into action. It did.

"Look, I don't know who you've been talking to, but I can tell you they don't know what they're talking about. Okay?"

Cane said nothing.

"I know you can't take my word for it. Why don't you help yourself to a cup of coffee over there and I'll see if I can find somebody for you to talk to."

There was a small coffee urn on a card table in a corner of the office, next to a filing cabinet. Cane picked up a paper cup, poured himself a cup of coffee, and sat on a folding chair to listen to Biff.

"Yes, I know. But he said he was filing the story for tomorrow's paper." Pause. "I already told him that, but he insists on talking with someone who was involved with the whole thing." Pause. "Wait a second, I'll ask him." Biff covered the mouthpiece with his hand. "Mr. Cane, what's your deadline?"

"I have until after close of business local time. I pick up eight or nine hours with the time difference between here and the West Coast. But the sooner the better."

He added powdered creamer to his coffee and stirred slowly. Biff hung up, waited a moment, and dialed again. He spoke quickly and hung up then dialed again.

Watching Biff struggle to line up an interview was fun, and

Cane smiled with pleasure. He was having a ball. Fribble finally hung up and looked at him again.

"Okay, Mr. Cane. I think we've got someone for you to talk with. But nobody here has any idea what you're talking about."

"Well, I've got some pretty good sources on this. So, who am I going to see and when?"

"I've arranged for you to talk with Colonel Rick Ridgeway. He's in the office of army intelligence. Everything relating to the army's part in this terrorist thing passed through his office. I know Colonel Ridgeway. He's a straight shooter. He'll tell you the truth. But this is strictly an off-the-record background interview. You can't quote him or use anything he tells you. He's only trying to help you get this straight. Those are the ground rules."

"Fair enough. When am I going to see him?"

"Well, he's tied up in meetings this morning. The earliest I could get you in was one-thirty this afternoon. Is that all right?"

"Okay."

The bluff had worked. He had the interview. If it didn't pan out, that would be all right. He'd done everything he could think of. He'd chased it down. But it just might work. Cane stood, pleased with himself.

"If you want, you can wait here in the office," Fribble offered.

"Thanks, Biff. But I think I'll wander around Heidelberg a little bit. It's a beautiful city and I haven't been here in a long time."

He signed out at the guard shack and had almost reached the car when he thought of the base library. He had the time, and it was nearby, just outside the base fence. He'd be foolish not to see what he could find.

Heidelberg had one of the best libraries in the army system in Europe. It had more resources and better references than most of the smaller branches scattered on posts from Turkey to England.

It took Cane less than five minutes to reach it from the front gate. He showed his press credential to the middle-aged woman sitting behind a cluttered desk that had a small sign,

REFERENCE, on the front. Of course he could use the library, the woman assured him. But he couldn't check out any books. Cane smiled easily and assured her, he just wanted to look at some back issues of newspapers.

He found the *Readers' Guide* and began his search. Fifteen minutes later he had more than a dozen references to the Red Army Faction spanning the last two years. As an afterthought he looked for the name Dietenbacher but found nothing. He checked earlier editions and eventually discovered one reference to a Fritz K. Dietenbacher in a *Christian Science Monitor* article written about five years earlier. He jotted down the information and returned to the reference desk.

The librarian smiled over her desk, its top almost invisible beneath a blanket of papers interspersed with small, ceramic figurines bearing cheery inscriptions.

"Find what you need?" she asked.

It took Cane almost an hour to read all the stories about the Red Army Faction. There were stories about their bombings and assassinations, about their roots in the Baader-Meinhof Gang, and one piece, quoting anonymous intelligence sources, about the gang's connections with the Middle Eastern terrorist organizations and the Irish Republican Army.

As he pulled the last spindle of microfilm off the projector, Cane was thinking that maybe he was right after all. From what he'd read the Red Army had connections with almost every terrorist group in the world. Maybe he had part of it right, but not all the pieces. He was still trying to make the puzzle fit his outline as he returned the microfilm to the reference librarian.

"Here's the *Christian Science Monitor* you asked for."

"Hmmmm? Oh, right." Cane took the paper, which was already open and folded to the proper page, and quickly scanned the article. It was a short piece about election gains by Germany's far right in Bavaria with a photo of Dietenbacher that was at least fifteen years old. There was no mention of a connection to other terrorist organizations, and Cane dismissed Dietenbacher, focusing his thoughts instead on the Red Army Faction.

He handed the paper back, thanked the librarian again for her help, and walked out of the library into the overcast morning. As he walked slowly to his car he was already planning some interesting questions for the colonel that afternoon.

TWENTY

Colonel Rick Ridgeway stared at the tidy stack of reports on his desk. Ridgeway was an orderly man, and the previous evening before leaving work he had planned this day's activities with precision: the reports to be written, read, signed, and forwarded. And now this.

It wasn't the interview that bothered him. It was the time. He estimated the meeting with the reporter would take no more than forty-five minutes. But he needed to reread reports and double-check the facts. He would not be caught unprepared.

"Jesus," he whispered to himself. The reporter's story was such an outrageous fabrication why even bother denying it? And now it was his job to convince him how wrong he was.

He flipped open a file, stamped TOP SECRET in red letters on its cover, and began to read. He read slowly and carefully, although he already knew everything in the report. When he finished he reached for one of the two phones on his desk but hesitated, his hand only inches from the receiver.

He hated to make the call. Asking such a question would make him look stupid in the eyes of an old friend. Still he wanted to say he had checked with everyone and been told in unequivocal terms that no one knew in advance.

"Jesus," he muttered again and grabbed the receiver.

His call was passed around the Frankfurt consulate, transferred from one extension to another before he finally reached John Herman, a buddy of Ridgeway from their days in Vietnam. Ostensibly an accountant who tracked NATO funds, Herman in reality tracked data on the Soviet military for the CIA. If anything was wrong, Herman would know.

But there was nothing to tell, Herman assured Ridgeway. No one in the CIA or anywhere in the government knew anything of the planned attack on the ammunition dump. The reporter's charges were wild, groundless. Herman give him his word on that. There was nothing to it.

"By the way, just for the record," Herman asked casually, "what's that reporter's name again?"

Cane arrived early for the interview. A large, middle-aged German secretary glanced up as he walked into the outer office. Without speaking, she pointed to a chair and resumed her typing. Her desk sat next to the colonel's door, which she jealously guarded with typical tight-sphincter German efficiency.

At exactly one-thirty the door opened and a short, thick man, with thinning hair and a neatly trimmed black mustache came out. The colonel extended his hand and Cane shook it.

"Mr. Cane, I'm Colonel Ridgeway. Won't you come in. Please, have a seat." He gestured to the metal folding chair next to his desk.

The office was small and sparse. A desk, filing cabinet, and two chairs were the only furniture. The desk top was almost bare: two telephones, and "in" and "out" baskets. No personal touches, no photos, no mementos. Behind Ridgeway on the pale green wall, in simple black frames, were the colonel's diplomas and awards, hung in two neat rows of four. There were no other adornments.

Cane noticed the folder marked TOP SECRET and suspected it had been left on the desk to impress him.

"I'm sorry I was late. I wanted to reread a couple of reports on the incident before talking with you." He kept his eyes on Cane, as if purposefully avoiding the folder that rested inches from his elbow.

"Good. I'm glad. I think it's quite important that I try to get some official reaction before I file my story tonight."

"Well, I don't know that I can be of much help to you. From what Mr. Fribble said, I think you've been given some bad information."

Ridgeway leaned forward and folded his hands together on the desk. His tone was friendly. And Cane knew he was trying hard to project the image of someone just trying to help. But Cane didn't buy it.

"Colonel Ridgeway, let me start at the beginning here—"

"Wait just a second," Ridgeway said, interrupting. "Mr. Fribble did go over the ground rules with you. This is a strictly off-the-record interview. It's for background only. You can't quote me or use anything from this interview. Is that clear?"

"I understand. If you confirm what I already know, it won't make any difference. I already have a great deal of information from other sources."

The colonel's smile tightened slightly but he said nothing and waited for Cane to continue.

"So, let me start at the beginning. I've been covering the terrorist attack in Ochsenburg. After it was over, a source, who is in a very good position to know, told me that the U.S. consulate in Frankfurt received a warning about a possible terrorist attack of this kind before it happened. Is that true?"

"No."

"Colonel, are you sure? I was given very specific information."

"Yes, Mr. Cane, I'm sure. And, I know." His eyes remained fixed on Cane. His hands were still folded. He made no movement toward the folder. "When I was asked to meet with you I talked to some very highly placed people who are in a position to know. I told them about the story you're working on and about your idea that the United States government knew in advance and did nothing. They think it's preposterous. And frankly, so do I."

"If that's true, then why were the nuclear explosives moved out of the ammunition dump the day before the terrorists attacked?"

It was a long shot, and Cane knew if they ever discovered that his "highly reliable source" for that precious nugget of information was a stoned painter he met in a bar, he would be laughed out of the office.

But he hoped that by using an exact time reference—one day before the attack—he might jar something loose from the colonel.

"What?" The colonel's surprise was authentic. He leaned back in his chair and folded his arms across his chest.

"Who told you that? That's the most incredible thing I've ever heard. Do you think that we let a group of Iraqi-sponsored terrorists terrorize this country just because we like to play crisis games here? That's the kind of reporting that you see in the *National Enquirer*. I thought you worked for a respectable paper."

Ridgeway's voice was rising and he struggled to keep control.

Cane too was struggling. He could feel his own anger rising. Military officers were all the same, he thought. They didn't really believe in a free press. Any time a story painted anything less than a rosy picture, they tried to tar the entire press with the *National Enquirer* brush. They thought everything ought to be government-approved before it appeared in the paper. The fucking fascists.

"So you deny the weapons were removed in advance of the terrorist attack?" Cane pressed for a straight answer.

"Absolutely." The colonel leaned forward quickly and lay his hands, fists clenched, on his desk. "That is a lie and whoever told you it is a liar and I'll tell them that to their face." The colonel's own face was tight with anger. The two sat in silence for several moments just looking at each other, and then Cane played his remaining ace.

"I find it interesting that you said the terrorists were Iraqi when I have it from an unimpeachable source that they didn't speak Arabic. In fact, I understand there may be a connection between the terrorists and the Red Army Faction, perhaps even the Stasi. Can you tell me anything about that?"

Ridgeway's eyes flared as he stared at the reporter. Cane could see the colonel was truly struggling to maintain his composure before continuing.

"Mr. Cane. I am an officer of the United States Army. I take great pride in that. I am also a man who places great value on integrity, my own personal integrity as well as that of the army. When I was given the order to meet with you this afternoon, I set aside all the other work I had scheduled for today and began checking. I didn't expect to find anything, but I checked anyway. I talked with people in the embassy. I even called an old friend at the consulate in Frankfurt who knows all about the incident. I have talked to some of the people here who were deeply involved in this crisis from the very beginning. No one I spoke with, absolutely no one, said there had been even a hint of a warning. To suggest we removed the nuclear explosives and then put them back just in time for the terrorists to seize them . . . well, frankly it astonishes me that anyone would believe that.

"Were they really Red Army Faction terrorists pretending to be Iraqis? Or were they really former secret police from East Germany? Did they speak Arabic?" His voice was rising again, despite his efforts. "Hell, I don't know, they might have spoken Hindi or Japanese. All the negotiations were done in English, so if someone told you they didn't speak Arabic, I don't think that person knows what he's talking about. And frankly I don't think it makes a damned bit of difference what language they spoke. Or even much difference who they hell they were. What mattered is they had nuclear explosives and were a God-damned inch away from blowing an entire German city off the map."

He paused for a moment, and when he spoke again he had regained control and his voice was soft, as though he were weary. "Mr. Cane, I think you should tread very lightly here. I don't doubt someone told you these things. But I give you my word, none of it is true. And believe me, I did try to find out."

Cane was now convinced Ridgeway was being as open and honest as he could be and he felt slightly foolish, and even a bit guilty. The man had gone to great trouble and Cane had only been bluffing.

"Can you tell me who you checked with?" Cane asked.

"No. I can't do that anymore than you can tell me who your sources are. But I can assure you I checked with some very high-ranking people."

"Well, colonel, I appreciate your time and help. I have a bit of a dilemma here now. I was assured the information I received was reliable. But I guess I need to do some more checking. I want to thank you again for your time and help."

"Does this mean you're not going to write the story?" Ridgeway asked.

Cane couldn't tell Ridgeway that any hope of writing a

story had vanished in the face of his strong denials. He had run a bluff and it hadn't worked and he couldn't tell him that either.

"Well, colonel, I don't know. Like I said, I obviously have some more checking to do. But I can assure you that I am a responsible journalist and I wouldn't write anything without being certain that it was correct. That's all I can tell you for now."

They shook hands stiffly and Cane left. At the front gate, he hurriedly scrawled his name and time of departure in the MPs' book and crossed to the housing area to find his car. He slid into the Taunus, leaned his head back, and stared at the roof. He was tired. He hadn't slept enough the night before. His earlier exhilaration was long spent, and the disappointing lack of success multiplied his exhaustion.

He knew he had done everything he could. He'd checked every possible source and angle he could think of. He'd tried as hard as he could. But somehow that just wasn't enough to keep the greatest story of his life from slipping through his fingers.

TWENTY-ONE

It would take close to two hours to drive back to Ochsenburg and Cane knew he should get started. The sun was finally breaking through the gray skies so at least it would be a pretty drive. The trip to Heidelberg had been a bust. Tomorrow, he would pack it in and catch a flight back to the States.

He took a long look at the community around him. It was all over now; the story, his trip to Germany, his touching base with the past. It would be a very long time before he visited a military housing area again and he looked slowly at the buildings, lawns, and cars.

In military housing the officers and enlisted don't live side by side, and it always shows. This was obviously officers' quarters. The lawns were just a little neater, the streets a little cleaner, no trash, no soggy candy and gum wrappers littered the grass. But, what really told the difference, Cane knew, were the cars.

He couldn't remember ever seeing a jacked-up car in the officers' housing areas, as if jacks and mechanical problems had to be checked at the gate. He had seen plenty of sports cars, weekend mechanics bent over them cleaning the engines or changing the spark plugs. But a car up on jacks so someone could crawl under and replace a worn-out muffler or rebuild a rear end, were unicorn-rare in the officers' housing area.

During his days at *Stripes* it had become a game with him. He would drive through a housing area and try to determine the status of the occupants by looking at the cars. He knew he was parked in an officers' housing area, but he unconsciously fell into the old game again.

That was when he saw the black Opel.

Opels were a common car among the American military in Germany. Officers and men alike bought them, but they favored the inexpensive models that provided basic transportation. No one bought the big, powerful models, which were not built to American specifications and couldn't be taken back to the States.

Cane saw the black Opel Senator, a sleek four-door sedan, parked about fifty yards behind him, near the end of the street. Its plates indicated it was registered in Frankfurt, and Cane knew instantly it didn't belong to a resident. Still, he paid little attention.

He was trying to forget the story he'd just seen go up in smoke. He eased his car away from the curb and pulled into the street.

Within minutes Cane was on the four-lane highway leading toward the edge of town and the autobahn. The Opel followed. Cane noticed the large black car turn onto the street behind him, but dismissed it: an insignificant detail in an already overcrowded, exhausting day. And again on the autobahn he saw it. And again he misunderstood.

Slow cars are not tolerated outside their proper lane on the German autobahn, and Cane settled into a steady grinding of the miles in the slow, right-hand lane. The Taunus, never built for speed and now well aged, couldn't do any better. Yet he didn't mind too much. With the sun out, the day turned warm. It wasn't such a bad drive.

Occasional breaks in the heavy flow of traffic allowed Cane to pull from behind trucks and make the long, deliberate run to overtake them and then duck back out of the way of the fast moving Porsches, BMWs, and big Mercedes.

And once when he pulled into traffic to escape the fumes of a slow-moving tractor trailor rig, he checked his mirror and spotted the black Opel overtaking a truck. Oddly though, rather than stay in the inside lane and pick up speed, it quickly slowed, merged to the right, and disappeared into the traffic.

A glimmer of suspicion began to form. Opel Senators are built for autobahn driving, where there are no speed limits.

As he stared in his mirror to catch another glimpse of the Opel he shot past the off ramp to a service station and restaurant. He had planned to stop, and now his bladder began to scold him for his inattention.

It was fifteen minutes later before he found a rest area and pulled in. Little more than a widened parallel road squeezed between the autobahn and a barren field, the rest area was sparse: parking places on the right and left, a concrete picnic table and benches on a small plot of grass to the right. Two trash cans near the tables were overflowing. On the left a thick row of tall bare-branch bushes with buds but no leaves formed a barrier between the parking area and the autobahn.

Cane pulled the Taunus to a stop facing the bushes and looked around: no rest room, no portable toilets. He had no choice but to relieve himself in the age-old fashion of male travelers everywhere. He moved to the bushes and turned his back to the parking lot. Cane heard the cars whoosh past just a few yards away, but they were impossible to see through the bushes. The sky began to cloud and the sun quickly disappeared completely. The air turned cold. A wind swept off the field across the rest stop, whipping at Cane's shirt sleeves and raising goose bumps on his arms. He shivered.

Finished, he turned to walk back to the car but stopped. There was the Opel. It squatted on the edge of pavement just off the autobahn facing into the rest area, overseeing all. Cane stared at the car.

Two men were in the front seat, and although he could barely see their faces he knew they had been watching him the entire time. He could feel it.

Neither man moved. They didn't study maps. They didn't look to the side or appear to chat. They didn't get out of the car to relieve themselves. They simply sat, watching.

Another gust of cold wind burst through his shirt, making him shiver again. He stared at the car, and for a moment considered simply approaching the men to face his fear head-on. But as he turned toward the car he decided he wanted only to leave.

Cane hurried to his car. He fumbled and dropped the keys to the floor. He rubbed his hands together to warm them and forced himself to move more slowly. He slipped the key in the ignition and turned it. The Taunus cranked but wouldn't fire.

"Come on, come on," he muttered. He glanced again at

the black Opel. It had not moved. Then the Taunus engine fired and a wave of relief swept over him. He backed up, quickly turned the car back toward the autobahn, and headed toward the rest stop exit, watching the Opel closely in his mirror. It hadn't moved. The autobahn entrance was less than thirty yards away now. Still the Opel sat. A small, nervous smile crossed Cane's face as he pushed the accelerator to the floor to gain the needed speed to enter the highway. A little more than ten yards now. He looked again. It hadn't moved. The autobahn was only a few car lengths away. He could feel the muscles of his neck begin to relax. He had been foolish. It was coincidence. There was nothing to fear. He eased the Taunus into the autobahn traffic.

The Opel began to roll.

A big truck closed quickly behind the Taunus, and for a moment Cane's mirror view of the rest area was cut off. He turned and looked frantically behind him. The Opel was gone.

Cane laughed, trying for levity. "I must be paranoid. This is crazy," he said very loudly to himself. But he didn't believe it.

Yet it made no sense, and Cane slowly marshaled arguments meant to banish the fear the black Opel had planted in him. Why would anyone want to follow him? he asked. There was no reason. Was the army so afraid he would write a damaging story that it was keeping tabs on him? But why would they do that? He believed Ridgeway, and he had practically promised he woudn't write the story.

Maybe the CIA found out about his affair with Maria and is afraid . . . of what? That didn't make any sense either. Unless they thought he was part of the terrorist operation from the beginning. No, that was too far fetched to consider.

As he drove he made up other scenarios, each more improbable than the one before, as if to prove to himself how preposterous the idea really was. There was no reason for anyone to follow him. There was no reason for fear. There was no danger.

Still, he constantly checked the mirror and without thinking pushed the accelerator close to the floor. He didn't look at the scenery. He no longer tried to enjoy the trip. He simply drove and scanned the mirror.

It was another hour before he reached Ochsenburg. His hands ached from gripping the wheel and his shoulders were hunched tight. He hadn't seen the black Opel again, but he had thought of nothing else.

TWENTY-TWO

Cane tried to rationalize his fears as flights of fancy. Maybe he was just overtired. Maybe he was making too much of all the questions, seeing things that weren't there. Just coincidence. He was pushing, trying too hard. His judgment was clouded. He was seeing ghosts.

Maybe being in Ochsenburg again and seeing Maria had been too much of an emotional strain. God knows he thought about her all the time. And each time that he remembered how much he loved her he also remembered anew he would never see her again. He was thinking with his emotions.

By the time he pulled the Taunus into the parking lot of the Engel, he was almost ready to believe the arguments. He got out, stretched, and looked around. The air was heavy and cool. The evening was still. He looked at the familiar hotel and felt his spirits rise. A hot bath, a beer and a schnapps, not necessarily in that order, were what he needed. He would feel better then.

His walked stiffly past the few cars in the lot, into the Engel and to his favorite corner seat. He gave Margaret a weak smile and mouthed, *"Ein Bier, bitte"* to her. But a few minutes later, when she set down his beer, she also lay a small piece of paper on the table with it.

"A Mr. Montgomery came by to see you early this morning."

He picked up the paper and studied it for a moment. "Montgomery. I don't think I know him."

"He said he was from the military. From the public affairs

[141]

office. He wanted to talk to you about interviewing that major's family."

He looked at Margaret and caught her unease. "Was he wearing a uniform?" The fear begin to rise.

"Yes. He said you should call him at that number in Frankfurt."

Cane looked at the piece of paper. The name "Capt. Montgomery" and a phone number were written in neat script. There was nothing else.

"Did he say what his first name was?"

"Ya. Ward. And, Herr Cane, he was here last night. But he didn't ask for you then. I remember him. He did not wear a uniform last night. And he drove a green army car like the one outside." She nodded out the window toward a green Chevrolet sedan in the parking lot, and then paused a moment. "I do not like him, Herr Cane. The way he looks," she added abruptly then turned and marched away.

The fear came back immediately. He had tried to convince himself his worrying was silly. Not now. He glanced around, looking at the five customers in the room. Did one of them drive a "green army car?"

Two of the men he knew as long-time customers. The other three were strangers. He rose slowly and walked to the small bar, where Margaret was drawing a beer. Leaning forward he spoke softly.

"Margaret, do you know all these men?"

"Herr Romy and Herr Kasier have come here for years, and Herr Schmitz started coming here about a year ago when the Turistenheim, the old hotel by the castle, closed. But the other two"—she motioned to a table on the far side of the room—"I have never seen them before. They came two hours ago and just drink beer."

He looked at the two men. One was blond with broad, powerful shoulders and big hands and closely cropped hair. The other was slight, almost skinny, with dark brown hair and a slight build. Cane watched them for a moment. The blond started chuckling, caught Cane's eye, then looked away; the other leisurely inspected his beer glass.

At the rest stop that afternoon Cane had given in to his fear and fled. But this was different. He was with friends. It was his territory and he had had enough. He turned from the small bar and walked toward the two men. They looked up and silently watched him approach.

"Pardon me, do either one of you drive the green Chevrolet parked outside?"

"*Bitte?*" responded the man with big hands. The other said nothing.

"*Sprechen sie English?*"

"*Nein. Nur Deutsch.*" (No, only German.)

Cane felt his fear and anger rise. "The Chevy outside, who does it belong to? What's this all about?" he demanded.

"*Wie, bitte?*" the blond responded casually.

Cane leaned close and lowered his voice so only the two men could hear. "What do you want with me anyway? Just what the fuck's going on here?"

In a split second the man's big right hand was around Cane's wrist. He squeezed it tightly. Cane tried to jerk away, but the man was too powerful and held him easily. He rose slightly out of his seat. His face was only inches away, his eyes fixed on Cane in a cold, unblinking, hate-filled stare. In a voice barely above a whisper he hissed, "*Es tut mir leid, aber sprechen Wir nur Deutsch. Verstehen Sie?*" (I'm sorry, we speak only German. Understand?)

He released Cane's wrist and sank back to his chair but didn't take his eyes off him. Cane moved backward, turned awkwardly, almost stumbling, and walked away from the table, fighting the internal voice urging him to bolt for the door. He forced himself to walk slowly across the dining room.

Rubbing his wrist as he climbed the stairs, Cane moved slowly up the steps and then down the hall toward his room. Suddenly he ran. He reached his room in seconds, unlocked and jerked open the door, then slammed it behind him.

His hands shook and he fumbled with the key as he slipped the lock closed. He sank to the edge of his bed, trembling. Questions flooded him. Why was someone following him? What the hell was going on?

He picked up the phone and tried to dial, but his hands shook and his fingers refused to cooperate. He breathed deeply and waited for his heart to slow. But there was no letup and finally, in desperation, he forced his fumbling fingers to dial the number.

Barbara answered on the third ring.

"Hello."

"Barbara, it's Cane."

"Hi. You okay? You sound a little weird. You been running or something?"

"No. Ahh, look, this may sound strange, but ah, did you see anyone following you when you and Maria came to the Zur Sonne yesterday?"

"Cane, what the hell's going on here?"

"Why?"

"Some captain came to the school today. He asked me questions about you and Maria and about yesterday. I didn't tell him anything. And I don't mind telling you I didn't like him very much. Cane, he scared me."

"Do you know who he was?"

"He said his name was Captain Montgomery, with army intelligence. I think he knows you saw Maria yesterday."

"Oh, shit. He told you he was from army intelligence? He told Margaret he was from public affairs. Barbara, I think I might be in trouble. Look, I'll try to call you later. One last thing. Is Maria okay?"

"I think so. I talked with her a few minutes ago. She and the boys are going home tomorrow. Woody's staying for a few days to finish the outprocessing or something. Cane, what's going on?"

"I don't know, I really don't know."

"Cane, I don't know what this is all about but I'm scared. You be real careful."

He hung up the phone and looked desperately around the room. An antique wardrobe was in the corner and the small writing desk and chair were against the wall. But his eyes came to rest again on the dark, heavily laquered door with its peephole keyhole. He stared at the door, expecting someone to kick it in at any moment. Was someone looking through the peephole right then? He wanted to look but was afraid of what he would see.

Suddenly he thought of the tiny balcony and whirled to look at the full-length windows that led to it. There was nothing, only the silhouette of the swaying trees outside the window.

As Cane struggled to control his fears, though, another emotion began to emerge. An anger began to build up inside him. Anger at the faceless men in the back Opel and the nameless men in the restaurant below. And above all, anger at himself for allowing them to scare him.

He pulled the slip of paper from his shirt pocket, grabbed the telephone, and dialed. Now he would know.

"Hello?" It was a man's voice.

"I was told to call a Captain Montgomery at this number."

"Who is this?"

"My name is Jonathan Cane. Who are you? And what the hell is going on here?"

"The captain is not here right now. I expect him shortly. I'll have him call you back. Where are you now, Mr. Cane? Are you at your hotel?" The voice was flat, remote, but tinted with a whisper of menacing urgency.

"Who are you? What office do I have? Who the hell is Captain Montgomery and why's he checking on me?"

The man ignored the question. "I'm sure the captain will be back in just a moment. Where are you now, Mr. Cane? At your hotel, in your room? It's important that you stay there, someone will be right up to speak to you. Mr. Cane?" the voice insisted.

Cane jabbed the receiver back on the cradle and sat staring at it. *Up!* They knew he was in the hotel, they knew where his room was, and the man had been too eager. Cane's muscles tightened with fear. He was quickly losing the tiny bit of control he had gained only moments before. He looked again at the window then whirled again to stare at the door. Again there was nothing.

He felt trapped. He looked at the phone and suddenly needed to talk with someone, to hear the reassuring sound of a friendly voice. He jerked the receiver off the hook and frantically dialed. The overseas operator put the call through immediately and a moment later Slovak was on the line.

"Don't tell me you need a couple more days. We've already had that conversation."

"No. No. That's not it. Something's going on here but I

[145]

don't know what it is. Look, Slovak, I went down to Heidelberg and talked with this colonel today and I told him I knew the government knew in advance that the terrorists were going to strike and that they weren't Iraqis. Shit, Slovak, these guys couldn't even speak Arabic. The colonel denied it, but some-one's been following me ever since, and now there's this captain who's looking for me. . . ."

"Hold on a minute, Cane. Hold on. What you're saying doesn't make any sense. You been smoking that wacko tobacco or something?"

"No. No. Slovak, listen to me. I really think there's some-one after me. Look, there's this captain who came to see me today. But I wasn't here. I was in Heidelberg. Checking out the Red Army Faction. . . ."

"Cane, what the *hell* are you talking about? Who's this captain and what the hell does he have to do with what you're working on? What *are* you working on? And what do you mean the government knew in advance and the terrorists were't Iraqis and the Red Army Faction is involved? That's a hell of a story. You sure about this?"

"I don't know, I just don't know."

Cane was losing his control again. But it didn't matter.

The line had gone dead.

TWENTY-THREE

It took Cane a moment to understand. He merely looked at the dead receiver in his hand. Then he heard several rapid clicks and in an instant it was clear. He dropped the phone and backed away from it. He bumped into the writing desk and tripped, catching himself on the chair. He sat and stared at the phone then looked quickly at the door. Were they outside now? Were they waiting in the hall, ready to burst in?

Daylight was disappearing rapidly. The room was in heavy shadows, almost dark. Fear overwhelmed him. He sat rigidly in the half light frantically searching for answers.

Instantly, he knew. He had to run, to get to the airport and fly home. He would drop the story. He could be home by morning. He would be safe.

Quickly he moved to the bureau, grabbed his backpack from the floor and stuffed his wallet, passport, travelers checks, a sweatshirt, and toothbrush inside. The sisters could throw the rest of his things away. He would write them later. They would understand.

He slung the pack over his shoulder and moved to the door. Opening it carefully, he peeked out. The hall was empty. He eased the door closed and was halfway down the stairs to the dining room when he suddenly realized the incredible error he was about to make.

They would be watching the hotel. He would walk right into them. But what choice was there? There were only two ways out of the hotel. How could he leave without being seen? He had no plan. He had no idea what he would do. He couldn't simply drive away. They would be watching the car. He fought back a rush of panic that welled up inside him and tried to think.

Could he climb out the bathroom window and shinny down the drainpipe? No. The drainpipe was too near the back door. Could he escape from the balcony of his room? No. They probably would be watching his room. Could he call the German police? And tell them what? Besides, maybe the men were part of the German police. He suddenly remembered his run-in with the officer in the forest.

Maybe he could get out through the building's adjoining wing, which long ago had been gutted and turned into small apartments. But there was no access from the hotel unless . . . unless . . . he went over the roof. Yes, of course, through a skylight. There were two, high on the roof's backside, away from the parking lot and not visible from the ground. It was the only chance.

He quickly changed his clothes, kicking off his tassled loafers and dropping his slacks in a heap. Cane put on jeans and running shoes. He was ready.

He climbed the stairs to the third floor, trying to move as quickly and silently as possible. At the top of the stairs he stopped dead. Herr Romy, one of the long-time customers, was in the hallway, locking his room. As he turned and saw Cane he seemed surprised. Cane's room was on the second, not the third floor. Cane smiled quickly, nodded, and opened the door on his right. The toilet room.

"*Besetz*," (busy) he said pointing down, indicating the common toilet on his floor was occupied. Herr Romy smiled in recognition and descended the stairs as Cane ducked into the tiny room.

It was little more than a closet with a toilet and a small, cold water sink. He flushed the toilet to justify his being there and realized immediately how silly it was. Turning on the water, he filled his cupped hands with water and splashed his face. He ran his cold, wet hands over the back of his neck, then rubbed his face furiously with the small hand towel and considered his most immediate problem.

Herr Romy's room was one of the two in the hotel with a skylight. Cane had seen him lock the door. There was only one room left to try.

[148]

He moved quickly down the hall to the last room, gently grasped the lever doorknob and pushed. The lever moved down but the door refused to yield. What would he do now? He let go and stood back. He looked nervously over his shoulder at the empty hall and turned again to the door. He had to get into the room. He jerked the handle down with all his strength and smashed into the door with his shoulder. It banged open and crashed against the inside wall.

He was sure the noise had filled the small hotel. His breathing was shallow and quick as he pushed the door closed. Sweat trickled down his sides. He breathed slowly and deeply, trying to regain control.

His eyes adjusted rapidly to the darkness. It was a sparsely furnished room. A single bed, marble-topped nightstand, and a small dresser were the only furniture. A suitcase lay on the edge of the bed, a shaving kit next to it. The room was occupied. He had to hurry.

He saw the skylight immediately. It was high in the sloped ceiling above the bed; too high for him to reach. Frantically, he shoved the bed aside and dragged the dresser under the skylight. Could they hear the noise downstairs? Was someone coming to inspect?

He grabbed the nightstand and hoisted it atop the dresser. He looked again at the skylight. He would never squeeze through wearing his backpack.

He was moving quickly now, all thoughts on escape. He grabbed the table lamp, ripped its cord free, and tied one end to the backpack and held the other between his teeth. He stepped onto the bed then scrambled onto the dresser. Forcing himself to move slowly, Cane stepped atop the nightstand. He squatted precariously, afraid he would fall if he stood too quickly.

A loud laugh rang down the hall, followed by the muffled sound of two people talking. Cane froze. His fingers hurt where he clenched the marble top. His knees ached. "God, don't let them come here, not this room," he prayed. Finally he heard a door close and the voices were gone.

He abandoned caution. He stood immediately, banging his head into the skylight's edge. Cane blinked and shook his head slowly then moved the latch on his window to freedom. It swung open easily. He stuck his head out into the cool night air, breathed deeply, and hoisted himself out.

The metal edges of the skylight frame cut into his forearms and he cursed the extra pounds he carried around his waist and his unfulfilled promises of dieting and exercise.

He pulled with his arms, wiggled his stomach over the edge, and slithered out, then pulled his backpack up behind him and slipped it on. Slow down, just slow down, he told himself. He raised his head and peered toward the edge of the roof. He appraised the short distance to the corner, where the two wings joined. If he moved slowly he could do it. If he hurried he might lose his footing and fall. From the roof it would be fatal.

He inched his way across the cool tile roof, eyes straight ahead, refusing to look to the edge. At the adjoining wing he moved quickly up the sloping roof and slid slowly down the other side on his rear, heels digging in hard. From the roof's edge, he climbed onto a tree and worked his way down.

Cane felt a rush of exhilaration as his feet hit the ground. He ran, fleeing into the woods, which grew almost to the edge of the building. Cane knew the forest well, but ran blindly. He missed the path he sought and had to double back. He found it and followed it through the trees, emerging near the road almost half a mile from the Engel.

And then he got a break. As he stepped from the forest, a bus pulled into a bus stop just ahead. He ran furiously and jumped on as the driver began to pull the doors closed. Moments later he sat, slumped in the back of the bus, fighting to catch his breath as the bus jostled down the road taking him farther and farther from the Engel.

Cane was the only passenger, but he still pulled the hood of his sweatshirt tightly around his head and slumped low in the seat. The other stops on the route were deserted and the driver pushed the bus hard through the narrow streets to the end of the line: Ochsenburg's main train station.

Cane stepped down and hustled across the small plaza to a bank of pay telephones. He fumbled with the coins but got them in the slot and, fighting for control, dialed Rick's number. The unanswered rings echoed in his ear like cries in the desert and finally he pounded the receiver down. He pulled a

[150]

five deutsche mark coin from his jeans pocket and fed it into the slot.

Quickly he dialed the American consulate in Frankfurt and asked for Simon North. The phone was picked up before he heard it ring. "Comm room, Winters speaking."

"Sergeant Winters, this is Jonathan Cane, I need to speak to Simon."

"He just stepped out. He'll be back in about ten minutes, maybe sooner. Want me to have him call you?"

"No. Look, can you give him a message please."

"Sure."

"Tell him to meet me at the Blick in Krausenheim as soon as possible?"

"The Blick, in Krausenheim, right?"

"Yeah, he'll know it. Tell him it's Frau Bauer's. He'll know."

"Sure, anything else?"

"Yeah, tell him it's an emergency and to get there as soon as possible."

"I'll see he gets the message. No problem. So, where are you now, you want him to call you?"

"No just give him the message."

In a straight line it is less than ten miles from Ochsenburg to Krausenheim, an isolated village that stretches along the floor of a steep valley. But the bus Cane caught at the station took nearly half an hour to wind through the hills to the ridge above the village. The intercity bus didn't make the side trip down the twisting road to the valley floor. So, when the American with the blue jeans and backpack signaled for a stop, the driver pulled the bus to the side of the highway and opened the front door to let him out.

Cane stood for a moment watching the lumbering bus pull away and disappear down the dark road. Then he started into the valley and toward the Begblick, which had been a favorite eating place of the Fast Track Patrol in earlier days. Nearing the village, he moved more cautiously, trying to stay in the shadows, out of the bright moonlight. Less than fifty yards from the restaurant, he moved to the doorway of an ancient brick building. He huddled there facing the street, studying the front of the restaurant. There were no cars in its small gravel parking lot. He had arrived before Simon.

The air was cooling rapidly, and Cane, in running shoes, blue jeans, a wool shirt, and a sweatshirt was ill prepared for a prolonged stay outside. He rubbed his hands and stamped his feet but didn't leave the protective shadow of the doorway. And he counted his blessings. There was no rain.

He heard the engine before he saw the headlights. As it grew closer Cane could make out the unmistakable whine of a VW bus engine. Then, as it drew closer, he flattened himself against the back of the doorway and watched as the van drove past.

It was Simon. He climbed down from the van and strolled into the restaurant. Cane controlled the desire to rush after him into the restaurant. He could make no mistakes. He had to be careful, to move slowly and cautiously, to make sure Simon hadn't been followed.

Finally, though, he looked at the aging van and knew it was his best, maybe his only, chance to get out. He stepped out of the shadows and walked slowly toward the restaurant.

TWENTY-FOUR

Cane slid onto a chair across the table from Simon and quickly inspected the room. A half-dozen men, villagers by their appearance, sat at the regulars' table. There was no one else and no one paid him more than a glance. He was safe.

"Hey, I was beginning to wonder if you were going to make it. I'm usually the one that keeps people waiting," Simon said.

Cane was about to answer when Frau Bauer, the long-time owner, approached. She wore a full white apron as ever, and despite her age, her black hair still showed no signs of gray. She looked at Cane for a second and then smiled as recognition came to her.

He smiled politely and nodded as she welcomed him back to Germany, assured him the awful winter was almost over, and said he really should have come a month or two later when the sun would be out. But when he told her they would be leaving quickly, she retreated to the bar.

"Go? You just got here," Simon protested.

"We've got to go. Now."

"Why? What's this all about, Cane?" His friend stared at him incredulously.

Cane gave a quick explanation of what had happened that day. "And now I just want to get the hell out of Germany. If you can take me to the airport, I'll take the first flight to London, or Paris or Amsterdam, I don't care. I just want to get out of here and then I'll catch a plane home from there."

"Sure, no problem. Here, you back the bus out. I'll pay for my beer." He tossed Cane the keys and went to the bar.

Outside, Cane hurried to the van. He ground the gears as

he rushed it into reverse. "Slow down. Calm down," he scolded himself.

But he didn't heed his own warning, and as he backed the van he heard a bang and a shout. Fear jolted through him. He twisted and saw an old, white-haired man standing by the rear the van. The man looked at the van, then down the street, and back at the van and waved slowly. At first Cane was simply too scared to comprehend. The man looked up and waved again, a come-hither motion, and finally Cane understood. The man was watching the twisty road to make sure Cane didn't pull in front of traffic. Cane backed into the street and eased the van to the curb.

The old man walked to the driver's window, looked in, and smiled. "Be careful young man. No sense having an accident," he said in heavily accented English.

"Yes, thank you," was all Cane could say.

The man disappeared into the restaurant just as Simon came out. Cane climbed over the gearshift to the passenger's seat as Simon got behind the wheel. He pulled the bus onto the road and they headed for the ridge. As they drove Cane looked back into the village to assure himself no cars were following them.

"Where do you want to go? You can't go back to the Engel."

"No. You're right. I hate to ask you this but could you drive me someplace where I can catch a train to Stuttgart or Munich? If I can get there I can catch a plane home."

Simon worked the Volkswagen bus through its gears, picking up speed through town before starting up the hill. The van quickly began to lose momentum as the road climbed. Simon downshifted, but still the van's pace slackened. Cane glanced again and again through the van's rear window to assure himself they were alone on the highway.

They were almost at the top—only two or three curves left to negotiate—and Cane began to relax. Then he saw a pair of headlights turn off the ridge above and head down the road toward Krausenheim.

His stomach muscles tensed instantly and he gripped the door handle hard. The bus continued slowly up the hill.

The headlights disappeared into a bend and Cane stared at the road ahead as the bus ground its way toward the same curve. A second later a speeding black Opel popped from the darkness of the curve, its headlights filling the windshield, momentarily blinding them as it shot past.

"Jesus Christ, it's them. It's them. It's the black Opel. We've got to get the hell out of here," Cane shouted. His fingers gripped the door handle and he jerked around to stare at the Opel's disappearing taillights.

Simon pushed the accelerator to the floor. The engine, already pushed almost to the limit, whined louder. The sound reverberated throughout the bus. There was no more power. It was only a few hundred yards to the ridge but the grade increased and gravity pushed hard on the bus. Cane rocked forward in his seat and pushed his right foot rigid against the floor, as if there were a second accelerator he could stomp on. His hand pressed frantically against the dash. The bus crawled toward the top, losing more speed. Cane fought the urge to throw open the door and leap clear.

"Come on, come on," Simon muttered as the growling engine pushed the bus toward the ridge.

The Opel slowed and turned sharply to the left. The car dove across the road and smashed into the hillside. The driver slammed it in reverse and the car jumped backward. The right front wheel climbed the side of the hill for a second before the car crashed to the road. Although beginning with a standing start uphill, the Opel quickly closed the gap with the Volkswagen.

The roar of the straining engine reverberated through the van as it moved up the last, short incline to the ridge. Simon sat on the edge of his seat, leaning over the steering wheel, almost standing on the gas pedal. The front wheels reached the ridge road and a second later the rear wheels. Simon turned left and flicked off the lights. Without thinking he shifted into third gear. The engine quieted and for a second the van lost momentum then began to pick up speed.

"I'm going for the logging road," he yelled.

It was a little more than a quarter mile to where a wide dirt road dropped steeply from the ridge into woods and eventually to the village on the other side of the hills. A main route for loggers, it was well maintained and a favorite route for Sunday hikers. Simon prayed he could reach it before the men in the Opel knew where they had gone. "Come on baby, come on," he muttered.

Cane's arms were rigid. The heel of his left hand pressed hard against the dash and his right held the door handle in a vise grip.

A moment later the Opel's headlights picked up the the back of the bus.

There was less than twenty yards to the dirt road when the Opel's hood pulled parallel to the rear bumper and with a burst of speed pulled alongside.

"Oh, God," Cane screamed as he rocked violently back and forth, trying to give the bus added momentun.

Simon stared straight ahead, searching for the entrance to the logging road. Suddenly, he slammed on the brakes and turned the wheel hard to the right. The bus lurched into a small rut, sending Cane flying up to the roof and slapping him back into his seat, then it was off the highway into the trees and heading down the dirt road.

Cane heard the Opel's tires screeching as the driver drove the brake pedal to the floor. He turned to look, and as he did the bus, heading down the steep hill, picked up speed. Too much speed. An instant later it hit something in the road, bounced, and the left front wheel slid off the side. Simon fought with the steering wheel, but the speeding van teetered, went off the road, and crashed on its left side. It bounced up, almost back to its four wheels, and then thundered down again, caving in the side. Propelled by its momentum it continued downhill, sliding on its side, leaving a raw swath across the forest floor. With a roar of tearing metal it crashed into a tree and stopped.

And there was silence.

Cane, his leg hooked around the gearshift, lay partially atop Simon, who was crushed against the door. Small chunks of glass from the shattered windshield had sprayed throughout the van.

Cane struggled to pull himself up. "Jesus, Simon, are you all right?"

Simon's crumpled body lay in a heap against the crushed-in left side of the van. Cane grabbed Simon's hand.

"Hey, let's get out of here," Cane said.

But Simon's arm was limp. Frantically Cane searched for a pulse. There was none. He pushed his ear to Simon's chest. Nothing. He put his ear to Simon's mouth, listening for breath. There was none. "Simon!" Cane screamed.

Through the stillness Cane heard the doors of the Opel on the road above him slam. There was no choice. He had to flee.

He flopped halfway through the gaping hole where the windshield had been. A piece of glass, embedded in the frame, dug deeply into his stomach as he slithered out of the wreckage.

He landed in the mud, his heart racing. He could smell the fumes of spilled gasoline and crankcase oil. Flashlights cut through the darkness above him on the hill. His backpack lay in the mud next to him. He siezed it, struggled to his feet, and ran down the logging road into the forest and away from the bus. His entire body ached, but fear and adrenaline powered his legs and the downhill slope of the road added to his momentum. He had covered less than fifty yards when speed overtook balance and he fell headfirst, sprawling on the ground. A second later he was up again, running blindly down the hill, thinking only of escape.

Within minutes he was exhausted and staggered to a stop in the middle of the road. Legs spread wide and bent at the waist, he gulped air. His lungs were raw. With each breath he thought he would puke. It took all his strength merely to stand. Move, his brain shouted to his body. Move or you'll die. Slowly he straightened up and began to jog. He could no longer sprint.

The blind fear that had propelled him began to ebb, replaced by exhaustion. He had to get off the main road. On the road he was still an easy a target. He saw a small footpath veering to his right. He followed it blindly into the trees. But it narrowed quickly and became overgrown. Branches slapped his face and hands until he was forced to hold the backpack in front of him to push on. Moments later his legs gave out and Cane fell. He could go no farther. He didn't have the strength to get up, and he lay listening to his own heavy breathing. The world seemed to swirl around him. He closed his eyes and waited to die.

TWENTY-FIVE

Cane lay still on the ground, unsure he had the strength to stand.

Ugly flashes of the drive up the hill, the chase, and the accident jumped into his mind like so many ghoulish jack-in-the-boxes.

He saw it all clearly. And he understand none of it. Who were the men in the black car? Why were they chasing him? Were they Red Army Faction, or renegade Stasi officers, or Middle Eastern terrorists?

Cane started to get up but hesitated. His ribs and shoulders ached from the crash and the fall during his sprint from the van. He took a deep breath and pain shot through his chest.

He knew he had to move, to leave the woods. The men could be looking for him now, methodically searching the woods. And unexpectedly he thought of dogs. They could return with dogs and track him down in minutes. The idea terrified him.

He moved to his hands and knees and felt a sharp pain across his stomach. Gently he touched his stomach with two fingers and discovered the cut inflicted by the piece of wind-shield glass. It had stopped bleeding, but the shirt was matted to the wound.

He stood unsteadily, and then moved stiffly back through the trees. He shuffled onto the road, stopped and looked for signs of pursuit, but he was alone. He turned and walked slowly downhill toward the village.

The logging trail left the forest to become a paved farm road cutting through still-fallow fields, rising and dipping over two small hills before finally ending at a side street on the edge of the village. As he moved through the small town Cane could think of only one thing to do, one place to turn for help.

He found a pay phone on the main street in front of a small neighborhood playground and called Rick Plummer. It seemed to ring forever before he heard Rick's muffled and grumpy "yeah, hello."

"Rick, it's Cane. I need help."

"What? What time is it anyway?"

"Rick, Simon's dead. They killed him."

"Simon? Who killed him? Cane, what the hell are you talking about?"

"Rick, I'm in trouble. I need help. You've got to come get me."

There was no levity in Cane's voice.

"Where are you?"

"I don't really know."

"Cane! Think man, think. How did you get there, where are you?"

"You know the road from Ochsenburg to Krausenheim? The ridge it runs along before you drop down into the village?"

"Sure. Of course. You in Krausenheim?"

"No. A village on the other side of the ridge. I'm by a phone booth on the main road. It's next to a small play area for kids. Right on the main road."

"I'll find it."

Cane pulled the door open, extinguishing the booth's overhead light, and hobbled across the wet grass to a large cement pipe, a huge toy common to so many playgrounds. He stooped and lowered himself onto the thin river of sand that had been transported in children's shoes and cuffs from the nearby sandbox to the pipe bottom. The big pipe offered little shelter from the night, and anyone seriously searching for him would find him easily. But for the moment Cane was only worried that someone walking home from an evening of beers and boasts at a local pub would see him and call the police. Besides, it was the only shelter he could find.

He leaned his head back against the cold, hard concrete and tried to remember the accident and the men in the Opel. Maybe, he thought, if he could see it more clearly he could find a clue. But concentration seemed impossible and he fell into a dazed half sleep.

When he first heard the unmuffled roar of the Fiat, Cane was unsure he could trust the sound. But as it grew louder he knew it was Rick. This must be the way soldiers in Nam had felt hearing the sound of choppers coming in to take them home, he thought.

Cane tried to stand, but his legs had grown stiff and refused to straighten or support him. As the roar of the approaching Fiat grew louder Cane was suddenly terrified that Rick, not seeing him at the phone booth, would drive away, stranding him in the village.

He fell on his stomach and crawled toward the pipe's mouth. The roar grew and then in an instant as Cane was at the edge of the pipe, he saw the small red Fiat speed past. Gripping the edge he pulled himself upright and began hobbling toward the phone booth. He heard the Fiat slow and then reverse course, moving more slowly this time. It stopped in front of the phone booth and Rick got out.

"Rick. Over here, man. Lend me a hand." His voice was weak.

Rick hurried across the grass, took Cane's arm, and draped it across his shoulders, and together they moved toward the car.

As Rick put his arm around Cane and helped him across the small playground, Cane felt a sense of relief and soul-deep gratitude swell within.

"Hey, man, you should have told me you were in such bad shape. I'd've brought an ambulance and a stretcher. As it is I'm going to need a shoehorn to fit you in the Fiat," Rick said.

It was a poor attempt at humor. But it was an attempt and Cane smiled.

Getting into the cramped Fiat was difficult, but Rick eased Cane down onto the seat and helped swing his legs into the car. A moment later the Fiat pulled a U-turn in the road and sped out of the village away from the hills, the ridge, and the road to Ochsenburg. The noise of its worn-out muffler echoed off the cement buildings in its wake.

Rick helped Cane out of the car and up the stairs into his apartment. He lowered him onto a beanbag chair. In the darkness he hadn't realized how bad Cane looked. Now in the light he began to understand. His shirt was soaked through with blood at the waist, a large bruise over his right eye had begun to swell. It was going to make a great shiner. His hands and arms with filthy and his face was streaked with dirt.

He wanted to ask about Simon but knew there would be time. First, Cane needed a hot bath and probably a shot of whisky. Rick left Cane in the chair and began filling the tub with steaming water. Then he moved around the aparment, gathering clothes and towels and clearing off the bed in his guest room before returning.

"You want a hand to the bathroom?"

"If you help me up, I think I can make it," Cane said and held up his arm. Rick pulled him to his feet then watched as Cane moved like an aged man to the bath.

Simon had been one of his oldest and closest friends. Rick had known him even longer than he had known Cane. He had an encyclopedia of memories with Simon: memories of times going back to when they cared so much less about the future and so much more about the present. The old times when they had shared the adventure and growth of youth and in recent years the quiet happiness of stability. He walked to his stereo, dropped a tape in the cassette deck, and punched play. *Sgt. Pepper* filled the room.

In the bathroom, Cane stepped into the steaming tub and gasped at the heat. His feet turned bright pink but he refused to retreat. Slowly he lowered himself into the water and straightened his legs. Finally he leaned back and let his body absorb the warmth. The tension slowly seeped away, and for the first time in what seemed weeks, not hours, Cane began to relax and feel safe.

He opened his eyes and looked down at his body, as if seeing it for the first time in years. His legs seemed skinnier than he remembered. And, was it his imagination or was there really less hair on them than there used to be? An angry red gouge cut across his middle. And his stomach seemed to float in the hot water like a blob attached to his ribs. He leaned his head back again and closed his eyes.

"I'm getting too old for this shit," he mumbled to cheer himself. But there was little humor in it because it was true.

"How you feeling?" Rick asked when Cane returned to the living room and sank onto the futon couch.

"Better. Thanks for coming to get me, Rick, I really don't know what I would have done. I don't understand any of this. I just don't understand."

"Cane, are you sure Simon is dead?"

"Yes."

Rick rose from his chair and left the room. Cane watched him and said nothing. Rick was a hard person to understand, and Cane wasn't sure he ever really knew him. Friends came easily to Rick. People found his charm, quick wit, and easy approach to life alluring and always wanted to be around him. And with Rick there were no such thing as an uninvited guest or too big a crowd.

Rick was like a man in a clear glass box. He was so easy to see and appeared so easy to touch. But when you tried to reach him your hand struck the invisible barrier.

Rick returned carrying a bottle of brandy and two small glasses. He poured some in a glass and handed it to Cane. Then filled his own and held it up.

"To Simon. The world is a lesser place now. We'll miss him."

"To Simon," Cane responded and drained the glass in a gulp.

Cane looked at Rick. He thought he had been crying but couldn't tell. The glass box was clouded over.

"Start at the beginning and tell me what happened," Rick said.

Cane spoke easily this time. There was no rush, no disorganization as there had been when he was talking to Slovak or to Simon in the restaurant. He told the story from his meeting with Von Stueben to seeing Maria to the visit to Heidelberg to the crash in the woods in a steady, even voice. But he spoke to the floor. A few minutes later, he finished and raised his eyes and looked at Rick.

The sparkle was gone from his eyes and his half-cocky grin had disappeared. And in that instant, Cane saw and truly understood for the first time that Rick had grown older. He too felt much older.

"Jesus, Rick, I hate to admit this, but I called Simon because I hoped he could help and he's dead because of it."

Cane fell silent again and lowered his eyes. He knew Rick wasn't judging him, but it didn't matter. He was judging himself and the verdict was a foregone conclusion.

Cane reached over and poured himself another shot of brandy, sat back and waited as Rick stared out the window into the darkness.

Finally he turned away from the window and looked at the glass in his hand. It was several minutes before he finally asked, "How did they know you were going to be in Krausenheim?"

"Shit, man, I don't know, maybe they followed Simon. Oh, yeah, I forgot to mention that I called the phone number this captain had left at the Engel. The guy that answered kept asking me where I was. That's all he wanted to know. Where I was. Jesus, Rick, what's going on?"

"I don't know."

"I mean, who the hell are these guys? Red Army Faction? East German intelligence? Arabs? Why didn't they just ask me? I'd have told them I saw Maria. Hell, we're old friends what's the big deal?"

"Be serious, Cane. If these guys wanted to play by the rules they would have."

Cane's muscles had begun to stiffen again and he felt an overwhelming exhaustion. He stretched his arms above his head then leaned back on the couch and stared at the ceiling.

"I don't know what they want, but whatever it is, it's not worth it. Maybe I should just call this Captain Montgomery tomorrow and ask him what the hell is going on."

Rick jerked his head around and stared at Cane. Could he really be that naive? Could he really, after all he'd been through, still not get it? Not understand what was going on around him?

"You're not really going to call this geek Montgomery are you?" Rick asked.

"No, probably not."

"Well, what are you going to do?"

"I don't know, man. I think the best thing is try to get out of here, to just go home."

"I think you should stay. Push it harder. Find out what's going on."

"What?" The idea stunned Cane. He had had enough. He wanted only one thing: to leave Germany, to go home and be safe.

"Look, if these guys killed Simon you've got to find out what the hell's going on here," Rick said.

"Yeah, and how am I going to do that? I already talked with Joe at *Stripes* and he couldn't help. The guy in Heidelberg denied everything. Maria is leaving tomorrow. I don't know anybody here anymore. I tried to get Simon to help me and now he's dead. How the hell am I going to find out anything?"

"I don't know, Cane, you're the reporter. I thought you knew how to find things out."

"Rick! These people are trying to kill me for God's sake. I don't want to mess with it anymore. I just want to catch the first plane back to the States."

"Jesus Christ, Cane!" Rick almost screamed. He slammed his brandy glass on the floor, cracking it off at the stem. "They killed Simon because he tried to help you. They're trying to kill you. You can't run. You've got to fight back. For once in your life you have to get off the goddamned fence and fight."

"Fence? What's that supposed to mean?"

"Oh, come on, Cane. That's probably why you're a journalist. You can flit in and out and never have to get involved. You get to stay objective. You never have to get your hands dirty. You never have to pay the price. It sure as hell is safe."

"That's bullshit."

"Cane, I don't know what the problem is. I don't know if you're afraid to fight or you really are so fucking idealistic that you still think the world is the way it's suppose to be instead of the way it really is.

"You told me one time that being a journalist made you realize there was no such thing as black and white, that everything was a shade of gray. That's real convenient way to keep from taking sides and getting involved. It's also bullshit. Sometimes things are black and white and we have to make a decision. Face it, Cane, at some point in our lives we all have to choose: be a whore or take the hemlock. It's your turn to choose."

Cane didn't respond. He didn't know what to say. Two days ago he would have denied it all and laughed off what Rick had just told him. Not now. Now he felt as though he were in a different world. Or was he just seeing the real world for the first time?

Either way, he knew Rick was right. He never had chosen. Part of being a reporter was being a professional outsider. Reporters weren't supposed to decide for themselves. They were supposed to be objective. He rose slowly, stiffly, from the couch and drained the last of the brandy in his glass.

"Let's talk some more in the morning. Okay?" he said, turning and walking to the spare bedroom, where Rick had cleared off the bed and thrown down a sleeping bag.

"Sure," Rick responded to the empty room, "let's do that."

TWENTY-SIX

The captain sat on the bench and watched the train glide to a stop. A second later the doors popped open and passengers began climbing down to the cement platform. No one noticed him, a dark-skinned man in laborer's clothes. He was unremarkable in every way. Yet he noticed everything. He saw every passenger boarding the outgoing train and when it pulled out from the station again, the captain was sure the journalist wasn't on it.

He looked again up and down the empty platform. The next train wasn't due for another thirty minutes. By then someone else would be there to watch. He couldn't wait. He had another, more important job.

In the station's rest room, he changed into uniform, becoming Captain Ward Montgomery. He carefully bundled his dark wool slacks and shirt into a bag. He stashed the package in the trunk of his green Chevrolet sedan and drove to the base.

A young soldier, in a freshly starched field uniform with highly polished boots and a glistening silver helmet, waved him to a stop at the gate. The captain rolled down his window and silently handed the young man his identification. The soldier studied it carefully, handed it back, and snapped a salute.

"Proceed, captain."

He parked the green sedan and glanced at the list of phone numbers again before leaving the car. He found the public information office easily. It was empty except for a young enlisted woman with dirty-blond hair and thick glasses who was pecking with two fingers at a typewriter. It was a perfect place to make his calls. He knocked gently on the door frame.

"Excuse me," he called.

The woman looked up. "Oh, I'm sorry I didn't see you. Can I help you?"

"Yes. I'm Captain Montgomery. I'm stationed in Frankfurt and was wondering if I could use your phone to make a couple of calls. They're all right here on base."

"Oh, sure, go ahead. Use that one." She made a limp-wristed gesture toward a desk across the room.

He glanced at a list he pulled from an inside pocket of numbers Cane called from the Engel during the crisis and dialed the number that appeared the most often. The phone next to the young woman rang. He hung up immediately. Of course, the public affairs office. It was obvious. That's where any reporter would call frequently. And then, on only the second call, he found what he needed.

"Engineers, Smith."

"Captain Barker please."

"Sorry, sir, there's no Captain Barker here."

"Oh, I'm sorry, I was told he could be reached at this number. Is this the Eighth Engineers Battalion? I was told he was assigned there."

"Oh no, sir. This is the Army Corps of Engineers. The Eighth Engineers are at a different number."

"Thank you very much, ahh, Smith? Did you say Smith?"

"Hey, no problem, I was just walking by and picked up the phone."

"Oh? Are you sure this isn't Captain Barker's line then?"

"I'm positive. This is Rick Plummer's phone."

"Sorry to bother you."

Rick. It was that simple. Barbara Darling had mentioned a friend called Rick. It was possible someone else had called Rick Plummer from the Engel. Or perhaps Jonathan Cane had just been trying to dig up information. But the captain doubted it.

The captain believed in his instincts and at that moment they told him he had found what he was looking for. Sometimes things were almost too easy.

TWENTY-SEVEN

Cane tossed fitfully, dragged toward consciousness by fragments of a bad dream. He was on the phone telling Simon not to bother meeting him. It wasn't important, he insisted. He'd changed his mind. There was no need to meet at Frau Bauer's place. It was nothing important, just stay in Frankfurt.

He jerked awake, and for a few brief moments of half sleep he clung to the idea that he actually had called Simon. Then the reality of the chase and crash flooded him and he was aware again that Simon was dead. Immediately he realized how sore he was. His entire body ached, as if someone had beaten him thoroughly.

He sat up slowly and swung his legs to the floor. As he did the gouge on his stomach sent a sharp pain across his middle. He sucked in his breath and waited for the pain to ebb.

He looked around the bedroom. It was as messy as the rest of the house. Clothes were piled on the dresser. Three skis and four poles stood in a corner. There was no system, no order.

The pain passed but Cane hesitated to make the final move and stand. He looked at the floor but instead saw the empty hole where the van's windshield had been. He saw himself squirm through the window and land in the mud. He watched himself struggle to his feet and run into the forest.

Someone, for some reason, had tried to kill him. They had failed and killed his friend. They would try again. There were no nuances, no subtleties, no intellectual arguments. Cane faced a choice. He had to fight or flee.

Yeah, but how the hell would I find out anything? he argued to himself. But the argument was weak and he knew it.

Because that was not the question. If he fought, he would find a way.

Again the captain went throught the drill. A young soldier waved the car to a stop as the captain approached the gate from the street. Security had been extremely tight since the terrorists had seized the ammunition dump. Every car was stopped. Every document inspected. The soldier looked carefully at the captain's identification, handed it back, and waved him through.

He drove up the slight cobblestone incline toward the main military headquarters for Ochsenburg and pulled his car into an empty spot marked "visitor."

"Excuse me, lieutenant," he called to a young officer walking by. "I'm looking for the Corps of Engineers. Can you tell me which building they're in?"

"The engineers? Right there," the lieutenant said and pointed, his fingers in the schoolboy form for a gun, at a small, square prefab building squeezed between two long three-story barracks.

The office was empty when Captain Montgomery entered. Two government functional metal desks were against the wall to his right and two drafting tables abutted the wall in front of him. The middle of the room was filled with a large table burried in blueprints.

"Hello. Anyone here?" There was no response. "Hello," he shouted again. No one answered.

He crossed to the twin desks and quickly glanced through the papers strewn across their tops, searching for Rick Plummer's home address. He found nothing and turned to the drafting tables. He leafed through the blueprints quickly but they gave him no help. He saw a filing cabinet near the door and had just stepped toward it when a middle-aged man carrying a soft-sided briefcase walked in. He had a barrel chest, sandy blond hair, and a face reddened by alcohol.

"Can I help you, sir?" He spoke with a thick German accent.

"I'm looking for Rick Plummer."

"Rick's not here. I think he was supposed to be at one of the sites today. Maybe I can help you."

"No, I need to talk with him, it's personal. I'll just try again later. Or maybe I'll try him at home. He still live in Krausenheim?"

"Krausenheim? No. Rick never lived there. He lives in Keilbach."

"Oh? Okay. What's the address there? I'll try his house, and if I miss him there I'll catch him at the site."

"It's on Benzmann Strasse. Number sixty-eight I think."

"And where's the site he's at today?"

"In Neiderheim, about eight miles east of here on Highway Twelve. You can't miss it. There's only one base and only one construction project. We're rebuilding the chow hall."

"Okay, thanks."

He let the door bang closed behind him. Keilbach. He remembered seeing it on the map. It wasn't real close, but he could be there quickly enough.

Cane gripped the footboard of the bed and using his arms more than his legs, got to his feet. By the time he reached the kitchen he was walking more than shuffling. Rick was drinking coffee at the kitchen table, where he had cleared two beach-heads among the clutter. He turned as his friend hobbled in.

"Hey, Cane, that's a pretty good Walter Brennan. How you feeling?"

"I feel a hell of a lot better than I did last night."

"You want some coffee and *brötchen*?" Rick asked.

"Yeah." He suddenly realized how hungry he was. He hadn't eaten since the previous noon. He moved to the table and was wolfing down a roll as he lowered himself to the chair.

Rick poured a large cup of coffee and waited while Cane spread butter and jam on two more rolls and quickly ate them. He didn't speak until it appeared his friend was slowing down.

"Good to see your jaw muscles are fully recovered."

Cane, his mouth full, just smiled and continued chewing.

"So, do you want me to drive you someplace today? I'll call in sick and we can easily make Munich in time for you to catch a flight home tonight. Whatever you want."

There was no judgment in his voice. Rick had had his say the previous night. There was no need to say any more. His offer was sincere. Cane didn't look up from his roll.

"No. I'm going to try to find out what the hell this is all about."

"How you going to do it?"

"I don't know. If I just show up at the embassy or the Frankfurt consulate these guys might nail me. I thought I might spend a little time here and try to sort it out."

"I don't think its such a good idea for you to stay here. If these guys are anywhere near as good as I think they are, it won't take them long to find out you and I are friends. They'll be around here pretty soon. I think we both should be gone."

"Yeah. I guess you're right. But I don't really know what I'm going to do."

"You know anyone in Heidelberg that can help?"

"No. I don't even know how I'm going to get around. I sure as hell can't go back to the Engel and collect my car."

"Use the Fiat. I just got a new starter put in. I'll catch a bus into O'burg and grab a staff car or borrow Roland's. It wouldn't be the first time I've had to borrow his car, believe me."

Cane smiled. He had little trouble believing the old Fiat was prone to breakdowns.

"Okay, if you're sure you won't need it today," Cane said.

"Look, I can get around. The thing is, you've got to be able to get around. You can't stay here. And if you want I'll try to lend you a hand today."

Cane put a half-eaten roll on his plate and looked at his friend. He felt a little odd about what he was about to say.

"No. Thanks, but no." He hesitated for a moment and then pressed on. "Look, Rick. I can't tell you how much your help means to me. I really don't know what I would have done. I might be dead by now."

"They killed Simon."

"Yeah, but you still didn't have to get involved in this. What happens if they find out about you helping me?"

"What's to find out? A friend called and said he'd been in an auto accident and needed help. Cane, I don't think these people are legit, you know what I mean? This isn't a routine investigation. They're not going to come ask me any questions."

"I guess you're right."

"Look, I've got to go if I'm going to catch the bus. Listen, don't stick around here too long."

"Okay. I've just got to figure out where to go and what to do."

"Leave first and then figure it out. I don't think it's a good idea for you to come back here, either. And another thing, you can't run around in those sweatpants all day. Grab some clothes from my closet. They won't be a perfect fit, but they'll be close enough. Let's get together tonight and you can fill me in on your progress. You remember the chicken house?"

"Oh, sure. I'm not sure I remember how to get there, it's kind of out of the way."

"That's the whole point. I'll see you there about six."

Rick picked up his briefcase and headed for the door. He stopped just in front of it, turned, and looked back into the kitchen.

"Hey Cane! Be careful. You've seen what these guys will do. See you at six."

"Thanks, mom. And you watch your own back."

When he heard the door click shut, Cane poured himself another cup of coffee then slowly added milk, watching the white fluid swirl around the cup, mixing and disappearing until the coffee was the proper blend.

Had it really been only days, not months, since he had arrived at the airport expecting to cover a great news story? And when had he seen Maria? Was it yesterday or the day before?

Barbara had said Maria was leaving today and taking her boys with her. He only hoped she had been spared the pain and suspicions their meeting had caused him. Cane looked at the clock and thought about her getting on the plane.

Rick had warned him to leave the apartment, but Cane found it difficult to move. The sun shone through the kitchen window and Cane could see the tree-covered hillsides. It was hard to imagine anything evil happening to him on such a day. Besides, where would he go? How could he learn the truth?

He stood slowly, stretched, and turned toward the hallway. Then he stopped abruptly and smiled. Suddenly he knew what he would do because he knew the answer to Rick's question. He knew how the men had found them in Krausenheim.

And now he would use that knowledge to gain his own edge. They had planned to kill him. Now he had plans of his own.

TWENTY-EIGHT

The captain flipped opened the folder and looked a last time at the photo of Jonathan Cane. There would be no mistakes. This time the right man would die.

He glanced at his watch. It was almost nine. Later than he wanted but Keilbach was not that far. Within minutes, he was on the edge of town, heading into the country. The two-lane road cut through an orchard on the verge of budding and passed through newly planted fields. The sun was bright. It would be a beautiful day in Germany.

The captain didn't notice. His mind was on Keilbach.

He had little, really, to connect Jonathan Cane to Rick Plummer. But his instincts told him the journalist was there, just a few miles ahead. He passed through a village. Then he saw the sign. Keilbach ten kilometers ahead. The captain's mouth twisted into a tight smile.

Rick's laissez-faire approach to housekeeping didn't stop at his bedroom door. Cane had to pick his way between clothes, books, and papers on the floor. The bed was unmade. The two top drawers in the dresser were halfway open. Socks and underwear spilled out. Cane worked his way to a large wardrobe. Shirts and slacks, still in their plastic wrapping from the dry cleaners, were neatly hung inside.

He found a pair of fatigue pants only slightly too small in the waist and an inch or two short. He picked out a shirt, pulled off the plastic wrap, dropped it to the floor, and then, almost as an afterthought, grabbed a windbreaker.

He carried the clothes to the spare bedroom, dressed, and

began his final search. He quickly rifled through the boxes and searched the desk. He was beginning to feel the urgency, to understand the need to flee. He moved quickly. He looked under the bed and in a trunk. He was ready to abandon the search when he found what he had been looking for.

The gun was neatly wrapped in a soft cloth, pushed far back on a shelf of a small wardrobe. He took it out, unwrapped it, and held it in his hand. It was cool and heavier than he thought it would be. He balanced the gun in his hand for a second more then slid it into his backpack.

The gun scared him. He knew nothing about guns and was unsure he would have the nerve to fire one. Still, when he put it in his backpack it seemed to solidify his determination. Now there was no question of what he would do. His plan was set. He would act.

On his way to the door he saw an MP's nightstick leaning in a corner and without thinking, grabbed it and walked out.

Rick stood over the large table in the center of his office, head bowed, looking at blueprints spread before him, and thought of Cane. He believed him. He was sure it had happened just the way Cane had described it. But why?

"Ah, here you are." Roland suddenly appeared from the next room.

"Hi, Roland. Sorry I'm late. Had car trouble. How are you?"

"Fine, fine. I thought you were going to Neiderheim today. That's what I told the captain who was here looking for you earlier."

"Captain? What captain?" Rick's stomach muscles knotted.

"I don't know. I thought he was a friend of yours. Maybe from the ski club."

"Did he tell you his name?" Rick's tone was insistent.

"No, come to think of it, he didn't. But he had on a name badge. Mant, Moe, no. Montgomery. That was it. Montgomery."

"You told him I'd be out at Neiderheim?"

"Yeah, but he said he might drop by your house. He thought you lived in Krausenheim. But I straightened him out. Did he come by?"

"Ah, I don't know. I came in on the bus."

Montgomery. Jesus. It was him. Rick grabbed the phone and frantically pushed the buttons. The ringing, as insistant and nerve wracking as the midnight crying of a collicky baby, went unaswered. "Come on, Cane, come on, come on. Pick it up, Cane, pick it up," he mumbled.

But he didn't pick it up, and Rick was left with nothing but the hope that his friend had left in time.

"Roland, Is there a car available?"

"Sure. Take the one I'm using. I'll be here the rest of the day. Just turn it in to the motor pool when you're done. It's right out front."

Rick took the keys and rushed toward the door.

"Hey, Rick, your orders are ready."

"Orders?"

"Your TDY orders. To Turkey. The inspection trip, you remember? Two weeks in beautiful Adana to inspect the building sites. You're supposed to go Saturday. I put them on your desk."

"Oh, yeah. Guess it slipped my mind there for a moment," Rick said.

In fact it had. He made the inspection trips twice a year to the outlying bases in Turkey and once or twice a year to other places. The trip had been arranged months ago, but with the terrorist incident and Cane's problems, Rick hadn't thought of it for days.

"So, you going to Neiderheim?" Roland asked.

"No, not right away. I've got a couple of other things I need to take care of first." His words trailed away as he hurried from the office.

"Okay, see you later. And don't forget to turn the car in," Roland yelled after him.

The captain found sixty-eight Benzmann Strasse easily. He parked across the street and studied the house. There was no sign of movement. The driveway was empty. The lace curtains on the downstairs windows were drawn. There appeared to be no curtains upstairs. He glanced in the mirror. The street was empty. Time to go.

He opened the glove compartment and withdrew the gun

and silencer. He attached the silencer and then put the gun in his waistband. His coat buttoned to conceal the gun, he walked briskly across the street to the apartment. The front door opened with a gentle shove. He glanced at the name on the bottom door, dismissed it, and cautiously climbed the white marble steps toward Rick Plummer's apartment.

He moved easily, silently, his shoes gliding on the polished marble stairs. At the top he pulled the gun from his waistband. The door was unlocked and he pushed it open slowly, entering in a crouch. He turned right and then left, but saw no one.

He flattened against the wall then pivoted into the living room doorway. He moved quickly to the bedroom then the kitchen and the second bedroom. The apartment was empty.

But as he looked, he became convinced the reporter had been there. In the kitchen two coffee cups and fresh bread crumbs were on the table. A pair of mud-caked jeans was on the floor in a bedroom.

In the bathroom he knelt to inspect blood-stained bandages in the waste basket. There was no question. Jonathan Cane had been there.

He had missed him. But now he knew the journalist had not fled. Karl had been right. He had looked for help. And now the captain knew from whom. Every step tightened the noose.

Once again the journalist had slipped away. Karl clenched his fist again, squeezing until his fingernails bit deep into his palms.

Months of tedious work and brilliant organization were becoming useless. Karl was forced to react to, not control, the events.

He looked again at a photo of Jonathan Cane. He hated the man in the picture thoroughly now. Despite his training and his knowledge, despite everything, it had beome personal. He wanted the man dead. He was an evil man who didn't deserve to live. Karl was beginning to feel the loss of control.

That all changed in an instant.

The phone rang and Karl answered it immediately, his voice cool, betraying no emotion.

"Yes."

"I just got a copy of the German police report on the accident," the voice said.

"And?"

"They've positively identified Simon North. But, they know there was someone else was in the van with him. A villager saw two men in the bus when it pulled away from the restaurant. They're looking for the second man. They want to talk to him. They think he might have been driving."

"Do they know who it is?"

"Yes. The woman who owns the place knew both of them. She's given the police his name and description."

Karl almost smiled at the irony. The German *Polizei* helping them find Jonathan Cane.

"Do you still have contacts with the police?"

"Yes, of course."

"Get them a full description, passport number, and photo of him. Make sure they get it, but that there's no way they can connect it with us. Tell them the army's criminal investigation divison wants him too.

"Tell them you're just helping out. Nothing official. Tell them it's part of an undercover operation. He's wanted for ah . . . drugs, for selling on the military bases. If they find him they're to notify you immediately. They don't even need to bother questioning him. He's considered mentally unstable and may be violent. Can you do that?"

"I can do it. But they may want to go through regular channels."

"Make them buy it. If they find him I want to know before anyone else. They must release him to us, do you understand?"

"Yes."

"I'll contact the captain. Can we get Interpol involved?"

"Maybe. I'll see what I can do."

True, it had moved beyond his immediate control, but that was less important now. Stopping Jonathan Cane was all that mattered. It didn't matter who did it.

Soon every police force in Europe would be looking for him. Every harbor, every airport, every border crossing, would be watched. And the captain could wait at the engineer's apartment.

Karl looked at the photo again. Try to run now, you piece of shit, he thought. Just try to run. You are mine and you are dead.

TWENTY-NINE

The library was quiet. Few people visited during a weekday. Still, Rick was unable to concentrate on the engineering book in front of him. Repeatedly he looked at his watch to find only two minutes had passed since the last time he looked. He was haunted by thoughts of Cane; visions of him sprawled on the bed, a bullet hole in the back of his head.

Again he considered his decision not to rush home when he'd heard that a man called Captain Montgomery had been at the office. He could do nothing, Rick knew. Cane was either dead or had left in time. Going home was futile. There was only danger in Keilbach. Danger to him as well as Cane. They had already found his office and home. Next they might look for him.

Instead of rushing home, he had decided to hide and what better place than in the open? In the middle of the library in the middle of the main base. It was perfect.

The sound of a cannon jerked him to the present. It was five o'clock and the color guard was lowering the flag. All traffic on the base stopped. People stood watching the ceremony, their hands over their hearts or saluting. The cannon sounded every day at five, just before the ceremony.

Moments later the flag was down and the base was moving again. A line of cars formed at the gate as the workers flooded out of the buildings and headed home.

Time to go. Rick left the reference books piled on the table and walked outside. But as he stepped from the building into the early evening, he saw Simon's van and stopped cold. It had been towed into the base and parked at the corner of the parking lot nearest the entrance. Anyone driving onto the base had to see it.

Lieutenant Colonel Anderson had ordered other wrecks parked in the same spot before as vivid reminders of the ultimate penalty careless or drunk drivers paid.

Rick walked to the van in a daze. Clumps of mud still clung to its dented side. The nose was crumpled. Two of the tires were blown. The windshield was missing. Rick looked inside past the steering wheel at the seat and the driver's door. The blood stains were still there. For a moment he felt numb and had to clench his jaw to hold back the tears.

"Really beat the shit out of it, didn't they?" a voice behind him said.

A flash of anger swept over him. Rick jerked around to face a young MP, probably a year from shaving, also examining the wreck. Rick's anger subsided. "Yeah, it's a real wreck, all right," he said. He didn't want to talk with the soldier. He wanted only to leave, go to the "chicken house," and learn if Cane was alive.

"They still haven't found the other guy, you know."

"What?" Rick asked, struggling to hide his surprise.

"The other guy. They figure there were two of them in the van. One's dead and the other guy just disappeared."

"How do you know that?"

"Trooper told me. She took the report."

"Oh, yeah? Where is she now?"

"She's in the office. Why?"

"No reason. I thought I might ask her something more about this van."

Her real name was Myrtle but everyone on base knew her as Trooper. She was almost six feet tall with broad shoulders and beefy arms. She had the voice of a chainsaw cutting sheet metal and a manner to match. More soldiers in Ochsenburg knew Trooper the MP on sight than knew Colonel Gill, the base commander.

Trooper was slouching against the counter, her back to the door, talking to a skinny sergeant seated at a desk when Rick walked into the station. Her arm was in a sling, the result, she was telling the sergeant, of breaking up a bar fight a few nights before.

"Excuse me, I had a couple of questions about the van outside," Rick said.

Trooper smiled as she turned and looked at him.

"You smoke?" she asked.

"Pardon me?"

"Smoke. Do you smoke?"

"No. I quit a few years ago."

"Well, go ahead anyway and tell me you smoke."

"Okay. Yes, I smoke." Rick could see nothing would be done until Trooper was ready. She stood at the counter, her hand resting on a small, painted, plaster figure of a horse that looked like a carnival consolation prize.

"So, you want a cigarette?" she asked.

"Sure. I'd love one," Rick said.

"Help yourself," Trooper replied. And as she spoke she pressed the ear of the horse down and a cigarette popped out its ass. As it came out, Trooper started laughing and a moment later was howling. Rick chuckled politely and waited.

"So, what can I do for you?" she finally asked, catching her breath.

"I saw the van out front. I heard the driver was killed. The van looks like one that a friend of mine drives and I was wondering if you could tell me who was driving it?"

"No, can't release the names until we get the word that the next of kin have been notified."

"Okay, I can understand that. How many people were killed?"

"Just one."

"Alone in it, huh?"

"No. We think there was someone else in there with him when it crashed. The other guy ran. But that don't matter. We got the guy's name and pictures and everything. Every cop in the country is looking for him. He ain't getting away."

"You mean the second guy in the van? You got pictures of him? How'd you do that?"

"That's police business."

"Oh, yeah. Well, good luck and thanks for the help," Rick said and turned to go. He stopped just before the door and glanced over his shoulder. "And, hey, I love the horse."

THIRTY

Cane drove aimlessly, following one road then another. He wandered past forests and farmland and through villages. Finally his route crossed over the autobahn and Cane turned onto the ramp and a minute later was headed toward Frankfurt.

Even before the opening of the East brought the world's capitalists scurrying to central Germany, skyscrapers and highrise buildings had crowded into the skyline of Frankfurt—a testimony to the city's prosperity. Old landmarks had disappeared and the streets were thick with cars, buses, mopeds, and taxis.

Twice Cane took wrong turns and had to circle before finally finding the right street. Two blocks away and unwilling to gamble on finding a spot closer, he squeezed the Fiat into a small space between a Mercedes and an Audi.

Simon and Ute lived on the twelfth floor of a eighteen-story rectangular apartment building in a thicket of symmetrically designed cement buildings. Cane stopped for a moment on the sidewalk outside the lobby door of their building and looked at the nearby housing towers. Their monotonous gray fronts were broken only by precisely spaced windows and balconies that stretched one above the other from the second floor to the top. They were, he knew, merely vertical versions of LA's infamous suburbs.

He studied the playground in the middle of the buildings carefully and slowly scanned the surrounding grounds. He told himself he was being cautious, making sure he wasn't being watched. But in truth he was stalling, avoiding facing Ute and telling her of his responsibility in Simon's death.

But when a young woman brushed past him and let herself in the main entrance, Cane moved quickly to grab the door before it closed behind her. The elevator jerked when it reached the twelfth floor, and Cane stepped out into a long hall. He tried to appear casual as he moved toward Ute's door.

He stopped again, just outside the apartment, hesitant to knock. What would he say? How could he tell her how sorry he was? And suddenly it occurred to Cane that maybe she didn't know yet. The thought of breaking the news terrified him. How could he tell her Simon had been killed?

But Ute already knew. The police had been there a few hours earlier, she told Cane as they sat at the small table in the tiny kitchen alcove. She seemed calm and at ease. But Cane looked at her red, swollen eyes and knew her tears could start again at any moment. She wore no makeup and her hair was pulled back in a severe ponytail. She was dressed in jeans and a large sweatshirt, no shoes. A small pile of tissue had already gathered on the table.

"Would you like some coffee? I made it for my girlfriend. You just missed her. She'll be back in just a few minutes," Ute said. She uncurled her feet from beneath her on the chair and moved to the coffee maker without waiting for a reply.

She was struggling to hang on, seeking stability in the familiar and the routine, Cane knew. "Sure," he said. She poured a cup of coffee and handed it to him without bothering to ask if he would like milk or sugar.

"Ute, did Simon tell you why he was going to Krausenheim last night?"

"No. I didn't talk to him. He left for work in the morning and . . . I never saw him again." She swallowed hard and turned her head as she struggled for composure. "He left a message on the machine saying he'd be home late. I thought maybe he was going to meet you or Rick." Her voice was flat, without emotion.

"Yes, he was. He came to help me."

"Help you?"

Cane looked at her for a moment then looked down. He breathed deeply. There was no retreat now. And he began, much as he had with Rick only hours before, to tell her what had happened.

". . . And then I got into a village and called Rick. I spent the night at his place," Cane concluded. Ute looked at him blankly, without expression, and for a moment he wasn't sure she had heard or even listened.

He sipped his coffee and when she still hadn't said anything he went on. "Ute, I feel responsible for this. If Simon hadn't tried to help me, he wouldn't have been killed. I know these guys are going to try to kill me again. That's why I'm here. I think I know how to stop them and make them pay for what they did to Simon."

"What do you want?" Her expression was cold and distant, and Cane couldn't tell if the anger in her eyes was aimed at him or the others. He spoke slowly, almost gently.

"Do you know a Sergeant Winters who works in the communications room with Simon?"

"Herman? Of course."

"Ute, I think he's part of this. I'm not sure how. But when I called the consulate last night to talk with Simon, he was there. I left the message with him. He's the only one who knew where we were going to meet. What can you tell me about him."

"He's German."

"He is? I thought he was in the army."

"He is. He went to the States in the late fifties and was drafted. He never got out. He made it a career. He's been at the consulate for maybe six years now."

"Where's he from in Gemany?"

"Leipzig."

"In the East?"

"Yes, of course. His parents came out through Berlin before the wall went up. He was still a teenager, I think." She was silent for a moment, staring into the distance, lost in her own thoughts. "But, Cane, I think you are mistaken. Herr Winters is a nice man. A gentle man. He always has a smile for everyone. He would not hurt anyone." Her voice trailed away and Cane remained silent, not sure what to say.

"We have visited his house once. It was after his wife and daughter died. Simon said we should go. He liked Herr Winters. He was so alone, so frail. I remember we sat there and he showed us their Hummel collection. His wife had bought one on each trip and at each special occasion. He told us they were his life now. They were all he had left of them. They were like photos. Each one with so many memories. He was so gentle. You're wrong, you must be."

She began sobbing again, and Cane moved awkwardly around the table to stand next to her and put his arm around her. She buried her head in his chest and cried for several minutes before choking back the tears and pulling away.

"I'm sorry, I'm sorry, I'm getting your shirt wet," she said and blotted her tears with a fresh tissue.

"That's okay. Look, I'm sure you're right about Sergeant Winters. But Ute, I've got to talk to him. I've got to know. Do you know where he lives?" He asked the question as gently as he could.

She rose from the table, walked to a desk, and thumbed through a small address book. "Here it is. We sent him a Christmas card. He lives at Eighty-four Hofstrasse. It's only a few miles from here." She wrote the address on a piece of paper, crossed the living room to hand it to Cane, then retreated again to her seat at the table.

He stood looking at the paper in his hand and wondering about the wonderful, gentle man that Ute had described. Could he really be the same man that had sent killers after Simon? He wasn't sure. But he did know Sergeant Herman Winters was from "over there," as the West Germans used to call the East. And again Cane wondered if perhaps he had been too hasty in abandoning his theory about the Red Army Faction and the East German secret police.

There was a soft knock at the front door. "I'll get it," Cane said and quickly moved to the door. He opened it to find a young German woman with a bag of groceries. She seemed startled to see him.

"I am Monica," she said but didn't offer her hand.

"I'm Jonathan Cane. I'm an old friend of Simon's. I, ah, just came by to give my condolences. I just found out."

Monica brushed past him, moved to the kitchen, and began emptying the bag of groceries onto a counter. After an awkward moment of silence, Cane walked over to Ute. She didn't stand and he bent down to give her a long hug.

"Don't worry, I'll make this right," he said in a low voice.

"I promise, Ute. They won't get away with this." At the door he turned and looked again. Both women sat silently at table. "Good-bye," he said. Neither one looked up.

He pulled the Fiat into an Esso station less than a mile from where he had parked and bought a Frankfurt map. Ute was right, Winters's street was on the same side of the city, perhaps three miles away. Still it took him almost half an hour to make the journey through the narrow, overcrowded streets.

Hofstrasse was quiet and suburban with sloped curbs, fresh blacktop streets, and new cement sidewalks. Sturdy, cement block houses with precisely manicured lawns were spaced evenly along its sides. Cane found number Eighty-four quickly, and it appeared he was in luck. An Audi with American forces plates was in the driveway.

Cane sat in the Fiat for a moment looking at the three-story triplex. But his thoughts were on the man who lived on the ground floor.

Who are you, Sergeant Winters? Cane wondered. Why are you doing this? Is it ideology, a commitment to a cause? Or is it simply money?

Suddenly he remembered a question he had started to ask Ute just as Monica knocked. How could he have forgotten? He had to have the answer before seeing Winters.

He got out of the car and walked quickly to a phone booth half a block away. Monica answered and only after Cane insisted did she give the phone to Ute.

"Ya." Ute's voice sounded thick and strained.

"Ute, it's Cane. I'm very, very sorry to bother you again. But I must know something. How did Sergeant Winters's wife and daughter die?"

"There was a plane crash. Everyone was killed."

"How did it crash?"

"Terrorists shot it."

"Where? Not here, not in Frankfurt?"

"Yes, here in Frankfurt."

"They were on the one that was shot down as it was taking off? That Pan Am flight a couple of years ago?"

"Yes."

"The one that Hamid al Hamani blew up."

"Yes."

"But that doesn't make any sense," Cane almost yelled. But Ute said nothing and Cane knew there was no point in going on. "Thank you, Ute." She hung up without saying good-bye.

He stepped from the phone booth onto the sidewalk and felt a drop of rain and then a second. A moment later it was drizzling. The sky was dark and the moisture began glistening on the sidewalks and blacktop street, scenting the air. But Cane was too involved with the puzzle of Sergeant Winters to notice.

If Winters helped the men who had killed Simon, that meant he had helped the terrorists free Hamid al Hamani. But what sane man would blackmail an entire nation to win freedom for the man that had killed his wife and only child? Yet it had to be Winters. No one else knew where Simon was going to meet him. Had he simply left a note for Simon that had been read by someone else?

Cane's head was wet and his clothes were quickly becoming soaked by the time he reached the Fiat. Without even considering his moves, Cane stuffed the gun in the back of his waistband and walked slowly to the building's front.

The door to the entrance hall opened easily and Cane rapped loudly on the bottom door. He waited a moment and then knocked again, more loudly. A minute later, a man who looked at least sixty years old appeared. He was short and thin. What hair he had was almost totally white with only a few whisps of redish blond.

"Excuse me, I was looking for Sergeant Winters."

"I am Sergeant Winters. How can I help you?" Cane looked closely and then realized the man was not as old as he first appeared. There was a weariness about him. His eyes were dark and sunken. His thin, almost frail, body seemed to sag onto itself.

"My name is Jonathan Cane. We spoke a couple of times on the phone." Cane saw a flash of recognition cross Winters's face. But there was more than recognition. There was a hint of something else.

"Yes. You're the reporter."

"That's right. Look, I'm sorry to bother you, but I've got a couple of questions I'd like to ask you." And Cane saw it again in Winters's eyes and this time recognized the look immediately. It was fear. Any doubts Cane had instantly disappeared.

"I'm sorry, but this is my day off and I have a lot of things to do today." Winters began slowly closing the door. Cane wedged his foot quickly in front of it.

"This will only take a minute," Cane said.

"No, I'm sorry," Winters said as he shoved the door, trying to close it. Cane's arm shot up then, striking the door with the heel of his hand and shoving it backward. The door jerked open, its edge smashing into Winters's head. He stumbled backward into the living room clutching his face, and Cane pushed into the apartment.

He pulled the gun free and pointed it at Winters.

"Sit down," Cane ordered. He shoved Winters backward with his free hand. The sergeant stumbled and fell into a sagging easy chair.

"You're crazy. Look what you've done to me. What the hell is this all about?" Winters blustered.

"It's about my friend Simon North, who's dead because you sent those men after us."

"I don't know what the hell you're talking about."

"Look, let's cut the shit, shall we? Who are they and why the hell are they after me. What do they want?"

"Who are who? I don't know what the hell you're talking about. I gave Simon your message. I didn't do anything more than that."

Cane didn't respond. He stood silently staring at Winters as he gently touched the bruise on his forehead. It was swelling rapidly. Cane grabbed Winters by the shirt and pulled him off the chair. Holding the gun only inches from his face, Cane whispered, "Simon's dead, you asshole. Just like you're going to be. Now tell me who they are and what they want."

"I swear, I don't know what you're talking about."

Now what? Cane knew he couldn't shoot the man, nor could he simply walk away. He had to know. Cane shoved Winters back onto the chair and stepped back and looked around the living room. It was small. One entire wall was taken by a free-standing bookcase in three sections. Its sides, top, and bottom were a dark veneer, and the shelves were enclosed by leaded glass doors. Winters sat in one of two side-by-side easy chairs in front of a small coffee table that faced a large television and inexpensive stereo near the front door. The room with its aging patterned wallpaper and thin carpet, had a sad, lifeless aura of well-ordered sameness, as though the drapes had never been cleaned and the pictures, ashtrays, and empty flower vases unmoved for years.

"Okay, I'll start at the beginning. Before you killed Simon by sending those goons after us you helped them when they broke into the ammo dump in Ochsenburg. I don't know what your role was. Probably facilitating communication. What better place to have your own communications center than right under their noses using the consulate's secure lines."

"You're crazy. Get the hell out of here. I don't have to listen to this," Winters screamed and started to rise from the chair.

Cane pointed the gun at him again and in a quiet voice, almost a whisper, said, "Sit down." He looked carefully at the bookcase then back at Winters and saw the sudden fearful recognition in his eyes.

"Let's try it again. Who are they?"

"I don't know."

Cane smashed the bookcase glass with the barrel of the gun, the door swung open and Hummel figurines tumbled from the top shelf and broke. Winter's eyes grew wide with panic. "Please, God, please they're all I have left of them. Please not the Hummels," he begged.

"Who are they?"

"I don't know."

Cane reached into the shelf with his left hand and swept it clean, sending the small elegant figurines smashing to the floor.

"Please. All I know is he said his name was Karl," Winters pleaded. He sank to his knees and slowly picked up pieces of glass, tears running down his face, dripping onto the floor. "Jesus God, they're all I have left. Please stop, please, please," he mumbled.

Cane reached into the second shelf, his arm behind as many figures as he could reach. He pointed the gun at Winters again. "But you know more don't you? You know who he is don't you?"

"No. I don't." Cane's arm moved forward slowly this time, sending only the few figurines closest to the edge to the floor. Winters looked up and spoke softly in a voice thick with tears. "Ya. I know him. I recognized him from the newspaper. It was Dietenbacher, the man who called himself the minister of war for the Republicans."

"But why did he do it? Why did he want al Hamani free?"

"I don't know. I swear."

Cane stared at the man kneeling in the spray of broken glass, trying to understand the madness. "Why would you help free the man that killed your family?"

Winters looked up at Cane then and suddenly the sorrow was gone, replaced by a fire and hatred in his eyes. "He's dead. I shot him myself." His voice was rising, filled with exhilaration. He almost shouted.

"Al Hamadi? You shot him?"

"Yes, I put the gun in his forehead and I saw the fear in his face as I told him who I was and why I was going to kill him. And he knew he was going to die. Then I shot him. And I shot him again and again until the gun was empty. They promised me I could kill him once he was free and they kept their word."

Cane slowly and carefully pulled his arm from inside the bookcase and simply stared at Winters, trying to understand the deepening insanity of it. "Why did Dietenbacher do it?" His voice was demanding.

"I don't know."

"Didn't you ask?"

"I didn't ask because I didn't care. All I knew was I could kill that bastard who had murdered my family."

"Where is he? Where's Dietenbacher now?"

"I don't know. We only met once in a park. I met the others in a forest after they had Hamadi. I never saw Dietenbacher after our first meeting."

"But you had to communicate with them. How did you do it?"

"By phone."

"How?"

"Cipher. We used the codename Cipher." Winters rose

from his knees and slid back into the easy chair, his hands full of small pieces of painted glass. His tears had stopped and he looked at Cane without expression. There was nothing else to ask, nothing more to say.

THIRTY-ONE

It was late afternoon when Cane pulled off the autobahn and onto a twisting two-lane highway. He drove slowly, thinking of the riddles he still had to solve. Winters had answered an important question for him. He now knew who the terrorists were.

But Cane wondered how much good it really did him. It all seemed a down-the-rabbit-hole puzzle where there was no logic. And Winters's answers didn't help. They only raised more questions.

Why had they demanded Hamid al Hamani's freedom only to turn around and kill him? Why go to the trouble of pretending to be Iraqis? Why not Red Army Faction or Irish Republican Army?

He slowed the Fiat even more to obey the speed limit as he entered a small village. "Jesus," he muttered and slammed his fist against the steering wheel. Well, he knew now why Simon thought the American government knew in advance. Winters was in on it. That explained the messages he had seen. But it also meant the U.S. government was caught as flat footed as everyone else. Fat lot of good that knowledge did him. He still didn't know why they hadn't fled with the weapons or even why they picked Ochsenburg in the first place.

He thought again of what Simon had said, going over the conversation slowly in his mind, trying to remember everything his friend had told him. And suddenly it made sense. "Of course. It's got to be," he mumbled. He pulled the Fiat to the curb at the outskirts of the village. The key *was* Ochsenburg. He sprinted half a block to a phone booth and fumbled with his wallet as he searched for the phone number of the one man he was now sure could tell him everything he wanted to know.

"Hello."

"Major?"

"Yes."

"Codename cipher."

"I'm listening."

"Heimstadt. Where the band practices. Tonight at ten o'clock. Karl said to tell you it's vital. Everything may depend on it."

"All right."

Cane hung up and walked slowly back to the Fiat. He leaned against the car and looked at his watch. Five hours to wait.

As he started to get back in, his eye was caught by a farmer across the road. The old man was trailing a plow horse as it dragged a rake across a plot too small for tractors. Cane watched the farmer guide the horse from one end to the other, breaking the large clods of dirt into a smooth surface beneath the rake. Back and forth, back and forth, they worked in a simple, repetitive rhythm. How many times in his life had the man followed a horse to rake the same piece of ground? Cane wondered.

He watched the man turn the horse at the far end of the field and follow it toward the road again. He watched the quiet spring ritual for nearly ten minutes, enjoying the idyllic eye in the middle of the dangerous storm that surrounded his life.

And as he looked at the farmer he wondered again how the hell everything had gotten so complicated. And now as he reconsidered it, even his plan to learn the truth seemed silly, almost ridiculous.

The "chicken house" wasn't much of a restaurant, just a small, brick building on the edge of the forest. It hadn't changed in the years since Cane was last there. A dining room, a later addition made of wood, sagged against the square brick structure. The shutters, opened wide before the building's one window, were a worn weather-beaten gray. The tile roof was covered with green moss and leaves, giving the building the appearance of a large, aging mushroom protruding from the forest floor.

Cane didn't know the restaurant's real name, or even if it had a name. He and the others simply called it the chicken house because of its limited menu: a grilled half chicken, french fries, red beet and green bean salad, and, of course, beer.

He climbed out and stood next to the car then slowly turned in a circle to examine the clearing and surrounding forest, searching for any sign that the restaurant was being watched. The forest and clearing were quiet and peaceful.

Still, Cane feared the men in the black Opel had learned of Rick's plan to meet him, and as he looked at the forest he searched for a hiding place. He found one almost immediately: a hunter's perch, just inside the edge of the forest. They were common sights in the German woods. Built like boxes on tall stilts, they offered hunters a lighthouse view of the forest and fields below.

Cane climbed the ladder to the bottom of the perch: a Lincoln Logs toy–like box big enough for two with a bench in the rear. He pushed open the trap door in the floor and climbed in. The roof was not quite high enough for him to stand. The front wall ended at his waist, a perfect place to hunt without having to exercise.

The perch gave him a great view of the forest, the fields, and the road from the village to the small restaurant in the woods. The bench was in shadow and Cane was confident that no one would notice him.

He looked at the lovely setting below him: precise, neatly plowed, fields surrounding the village of red-roofed houses in the distance. But Cane drew little pleasure from it. He could not forget why he was there.

He sat without moving, watching the village and road that led to the clearing. And he played in his mind the closed loop video of events. As the hours passed Cane began to accept a different understanding of them. Yes, what had happened was unfair. Yes it was wrong. But that was irrelevant. He had already locked his sense of fairness away. His threats to Winters proved that. He couldn't afford ambiguity or subtle arguments about ideals and dogma. His existence had been reduced to two things: discovery and survival.

THIRTY-TWO

The sun had already disappeared when Cane saw the headlights of a car as it turned off the main road. He watched it make its way past a sparse orchard and a fallow field toward the restaurant. It disappeared for a moment in the trees and reappeared in the clearing below. As it swung into the parking lot Cane made out the outlines of an American military sedan. He pushed himself back into the farther corner of darkness in the small hut on stilts. A moment later the sedan's door swung open and Cane saw Rick get out and walk into the restaurant. He waited a few moments longer but no other cars ventured off the main road below.

Certain that Rick hadn't been followed, Cane climbed down and went into the restaurant. It was small, sparse, and functional. A small bar ran across one side of the room and behind it was an alcove kitchen. There were a six tables, twenty-four chairs, and one customer. Rick sat at a table near the bar, facing the door.

He smiled broadly as Cane walked in. "Hey, sailor, buy you a beer?" he called.

"Sure, thanks." Cane set his backpack on the floor and pulled out a chair.

The old proprietor, looking not a day older than he did the last time Cane had visited, more than six years before, shuffled to the table and stood without speaking, awaiting their order. Without consulting Cane, Rick asked for two beers and two chicken dinners.

"That okay with you?" he asked as the man moved away from the table.

"Sure. What other choice is there?"

They fell silent, each waiting for the other, until Rick finally spoke.

"I'm glad you're here. I wasn't sure you were still alive."

"Well, I am. At least for now," Cane answered with a chuckle.

"No, I'm serious. That guy calling himself Captain Montgomery came to my office today." He let the idea hang between them for a moment. When Cane said nothing he continued. "He got there before I did. He talked to Roland and found out where I live and then left. I was afraid he would get to my place before you left."

Cane thought of Rick's gun in the backpack at his feet but said nothing about it. "I left right after you did."

"Good. I haven't been home since this morning. I tried calling but there was no answer and I had visions of you . . . ah, having met with an awkward demise in my living room. Hell, the place is messy enough already. Anyway, I didn't dare go home, so I spent the day in the library to avoid running into that guy. Did you have any luck?"

"Yes. I got some answers. And now I've got a lot more questions than before. But it doesn't matter. I'll have the answers in a couple of hours."

The flatness of Cane's tone, as much as what he said, caught Rick by surprise. His voice seemed to have changed since the last time they talked. But the change was elusive, hard to describe. There had always been an edge of bright energy that spoke of optimism, or what Rick often thought of as naivete, behind Cane's words. Suddenly it was gone, replaced by a remoteness that made him want to wave his hand in front of Cane's face to make sure he was listening.

"What do you mean? What happened?"

"Before I tell you, you've got to tell me something. Okay?"

"Sure, what?"

"Do you know Major Henry?"

"Yeah. Why? What's he got to do with this?"

"Look, first you tell me about him and then I'll give you a complete rundown on my day."

"All right. Well, old 'Two-Second Woody' and I were at West Point together. He's a hive."

"A hive?"

"Yeah, at the academy there were goats and hives. The hives were the real engineer types, spent all their time studying and getting good grades. He was hive. His father went to West Point and became a general. So did his granddaddy, I think. The goats were the ones at the other end."

"Which were you?"

"Are you kidding? You've seen my apartment."

"Oh, yeah, I see what you mean. But why did you call him Two-Second Woody?"

"It's sort of a long story."

"Tell me. It might help to know what he's like."

"Actually, you're probably right. It does say something about the man. Woody did everything by the book. Everything for the greater glory of God and Country. He's a fierce patriot with a deep seated hatred of the Commies. He fit in great at the Point. Like I said, he was a hive.

"Don't get me wrong. It's not like the minute you meet him you hate him. In fact, he can be very charming. But after a while he really begins to bug you. He's an arrogant bastard. He knows the way the world should be run. And he's so damned sure of it. There's no room for error.

"Well, when we graduated, I got sent to Korea. Woody drew Nam. He was really looking forward to going. He ended up as a platoon leader; replaced some guy from Ohio State. The way I hear it Woody had great plans for the unit. Going to be covered with glory." Rick grunted a half laugh.

"It's almost funny. A smart guy like Woody with a million-dollar education and he never did get it. And this guy he replaced, some ROTC yahoo from Ohio State, figured it out the first couple of days there. That whole war was about just one thing: staying alive, man, just staying alive." Rick laugh-grunted again and took a long drink of beer.

"This other guy was platoon leader for almost a year and they didn't lose a man. Not one. He never volunteered his men for anything. Always did just what it took to get by, nothing more. And he learned survival real quick and taught his men everything he knew.

"Like one thing he taught them was you never walk down a blind path. Always make sure you can see into the brush on both sides. Great ambush spots. In that country that was pretty hard to do sometimes. But, he wasn't as interested in the mission as he was in coming out alive.

"So this guy rotates and Woody arrives. It was bad from the beginning. The first thing he does is volunteer the outfit for some patrol or something. Man, the last thing these guys wanted was to go on patrol, especially when they don't have to. But what the hell were they going to do? Maybe Woody was trying to impress the brass. Maybe just figured it was the right thing to do.

"And that was just the beginning. Woody keeps volunteering them, and pretty soon they're out in the jungle all the time and all the men hate him. And I've got to believe Woody didn't like them much either because they weren't gung ho about going out and killing Charlie. Just imagine it: a stiff, arrogant West Pointer in the middle of the jungle trying to tell some street-smart blacks and a couple of redneck cowboys from Montana what to do and you'll get the picture.

"One day they're out on one of their patrols, and they get a message they've got to be at some spot to be picked up by choppers at three that afternoon. Headquarters is planning some massive saturation bombing in the area and they want every GI out of there. And man, let me tell you, those B52s could lay down some massive shit. You don't want to be anywhere nearby when they start sending that hardware down.

"The guys were pissed off right away. Turns out the pickup spot was near a place they were at earlier in the day, which was just about as far as they were supposed to go. But Woody'd been pushing them to cover even more ground. And now they've got to go all the way back. Well, its a pretty good hike, so they pack it up and start humping.

"It was almost the end of the summer—hot, humid, and mosquitoes everywhere. Woody won't let them stop and rest. Just kept on pressing. Can't keep those big birds waiting on the ground.

"They're dying of thirst, covered in sweat and mosquitoes, and nobody's saying a goddamned word. They're just hustling to get to the pickup point. Pick em up and put em down, move, move, move. And the whole time they're thinking if they'd just been a little slower out the gate that morning, if Woody hadn't been so damned determined to shine for the brass, they wouldn't have to be doing all this.

"Finally, they get real close to the pickup spot. The choppers are due in a few minutes. And they're ready to go. They're on a little hill and they can see the landing area, it's just down this path a little ways. But on both sides the jungle is high and thick. You couldn't see two inches into it.

"Woody says 'let's go,' and they just look at him. It was like that was the last straw, you know. They didn't go through all that shit and bust their butts to get that close to being picked up just to go walking down some path and get all shot to hell. One of the guys just says no he ain't going down the path and the rest just stand there. So Woody gives them an order: go down the path. As if an order is going to do any good. They just stare at him. They flat refuse to go.

"Woody must be thinking about those bombers revving up on the runway or halfway there and how the choppers are going to be there in a minute and how the mission is going to be scrubbed or something and he's going to get blamed and how these bastards who he hates anyway are disobeying orders and he just sort of loses it.

"He whips out his pistol and grabs the guy that said no and puts the gun to his head and says something like 'I'm giving you a direct order to go down that path. If you don't I'll shoot you and I'll shoot every damned one of you who won't go. Now move it.'

"They went. They didn't get shot and the bombing mission went off just as planned. And they get back to base and Woody acts like there's nothing wrong, like he had to be stern so he was, and now it's over and everything is fine again. By now, though, they're sure it's just a matter of time until he gets them all killed. So they decided to frag him.

"They put a bomb in his tent with a remote detonator. They put a spotter on a nearby hill watching through field glasses and when Woody gets to the tent, the spotter's supposed to signal the guy to let it rip. Well, Woody walks up to the tent, starts to open the flap but turns and starts walking away for some reason. Only the spotter stopped looking when Woody got to the tent. He turns and gives the signal and the guy touches it off. But Woody is walking away from the tent. The blast knocked him for a loop and he broke his leg or something and he ended up in the hospital. They didn't kill him, but he never came back to the unit either and no one checked too close about the explosion. They figure he was probably two seconds away from dying."

"And that's why they call him Two-Second Woody," added Cane.

"You got it. Now you tell me why you're so anxious to know about Woody Henry."

"I'm going to see him tonight. And he's going to tell me the truth." Once again Rick was startled by the cold, distant tone in Cane's voice and he looked closely at his friend. His once bright, sparkling eyes were dull and clouded.

"Cane, what the hell's going on?"

"He's the man who has the answers. It's so obvious it's almost funny." He paused for a moment, and then in a slow monotone told Rick of visiting Ute and his confrontation with Winters and what Simon had told him about the messages he'd seen.

Rick saw the simple logic of it but was deeply worried nonetheless. Cane's flat, cold tone concerned him. It spoke of a grim, nothing-to-lose determination that could be very dangerous. And there was something else. Something even more disturbing.

Cane would be carrying excess baggage to the meeting. Simon's death and his own fears were no longer his only motivations. Long-ago wounds were propelling him and it scared Rick.

"And then what?" Rick asked when Cane was finished.

"Once I know what happened, I'm going to have to get back to the States. I've got to get to the paper. If we can get the story in print, I'll be safe. I mean, what could they do? Can you imagine what kind of shit they would stir up if the reporter who had just blown the cover off something like this, whatever it is, were suddenly killed? Even in an accident? No, the shit would hit the fan. I get it in print and I'll be safe. Hell I might even win a Pulitzer. It's the only way out that I can think of."

"Yeah. But you may have some problems there."

"Why?"

"We've got problems, friend. Somehow the German police

know you were in the van with Simon. Now they're looking for you too."

"Jesus Christ," Cane sighed and shook his head slowly. "What the hell's next? I suppose the MPs are after me too?"

"I suppose. But I wouldn't worry too much about them. They couldn't find their ass with two hands and a search warrant. But its going to make it harder than hell to get home. You can't just walk up to the Pan Am ticket counter and slap your passport down and buy a ticket. Look, whoever these guys are they're going to be watching all the airports. And now they've got the German police looking for you too. Shit, man, every goddamned railroad station in the country is probably being checked."

"Okay, so I'll slip over the border into France, or Italy or Holland and catch a flight from there."

"Maybe. I don't know, Cane, it's dangerous. For all we know they've alerted Interpol. Besides the longer you stretch it out, the more of a trail you leave and the easier it's going to be to catch you. I don't think I can help you much. They already know who I am and they're probably watching Barbara Darling's place too."

The old man shuffled up to their table and put a heavy, white glass plate loaded with food in front of each man and walked slowly away to get their beers. Cane burned his mouth gobbling food and waited impatiently for the man to meander back with two short, empty glasses and two bottles of beer. Cane drank straight from the bottle, allowing the clear malty liquid to soothe his burning palate.

The two men ate without speaking, each silently addressing the same problem. How could Cane get out of Germany? Was there any way to escape?

Cane had always assumed he would merely fly home. It had never occurred to him they would watch the airports. Could he slip into Italy or take a train to France or Spain and then catch a flight home? Maybe. But Rick was probably right. The farther he ran, the more of a trail he left and the less chance he had.

Maybe he could just call the story in. But what if the lines to the paper had been tapped? Could they trace the call all the way across the Atlantic back to him? Probably not. But he couldn't risk his life on it.

Besides, he had to get the copy into Slovak's hands. He had to be there to convince them if the editors suddenly turned soft. It was a hell of a story, and they'd want more than just a fax before running it. But if he were there it would be okay. All he had to do was get back to LA. But how?

And suddenly Rick laughed a full deep-throated laugh that was almost a howl.

"What?" Cane asked.

"I think I know a way. It's just beautiful. Just flat-out brilliant." And he laughed again.

THIRTY-THREE

Cane gunned the Fiat to life on the first try then switched on the high beams. Letting the engine idle, he got out and knelt in front of the headlights to study the map once more. He looked at it for only a moment then stuck it in his rear pocket.

But as he stood, the headlights shone off his face and he saw himself reflected in the windshield. His hair was disheveled, and he had not shaved that morning. He looked thinner and almost devoid of color and life. His eyes were empty.

He stared at the distant and indifferent image but refused to acknowledge the man in the windshield. From the moment he had seen Ute he had slowly walled off every feeling within himself until he cared only about discovery and life. And he would allow nothing to distract him now. Nothing would challenge his new convictions.

Later, when it was over, when he had the luxury of time, when he knew the answers, he could think about what he had become in order to survive. Later he would think. Tonight he would act.

Moments later the Fiat was bouncing down the road toward the main highway that led to a second highway which would lead to a village where a group of men gathered in a *Gasthaus* once a week to play music and drink beer.

And that evening Major Woodrow Wilson Henry would show up. And this time Cane would act. This time he wouldn't merely sit and watch the man cheerfully leave the *Gasthaus*, walk to his car, and drive away as he had done years ago.

The memory of that night was a chronic virus he had lived with. It still flared, hurting him occasionally, but with the years the attacks became less and less frequent, and for a while he actually began believing he had made the right decision years ago. Now he doubted it anew.

He and Maria were to have lunch at the same park where he had first put his arm around her. This time, however, she was the first to arrive. Cane was so used to being first, he parked his car and didn't even bother to look for her car. When he saw her walking slowly toward him he got out and waved.

Immediately, though, he knew something was wrong. He had known their relationship could not last forever as it was. But afraid of what Maria would decide, he never pushed it, never demanded she choose between him and her husband. Indeed, he never spoke to her of the need for a decision. Besides, she was in love with him, and although he didn't push it, he felt she saw the world differently now. She could never go back to the geek in the uniform. Not now. Not after everything they shared.

Maria looked pale and shaken as she approached the car.

"What is it, what's wrong?"

"We got our orders."

Cane's stomach twisted. It was too sudden. Too unexpected. They were supposed to have lunch and go for a walk in the park. They loved the park. It was "their" park. Now she was telling him about orders. And the way she announced it, in a flat, emotionless voice that said it was final, there could be no discussion. It answered all his questions, defeated all his arguments before he could make them.

He felt faint and disoriented. He knew what she was trying to tell him, but he had to be certain, to eliminate any doubt.

"What are you going to do?"

"I'm going too."

"But Maria you can't. You can't just leave. I love you. You love me." His voice was becoming thick.

"Cane, I can't leave Woody and go with you. I've tried to tell you that before, but you wouldn't listen to me."

"Don't you love me?" The woman he loved more than anything in the world was leaving him, and yet he felt weak, unable to fight. She had defeated him with three simple words,

"I'm going too," and his response came as a collapsing whimper, almost a plea. "Don't you love me?"

"Yes. More than you'll probably ever understand. But I love Woody too. It's different with you. I love you very much. But I am married to him. It's who I am. I can't leave him."

"Of course you can. Just do it. We'll leave Germany. I can be out of here in two weeks. Maria, I love you. I'll do anything." Desperation seeped into his voice as he began to more fully understand the terror of losing her.

"No. Cane, it has to end." She put her arms around him and hugged him deeply. He could tell she was was crying too. "I love you. I will always love you. I can't see you again. Ever."

She pulled away, turned, and left. He could still see her walking away from him. He remembered her dark blue skirt, her yellow blouse, and her canvas shoes. He could still see the red belt that matched the red stripes in her shoes. Despite the years the image was sharp.

He had driven to the village that night years before, knowing only vaguely that Woody Henry played in a band there. He had no idea which *Gasthaus* it was. But as he rounded the bend in the road he saw their car in the gravel parking lot and pulled in. He parked as far away from the other cars as he could and waited to speak to her husband.

Certainly, Cane had told himself through his grief, her husband had figured out there was another man. Certainly he knew someone else was capable of making her so much happier than she had ever been. He would approach her husband as he left the *Gasthaus*. They would be on neutral ground. It would be a reasonable discussion. They would talk like gentlemen. He would see Cane's point and bow out. Certainly, if he loved her he would want her to be happy. And if he didn't love her, then he would never stand in the way of her happiness.

Woody had been almost the last to leave that evening. He walked to the trunk of the car and opened it and stowed his instrument case. He was whistling, as if he had no cares. Cane could still hear the whistle.

Cane reached for the door handle but didn't open it. He could still see her husband carefully close the trunk and walk to the side of his car, casually unlock it and get it. Cane watched him, heard him whistling, but didn't move. His resolve, his plans and hopes, crumbled further with each move that Woody Henry made. He had never understood why, had never been able to know himself well enough to know why he had sat there in the dark and cold and been unable to open his own door and walk the few yards and confront the husband of the woman he loved.

He still didn't understand. But it didn't matter. This time he would get out of the car.

The restaurant was on the edge of the village but Cane drove past it. The major wasn't due for two hours and Cane slowly cruised the hamlet's few streets, searching for evidence of the black Opel or other cars filled with waiting men. Finally he parked in front of a small grocery store. He dug the pistol from his backpack and put it in his coat pocket then grabbed the nightstick off the backseat, got out of the car, and walked the two hundred yards to the restaurant. He stopped across the street from the restaurant for a moment, then turned and walked up a narrow side street, little more than an alley, that twisted and turned as it ran away from the highway. He followed the street to the second curve and stopped. From where he stood he was nearly invisible to cars passing on the highway yet had a good view of the parking lot. He stuck the nightstick through his belt and leaned against a high brick wall surrounding a courtyard and stared down the road at the restaurant. Twice, cars pulled into the parking lot and Cane tensed. But neither was the major's.

Cane had made no specific plan beyond confronting the man. He was unsure what questions he would ask or even what he would do if Henry demanded proof that he was from Karl. And what if he refused to answer any questions? What would he do then?

Just after ten a Chrysler Le Baron convertible pulled into the lot and stopped. Cane stood straight and stared at the car. His stomach muscles tensed and his heart, fed by adrenaline, began to beat more rapidly. His hands were sweaty and he repeatedly grasped and released the handle of the nightstick. Cane stood absolutely still and watched as Major Henry got out of the car and looked around him. Cane moved slowly down the narrow street toward the restaurant, trying to move

[210]

with an air of nonchalance. He was unaware of his own move-
ments and later he would not remember crossing the street
and parking lot or approaching the major as he stood near his
car.

The man was taller than Cane remembered. But he could
see his dark hair was still neatly trimmed, with half moon
circles of white skin over his ears. The major watched him
intently as he approached but said nothing.

Cane stepped close and spoke in a very low voice. "Major
Henry, I called you today."

"Who are you?"

"It doesn't matter. There's been a leak. Karl sent me to
ask you some questions."

"He said there would be no more contact." He made no
effort to hide the suspicion in his voice and Cane knew he had
to move cautiously. "What kind of questions?"

"Did you talk to anyone about this, about your involvement in a special project or anything like that?"

"Of course not."

"Why do the Americans think the men were Iraqis? What
did you tell them?"

"What's this really about? I didn't leak anything. Karl
knows that."

"And the explosives are all still there? They've checked?"

The major's jaw stiffened and he squinted, creasing his
forehead as he stared at Cane. "Who are you?" he demanded
suddenly.

"I told you Karl sent me. We think there's a problem."

"Karl knows the answers to these questions. Besides he
wouldn't contact me like this. He wouldn't just send someone
to meet me. This doesn't make any sense." Anger, touched
with fear, had replaced the open suspicion in his voice.

"I told you. There was a leak. We think it might be
Winters." Cane struggled to remain calm, reassuring.

"Who? I don't know Winters." Of course, they would have
used codenames. The realization came to Cane suddenly. But
it was too late. The major had stepped back. "Something
stinks," the major said and he started to turn away.

"Wait. You can't go. We're not finished. I have to know."

[211]

Cane was almost shouting. He reached out and grabbed the major's sleeve.

"No. Whoever you are, we're done." He spoke angrily through clenched teeth and jerked his arm free.

"But you don't understand—"

"No, *you* don't understand. I said this is over. I don't know what this is about but I'm not talking to you. Now get the hell out of my way, I'm leaving."

As he moved toward the driver's door, Cane could feel him slipping away, again. In a moment he would be gone.

The nightstick made a dull thud as it hit the major's head. Cane had swung it wildly but with all his energy. The major's head jerked sideways and his knees buckled. Cane felt nothing, no remorse, no guilt as he swung the nightstick again. The major had begun to recover when the second blow struck his ribs. It hit with a sickening thud, and there was a snap as if the bones were broken. But he was still conscious as he slumped to the ground. Cane swung again but missed, and the nightstick smashed the side window of the car door.

The major moaned as he lay on the ground. Cane dropped the nightstick and pulled the gun from his pocket. He fell to one knee and pointed the gun at the major's head.

"This is for Simon and Maria and all the others. You bastard. You fucking bastard, now you're going to die."

The major looked at him through glassy eyes. Blood streamed down the side of his head and trickled from the corner of his mouth. He made a gurgling noise as he tried to breath.

"Who are you? What do you want?"

And suddenly Cane understood what he had been about to do. He didn't really understand what had happened, how he had come to be kneeling beside Maria's husband, pointing a gun at his head. It was all bits and pieces, as if he were looking at the past few moments through a shattered windshield.

But he felt no sorrow for the bleeding man in front of him. He felt nothing. Empty. He kept the gun pointed steadily at the man's head and made one demand.

"I already know most of it. Now you're going to tell me the rest. If you lie, I'll know and I'll kill you."

The major had to struggle to answer, and one time his eyes

began to glaze and Cane feared he was slipping into unconsciousness. He slapped him across the face with his open hand. "Answer the fucking question you asshole," he yelled. The major's eyes cleared and he mumbled a response.

In the end, it was enough. Cane finally understood. He had all the pieces. He put the gun back in his pocket, stood, and walked slowly toward his car. Major Henry rolled onto his side and then struggled to his hands and knees.

"Whoever you are, they'll find you. You'll die," he managed.

Cane stopped and looked back at the man kneeling on all fours in the gravel parking lot. He thought of the evening years before when he sat in his car unable to move, and he thought of Simon who had died only the night before.

"Maybe, but I don't know that it matters," he said. He walked up the street to the Fiat and drove away.

THIRTY-FOUR

Rick's plan to get Cane out of the country was simple, almost foolish. But Rick was sure it would work. And no one would discover what he had done until it was too late, if ever.

Still, it was risky. If it failed he would be involved. Perhaps not right away. It might take a few days, or perhaps a week, but someone would trace it back to him. It could cost him his job, his career. Maybe his life. But he had to take the chance. He was already involved.

Rick stood next to his car, looking at the surrounding trees in the warm moonlight and thought about it for a moment longer. No, there was no choice. He got into the car and headed down the bumpy road away from the chicken house. Twenty minutes later he was at the office.

He unlocked the door, switched on the lights, and quickly moved to a green metal filing cabinet near his desk. Pulling out the top drawer, Rick rapidly flipped through the folders until he found the blank forms he needed. It took a minute more to sift through the papers on his desk and find his own completed forms. Then he was almost ready. He dug a bottle of Liquid Paper from the back of the desk drawer and sat down to type.

He was a two-fingered typist and after the fourth mistake on the first line, he ripped the form from the typewriter and started again. He blew his second attempt as well and again put a fresh sheet in typewriter. On the third try he hacked out an acceptable job. Forging the signature was easy. He studied the legitimate forms and tried a few times on a piece of scrap paper until he was sure it was illegible but still resembled the name he had typed. He signed with a flourish and ran off a dozen copies.

He paused by the door and admired his handiwork. It would work. No one would ever know. He flicked off the lights and left.

Cane was running again. And again he needed somewhere to hide.

He remembered little of what happened only minutes before. He recalled approaching the major and saying something. But after that, he wasn't sure. One thing, though, he remembered very clearly. Cane saw himself kneeling beside the bloodied major, pointing a gun at his head and cocking it.

He looked at the gun on the seat beside him and shivered. That it had ever given him a sense of excitement or power amazed him now. Suddenly a wave of nausea swept over him. He swerved onto the shoulder and skidded to a stop. Pushing open the door, he crawled out. All he could see was the major, blood streaming down the side of his head, his breath labored, lying in the dirt.

A second rush of nausea swept over Cane and beads of sweat covered his forehead. A moment later it passed. The image of Major Henry was still there. But so too were his words. And thinking of them again, Cane felt better.

He sat for a moment, to enjoy the cool air, then got back into the car and headed for the rendezvous point. He might as well go there, he thought. It would mean sleeping in the Fiat, but he would be safe.

There are no guards and no gates at the U.S. forces campground across the autobahn from the Frankfurt Airport. And with the camp directly under the flight path of the Frankfurt civilian airport and the U.S. Air Force's military air terminal, there are few overnight campers.

Rick had been right, it was probably the last place anyone would look for Cane. He parked the Fiat on the far edge of the campground and stretched out, sticking his feet around the clutch and brake pedals. Folding his arms across his chest, he leaned back and tried to sleep. A jet roared in low.

Sleep seemed impossible. Noise from the jets mingled with

images of the major and Maria and Simon that played contin-uously in his mind. Again and again he heard the major's words and his declaration that Cane would die.

Cane now knew the secret that men were prepared to kill to protect. He understood why they had followed him. He knew why Simon was dead. He knew why they had chosen Ochsenburg and why they had freed Hamid al Hamani and why they had sat in the igloo surrounded by hundreds of soldiers. It all made sense. It was everything he needed. It would mean his safety. It would be the biggest story of his life. It could mean prizes, perhaps even a Pulitzer—or it could mean his death.

But he'd paid a price for it. He had attacked a man and come close to killing him to get the story. As Cane thought about it, though, he felt no shame. He felt totally detached. And he knew that too was part of the price.

Then, still convinced he could not sleep, he closed his eyes and immediately fell into a deep slumber as another jet came in for a landing.

Karl sat alone in total darkness and thought of the mission and considered how to save it. There was no question. The reporter had it all now. Before he had only pieces, just guesses and hunches. Not now. Not after he had beaten the major and trashed Winters's precious Hummels. Now he knew and he could destroy everything.

He had to think, to plan. He forced himself to ignore the headache that was spreading to the base of his skull from his taut neck muscles and consider the problem. Above all else, the reporter had to be stopped in Germany, he knew. He must not get home. Who knew what damage he could do if he got back to the States?

But there were other, more immediate, questions he had to answer. Where was the reporter now? What would he do next, where would he go? The captain was sure he had been at the engineer's house earlier. Would he return? The captain was waiting. If he returned, he would die.

Others were watching the teacher's home. Her phone was tapped, so was the engineer's. The airports were covered. So was every train station near Ochsenburg.

Could he escape? There seemed no chance. But too many times in the last days he had waited confidently to hear of Jonathan Cane's death only to learn he had slipped away. This time there seemed to be no place left to hide, no way to escape.

Karl switched on the desk light and slid the photo of Cane and Maria into the small circle of light. He looked at the reporter and felt the intense pain in his neck and head. Only when Jonathan Cane was dead would it stop, he knew.

"Hey, Cane, wake up, man."

Cane opened his eyes. Rick was leaning in the passenger's side, shaking him.

"Come on there, wake up. It's time to catch your plane."

"What time is it?"

"It's about six, but you've got to check in two hours in advance if you're going to catch that flight."

"Okay. Here are the keys. You mind driving?" He pulled the small key ring from his pocket and handed it to Rick.

"Thanks, but let's take the staff car I brought. It's a little less conspicuous."

Cane followed Rick to the green Ford sedan and got in the passenger side.

"Well, how did it go last night?" Rick asked.

Instead of answering, Cane simply reached into his backpack and pulled out Rick's gun. "Here. It's yours. Look, I'm sorry I took it. I just thought I might need it. I took a nightstick I found in your place too. I think I dropped it somewhere, I really don't remember."

"God, Cane, what the hell happened? What did you do?" Rick asked the question quietly and gently.

"Don't worry, I didn't shoot him. I hit him with your nightstick, though. I don't know what happened exactly. I really don't remember every detail. I know I hit him. I hope he'll be all right but I don't know, I hit him pretty good. I may have busted a couple of his ribs. But I found out what the hell this is all about. You won't believe it."

He told the story slowly, several times going back to fill in details as he remembered them. When he finished the two sat in the car silently until Rick, in a low voice, said, "That's absolutely unbelievable. I mean that's really unbelievable."

[218]

"It's funny, if someone had come up to me my first day back in O'burg and laid all this out in front of me, I wouldn't have believed it, either. I guess I was too trusting. I'm beginning to think I've been a fool all my life."

"I don't know, Cane, I don't think it's a matter of being a fool. No one would have suspected something like that was going on."

"You know, Rick, one thing I don't understand is how she could be married to him."

The sudden transition didn't surprise Rick. He knew Cane couldn't separate his feelings about Maria from his emotions about the incident in Ochsenburg and what had happened in the past days.

"Don't judge her too harshly," Rick said. "We make decisions when we're young that we try to live with for the rest of our lives. She's no different."

"No, you're probably right. But Jesus, how could he . . . ah hell, who knows?"

"Look, we'd better get going," Rick said. "But first, why don't you change your shirt. That one still has blood on it. Must be Woody's. I brought a fresh one I borrowed from Roland. I spent the night at his place."

Rick reached onto the backseat and handed Cane the fresh shirt then waited as Cane pulled the other one off. "Here, I'll wrap the gun in this one and hide it. I can't take a chance on carrying it in," Rick said.

He wrapped the gun in Cane's bloodied shirt and hustled from the car to a small group of trees on the edge of the campground. He brushed aside the leaves and dug a shallow hole with his hands to bury the gun. He got back to the car, opened the trunk, and pulled out an old, pea green plastic suitcase. He tossed it over the front seat to the rear and slipped behind the wheel.

"Got that from Roland too. It really has clothes in it. They probably wouldn't fit, but hell that doesn't matter. At least you'll have a suitcase. It might look funny if you tried to check in without at least some luggage. No sense taking chances."

"Looks like you've thought of everything."

"Hell, boy, I'm an engineer. I'm supposed to think of details."

Cane just smiled.

They were at the front gate of Rhein Main Air Base in minutes. A half-dozen cars were backed up single file at the entrance, waiting for the security guard to wave them forward one at a time.

"Here are your travel orders," Rick said, handing Cane a small pile of forms. "It says you're a civilian consultant working for the engineers. You've been called home on emergency leave. If anyone asks too many questions, try to be vague. You know, overcome with grief. All you need are the orders and your passport."

"Yeah, just like when I worked at *Stripes*. But are you sure they won't be looking for me here?"

"No, I'm not sure. But it seemed like the best shot. Besides, just because the army's looking for you doesn't mean the air force knows anything about it."

The cars in front of them had passed onto the base and the security guard waved the sedan forward. Rick pulled to a stop next to the guard tower that divided the highway: incoming traffic on one side, outgoing on the other. The young airman, a pistol on his hip, leaned down to the window and asked for their identification. Rick handed him his official ID card and Cane passed him his passport with a copy of his orders folded in the middle.

The guard glanced at the ID card, studied the photo, and looked at Rick, then scrutinized the travel orders and the passport Cane had given him.

"Catching a flight?"

Cane tried to look at the airman with a sad expression. "Yeah, got to get home," he said.

The airman smiled. "Well, have a safe trip, sir," he said. He returned their papers and waved the car through.

"So far so good," Rick said. "In a few hours you'll be home and you can write the story."

"But what about you? What are you going to do?"

"Oh, I'll lay low for a couple of days, call in sick or something. Then I'm off to Turkey for an inspection trip. If I want I can find enough work there to justify extending my trip for an extra week or two. Roland will help me fudge the paperwork on this end if I need to."

He drove at a leisurely pace past the base exchange, recreation center, hangars, and barracks until he pulled to a stop in front of the terminal and they got out. Rick pulled the small suitcase off the backseat, set it on the curb, and stuck out his hand.

"You know the routine from here. Good luck."

"Thanks. I mean it. Thanks for everything."

"Don't mention it." He laughed. "And I mean *don't* mention it."

"Thanks, Rick."

Cane picked up the suitcase and held it at his side as he watched Rick drive through the parking lot and back onto the road. Then he turned, walked into the air terminal, and joined the line of people waiting to check in for the 8:30 A.M. flight to Fort Dix, New Jersey.

THIRTY-FIVE

The apartment was dark. Only the circular light from the desk lamp kept it from being totally black. Karl sat just beyond the ragged edge of the white light. He held the telephone lightly in his right hand.

"Yes. I understand," he said. His voice was cool, betraying no emotion even as his free hand dug at the knots in his neck. "Are you sure? There's no mistake?"

The U.S. Air Force. Damn. It was a brilliant move. He hadn't thought the reporter capable of such a ploy. He must have had help. Someone who could get him on the flight, probably the engineer. But Karl knew such speculation was irrelevant. All that mattered was what happened next.

"No one thought to watch the military flights until just now. The flight left about an hour ago." Winters sought to explain and reassure.

"Yes, of course," Karl answered absently. His mind was racing elsewhere, already planning the next move. Now it would have to be the final step.

"What do we do now?" Winters asked.

"There's no choice. The captain and I have to go to LA. There's a flight in two hours."

"Can you use the captain there, in the States? I mean, is it wise?"

"Perhaps. I think there's another way. But I'll have to meet with him."

"Meet him? You can't be serious?"

"It's a risk. But there's little choice. And I'm sure I can convince him to do nothing."

"How the hell are you going to do that?"

"I'll tell him the truth, of course. He already knows most of it. But he doesn't understand the consequences," Karl said. "In the end he'll understand that he has no options except to forget. He'll see the way it is."

"Okay." Winters hoped the skepticism hadn't seeped into his voice. He did not want to incur the wrath of Karl, not even this late in the operation. "What should I do?"

"Nothing. Forget everything. It will all be over soon."

Karl hung up and looked at a thin briefcase on the edge of the table, barely visible in the half light. He considered the various passports and identifications within the case. Who should he be? Who should confront the journalist? Who best to offer the blend of fear and persuasion? Perhaps an emissary from the National Security Council or the Defense Information Agency or even the German government. No, the Central Intelligence Agency. Of course. That would be much better. It might just give him an edge with the reporter.

He held his hands in the circle of light in front of him. He knew people though him an eccentric—a crazy man who haunted the fringes of society. He knew their names for him and how they laughed at the mention of him in the beer halls. The country's leaders, in their rush to reunite, dismissed his ideas and his worries. They didn't see the dangers. They didn't understand the terrible risks they were taking. And so few understood the glory that was possible for the new fatherland. But a reborn Germany could not follow in the wake of other nations, like some duckling waddling after its mother.

Deutschland would be its own power once again. It would have the glory and position it deserved. He would see to that. When the country needed him, he would be ready. That was the reason for the plan. He would be strong when the need came. Then they all would understand what a patriot could do when he was given the freedom to work.

First, though, there was one man he had to convince.

The jet lumbered in low over Los Angeles, dropping out of the brilliant clear blue sky and disappearing into the brown smog that hugged the earth, held there by the hotter air of the upper atmosphere. Cane peered past the young lady next to him and out the window. He could make out only the faint outlines of downtown and Century City and other landmarks until just before the jet crossed the 405 Freeway and touched down.

At first he had been scared, certain someone would discover him. At Fort Dix he had hurried off the jet and through the terminal, not bothering to fetch the suitcase Rick had given him. Only after the bus left the base and slipped into traffic on the highway headed for JFK did Cane begin to feel safe.

And now he was home, back in LA, and the bastards probably thought he was still hiding in Germany. As he sat waiting for the aisle to clear, he thought about the story he had. Nothing could stop it now.

Finally, the last one off the plane, he walked to the long line of cabs outside and climbed in the backseat of the first one. The cab driver looked quizzically at the man who needed a shave and shower so desperately and carried no luggage, but said nothing. He just turned the air conditioning up a notch and pulled into traffic.

Throughout the ride, Cane tried to think of exactly what he would write. He worked on the lead and tried to force himself to organize his thoughts. But he couldn't get past the first sentence before his thoughts would move back to Maria or to Rick, or forward to walking into the newsroom.

What would the other reporters say when he walked in? Would they congratulate him on his coverage of the terrorist incident? Maybe tease him about finally being back. Or would they simply look at him and wonder what the hell happened to him? He touched the bump above his eye. It was smaller today but he knew it was terribly bruised.

The cab stopped with a lurch. "Here you are," the driver said and leaned over the seat to collect his fare. With the last of his travelers checks, Cane paid the bill and added a hefty tip. He got out and paused for just a moment on the curb and smiled broadly.

He'd done it. He was home with the biggest story of his life. Maybe a Pulitzer. He pushed through the revolving door into the lobby and headed straight for the elevators. A few moments later the doors swooshed open and he walked into the main newsroom.

He saw Slovak at his desk, staring intently at a computer terminal. A couple of reporters yelled greetings as he walked in. Slovak looked up and smiled.

"Cane!" He seemed genuinely pleased to see him. But the impression was fleeting. "Where the hell have you been? You look awful. I hope the other guy looks worse."

"It's a real long story."

"I'll bet it is. I was beginning to wonder if you were still alive."

"Oh, I'm okay. And I've got a hell of a story. You're not going to believe it. It's the best thing I've ever had. Maybe the best thing the paper's ever seen."

"After that last converstion, it ought to be good. But don't tell me about it, write it."

Slovak turned and walked away. Cane smiled. Some things don't change. God, it was good to be back.

He walked to his desk and signed in on his terminal. He thought for a moment and typed *terrorists* on the screen. Now the story had a name.

He began typing. Slowly at first then in an easy rhythm. It wasn't difficult. Less than two hours later, when Slovak approached, he was almost done. It would need editing and a little polishing, and the paper's attorneys probably would want to see it. But it was good. It was damned good. He was flying, full of confidence and inspiration.

"How's it going?"

"Great, Slovak, I'm almost done," he said without lifting his eyes from the screen.

"Well, take a break for a couple of minutes, okay?"

"No. I'm rolling, I want to finish."

"Close it up, Cane."

It wasn't his words. It was the tone. Cane stopped typing and looked up. "Why?"

"Josh Lobo wants to see you. He called himself. He told me to send you to his office the moment you got here. I told him you were already here and he said to go up right away. Something to do with your stories from Germany."

God, could it be? Could they already know he was back? It

had to be. Why the hell else would the owner want to see him? The euphoria evaporated, replaced instantly by an overwhelming sense of fear.

"What about my story? Does he know I'm writing something?"

"Hell, Cane I don't know. All I know is that he just wants you there now."

Cane punched the keys to store his story in the computer then rose slowly from his chair and walked toward the elevator that would take him to his final confrontation.

THIRTY-SIX

Josh Lobo was a short, nervous man who seemed lost in his own thickly carpeted and richly paneled office. A softspoken man trapped in a decorator's version of old wealth: leather-bound books, a regulator clock, porcelain hunting dogs, and a cigar store Indian to guard a corner.

Lobo had inherited the paper from his strong-willed father and generally had the sense to let others run it for him. He spent his days instead on philanthrophy and civic projects. Occasionally, though, he played publisher in an effort to prove himself worthy of his patrimony. The staff had largely learned to weather the infrequent intrusions, but when he was determined, Lobo could be stubborn and demanding.

As Cane entered, Lobo rose from his high-backed leather chair behind his polished cherry wood desk, which Cane noticed was free of papers, and held out his hand. "Jonathan. It's nice to see you again. I enjoyed your coverage from Germany. I thought it was excellent."

"Thank you, Mr. Lobo. I just got in, haven't even been home to change," Cane said as he shook the owner's hand.

"No, no never mind. There are two men here I'd like you to meet. Ah, Jonathan this is Neal Williams, and Jack Macy, his assistant. They're with the Central Intelligence Agency."

Cane looked at Williams and recognized him instantly. He was much older than the picture Cane had seen in the Heidelberg library but there was no question. It was Fritz Karl Dietenbacher. The years had treated him well. His face was still thin, but his hair was longer and white at the temples, giving him a distinguished appearance. He was elegantly dressed in an expensive, charcoal gray wool suit with a white shirt and subdued tie. Dietenbacher held out his hand and smiled warmly.

Yet when Cane looked at the man he was drawn to his black eyes. He saw the cold emptiness of an arctic wasteland in them and wanted to shiver. He merely nodded his head instead, keeping his hands at his sides.

The second man, the one Lobo had called Macy, had broad prowerful shoulders and thick black hair. He stood near the window, which offered a view of LA's smog-shrouded mountains, silently staring at Cane. He made no effort to shake hands.

"Mr. Williams and Mr. Macy came to me just about an hour ago and said it was very important that they talk with you," Lobo continued. "Mr. Williams gave me a little background on the situation, but not a lot. He did say you might have some information regarding a matter of vital importance to national security."

Cane looked from Lobo to Dietenbacher and suddenly realized that except for the German he probably was the only one who knew the truth. Even Major Henry hadn't understood.

"Mr. Lobo, I think you should know these men were involved in the terrorist attack in Ochsenburg. Their real names aren't Williams and Macy anymore than my name is Shickelgrubber."

"Well, yes, Jonathan, that's not really surprising, given their jobs, is it?" Cane detected a trace of condescention in Lobo's voice and looked at him.

"No, I mean these men did it. They're up to their eyeballs in this whole thing. These guys are not CIA. They're Germans—"

"Jonathan, I don't want to know anymore about this right now. We can talk about it later. In the meantime, I told these men the paper would cooperate in any way possible. If we can help catch these terrorists, it's our duty to do it."

"But, Mr. Lobo, these guys—"

"Jonathan!" Lobo held up his hand, a cop signaling traffic to stop. "We can talk about this later." Cane merely stared at Lobo. Jesus, he thought, he's decided to play powerful publisher and he's got it all wrong. "Now, Mr. Williams asked to speak to you privately. I have a meeting across town and I told him he could use my office. Stay as long as you wish. I'll be glad to discuss this with you later."

"Mr. Lobo, you should stay and hear this, or at least get Slovak up here."

"We can discuss it later. I assured Mr. Williams he could have a private meeting with you." His voice was hard. There would be no change. "Now, as I said, I have a meeting."

The dark haired man moved quickly to the door and opened it for Lobo. He closed it softly behind him and then stood in front of it. Cane turned and looked silently at Dietenbacher.

"I won't waste your time, Mr. Cane," Dietenbacher began. "I know you know most of what happened. But first, Mr. Cane, I heard about what happened to you and to Simon North and I want you to know that I'm very, very sorry about your friend's death. It was an accident. It was never intended to happen."

"Sorry? You're sorry? What the hell good does that do anybody?" Cane shouted.

"You're right, of course," Dietenbacher's voice was smooth, easy, and reassuring, filled with an undertaker's sincerity. "My apologies are little more than words, but they are genuine nonetheless. But, Mr. Cane, I'm here to talk to you about something much more important. I must talk to you about the story you obviously plan to write." Dietenbacher moved slowly from the front of Lobo's desk to the back and stood behind the publisher's high-backed chair, his palms resting lightly on its top.

"You're right, I'm going to write the story. I think the world should know the whole thing was a fake. There never were any nuclear weapons in that depot. Codename Cipher," Cane grunted a half laugh. "Of course. Cipher. It means zero, doesn't it? Empty, nothing there, that's it isn't it?"

"Yes. But it's not quite true the explosives weren't in the storage areas. They were there only a day or two before. In fact, they were there when we left. We had merely removed the atomic cores from several of them when the hut was emptied for painting." He moved slowly to the chair's side and doodled on the desk top with his fingertips. "The painting was a stroke of luck, actually. It made everything a lot easier."

"Yeah, I got that much from the major. Only he really believes he's part of a top secret White House mission to send the explosives to Israel without Congress finding out. What a fine patriot he is. Only in this country we call men like him fascists. But then you just call them heroes, don't you? *Sieg Heil!*" He clicked his heels.

Dietenbacher looked at Cane calmly and smiled. "The major is an enthusiastic fool. You can call us what you like, Mr. Cane, but those nuclear components are vital to the future of our country and yours as well." He leaned forward, his palms now resting on the desk. "The world is a dangerous place, Mr. Cane. You Americans never seem to understand that. You think that because Mikhail Gorbachev tells you that the Russian bear is now a house pet the world is safe." A touch of scorn tinged his words. "I know the Russians. What about five years from now, or ten? What then? What will happen when the grand experiment fails and there are bread riots in the streets of Leningrad and mobs in Moscow? Who will be in charge in Russia then? Will it be a reformer, or will it be a general who yearns for the good old days of Russian power and empire? Can we take the chance? You, of course, will be huddled behind your oceans, but we Germans will be only a few days march away."

He stood straight and moved from behind the desk, standing at its end and looked out the window. When he continued, his words were barely above a whisper. They came slowly, with a soft reassuring tone, as though explaining a highly personal code of honor. "Mr. Cane, NATO is collapsing. Five years from now there will be no NATO. Germany will have to stand on its own." He stopped suddenly then and looked directly at Cane.

"Germany will again become a great power. It will be a leader of Europe, a line of defense against the resurgence of communism." His words came quickly and with force now. "But a strong, powerful Germany must have its own weapons. Then, we will be safe from the Communists forever. That is why we stole the explosives. A strong Germany will once again become the protector of freedom and order in the world."

Cane stared at the man and struggled, despite all he had learned in the last days, to believe he was real. "You're mad.

Even if you succeeded, you'd never build the new Reich with one or two explosives."

"No, you're wrong." Dietenbacher answered quickly, as if Cane's words had pulled him from a faraway place. He glided to the front of the desk and leaned back against its edge.

"It is true, we are still a small organization." The smooth, reasoned tone was back. "But with nuclear explosives even a small organization is a powerful one and a small country becomes a powerful one. There are hundreds of ways we can use the explosives for the glory of the fatherland."

Cane shook his head, blinked, and stared at the man again. "You're no better than Hitler. You're a butcher dressing up in rhetoric."

Dietenbacher waved his hand and ignored the remark. "This may be hard for you to accept, but we don't feel the damage was too severe, and the original purpose of the incident was served."

"Purpose? What the fuck purpose is worth killing an innocent person for? Just to play out your stupid fantasies about power. You people are sick."

"Mr. Cane, Major Henry helped us remove the nuclear cores from the explosives and replace them with lead before our little attack. But we had to convince everyone, even Congress that the explosives were still there. That they were whole. What could be more convincing than their own decision to release Hamid al Hamani?" A small, hard smile stretched the corners of his mouth.

"But they'll find out what happened," Cane said. "They're not fools. They'll find out that the atomic part is missing. And then, they won't rest until they find them. They'll hunt you down," he hissed.

"No, Mr. Cane, you're wrong. After all, for all intents and purposes the weapons are still in the storage site, just as they have always been. They all still look just like they did before." Dietenbacher spoke as if addressing a child. "But what if they do discover the deception? What will it matter? They won't look too hard for them. They know who took them and they know they'll never find them. That's why we had to free Hamid al Hamani, not an Irish or Basque terrorist. Those organziations can be tracked, infiltrated. But an unknown terrorist group working for Iraq, a country where you have no spies?" He shrugged. "Oh, eventually the story may get out and Baghdad will deny it stole them. But who will believe the Iraqis? They're desperate to get nuclear weapons anyway. As I said, Mr. Cane, I've thought of everything."'

Cane stared at the man in front of him who spoke so easily of life and death and nuclear blackmail. He squeezed his eyes shut, as if to banish the nightmare in front of him, and slowly inhaled a deep breath. And in that instant Cane realized that he alone knew who the men really were and understood they could kill him there in Josh Lobo's office and simply walk away. He wanted to look over his shoulder to see if the man called Macy was still guarding the door, but he kept his eyes on Dietenbacher.

"Major Henry helped us fake the photos. The whole thing had to look legitimate. I even planted all those stories in the *Tagesblatt*. I've thought of everything, you see," Dietenbacher said.

As Cane looked at Dietenbacher, a man supremely confident and satisfied, he saw again the oveturned van and Simon's limp body against the crushed door.

"That's where you're wrong," Cane barked, banishing his fear of the man at the door. "I know the truth. And I'm going to write the story. I don't buy your Nazi propaganda, your fear of the Russians, and the greater glory of the Fourth Reich. We stomped your kind into the ground once and I'll be damned if I'll stand by and let you climb out of the slime and infect the world again. When this story hits you're history."'

"Mr. Cane, I'm asking you for the future of Germany not to write the story." The tight smile was gone. He stood straight again and looked hard at Cane.

"I've only got one thing to say to you: go fuck yourself. I've already written the story. I don't know what the final consequences will be, hell, you can kill me here. But it won't stop the story. It's too late for that. You're already finished. You just don't know it."

For an instant Cane though he saw a flicker of fear or anger flash through Dietenbacher's eyes, but it was quickly gone.

"I'm very sorry to hear that, Mr. Cane." He turned back to Lobo's desk and trailed his fingertips across its top to an ornate stiletto letter opener. He picked it up and examined it carefully, as if suddenly fascinated by its fake jewel handle and long thin blade.

"Mr. Cane, I had hoped you would listen to reason. Now I see you are determined. That is a shame. I wanted to avoid the rest of our discussion."

There was a sudden coldness to the man's words that startled Cane. He glanced over his shoulder at the man near the door and realized with a jolt that the man was staring at him with utter hatred. As Cane watched, Macy moved slowly toward him, his eyes never wavering, and stopped not a yard away. He appeared coiled, as if ready to leap across the small space that separated them.

"Oh, you going to have your trained killer here come after me?" Cane said, turning back to face Dietenbacher. "After my piece gets in the paper you'll be too busy running for cover to do anything else." His bravado sounded false even to him.

"No. Mr. Cane, we're not threatening you with violence." He paused, toying with the stiletto and let the lie hang in the air between them. "Mr. Cane, if that article is published, we will deny it totally and I think the world will believe us. Who, after all, would believe you. You'll be standing trial in Germany."

"Trial? Why? Is Jack Macy here, or should I call him Captain Montgomery, going to charge me with slander? Get serious."

"Mr. Cane, if I make one phone call you'll be a wanted man in Germany. I think manslaughter and attempted murder will do for openers. Perhaps you've forgotten that just a few minutes before your van crashed and killed your friend, you were seen in the driver's seat. Can you convince a judge that Mr. North took the wheel from you? I doubt it."

Cane suddenly remembered the old man who had banged on the rear of the van and helped him back into the street.

"And I doubt they'd have any trouble convicting you of attempting to kill Major Henry. You left the nightstick behind. It was very careless of you. It has your fingerprints on it and is covered with Major Henry's blood. The German police have it, and we can give them a copy of your fingerprints. And I'm sure

[235]

Major Henry will have no trouble identifying you as the man who attacked him for no reason.

"Now, do you really think the world will believe a reporter who killed his friend by his own careless driving and then attacked a U.S. Army officer who, it just happens, is the husband of his lover? Tell me, Mr. Cane, did you beat him just because you were jealous? Was Major Henry becoming too famous?

"Think of it, Mr. Cane. You'll have no credibility. You beat Major Woodrow Henry, who had just survived days of captivity with terrorists armed with a nuclear bomb. You beat him unmercifully until he told you whatever you wanted to hear, just so you could get a scoop. Funny, how no other newspaper in the world discovered the plot, isn't it? Only you, Mr. Cane, got the great scoop. How the Germans blackmailed themselves into turning a terrorist loose so they could shoot him. Great story, Mr. Cane. And all it took to get it was a billy club."

The sarcasm stung, but Cane said nothing. He was reeling, trying to think of a response.

"Frankly, I doubt your own paper would even publish the article, once this is known. Mr. Lobo has agreed to have a chat with me before the paper runs anything more you write about the terrorist attack in Germany. I haven't told him anything yet. I saw no reason to ruin your reputation needlessly. And you can say whatever you want to him, but my CIA credentials are masterpieces. He'll believe me. He wants to cooperate, to be helpful."

Cane focused on the man's dark eyes as his mind searched frantically for an argument, a reason why what the man had said wouldn't work. But it made some kind of awful, twisted, distorted sense. No one *would* believe him. He might, just might, be able to convince Slovak. But Lobo? Probably not, not when he admitted he had indeed attacked Woody Henry. And, Jesus, what kind of impression had he made on Lobo when he walked into the office a few minutes ago? He looked like a street bum, and he knew it. And Lobo had seen it too.

How could he explain it? How could he say, yes, he and Maria had been lovers but he hadn't seen her in years, and, yes, he had seen her again in Ochsenburg but they had only talked. And how could he convince anyone that he didn't really know why he had attacked the major. Yes, it probably had something to do with Maria, but what the major told him was true, he was sure of it. It probably would make no difference. When it came out that he had first suspected the Red Army Faction and later switched to the neo-Nazis, he'd look like a zealot. He would end up totally discredited and probably spend years in a German prison.

"You're sick. All of you," was all Cane could say.

Dietenbacher stepped close and spoke in a voice so low, Cane had to strain to hear.

"Don't go where you don't belong, Mr. Cane. This is beyond you." He stepped backed suddenly, dropped the letter opener on the desk, and smiled another terrible hard smile. "We have to go now. I'm sure you understand the wisdom of not trying to write anything." The two men moved toward the door but stopped just short of it.

"Oh, yes, I wouldn't try telling your story to any other paper, like the *Washington Post* or the *New York Times*. They'll never run it without trying to check it out. And, of course, since no one knows what really happened, it'll never check out. But the word will get back to me and the consequences will be the same for you."

He pulled open the door and was gone.

Cane stared at the closed door, unable to comprehend what had happened. A frustration swept over him, fueling his rage. There had to be something he could do. But there was nothing. He was defeated, and suddenly, surprisingly, he felt deeply embarrassed.

Less than an hour ago, so confident, so sure of himself and his abilities he had dared to dream of a Pulitzer prize. Now he understood he was an amateur who thought he could handle the pros. They had won. He had been nothing. His anger, his promise to Ute, none of it mattered. All he had managed to do was save his own life. But he would not avenge Simon. Again the rage swelled within him and again it quickly collapsed upon itself.

He walked slowly to the door, through the outer office, and took the elevator down to the the newsroom.

"Jesus Cane, what the hell happened up there?" Slovak asked.

"Nothing."

"You feeling okay? You look worse than before."

Cane didn't answer. He just walked to his desk and typed the word *terrorist* on the screen and punched the kill button. Instantly all traces of the story were gone.

He paused at Slovak's desk. "There's no story," he said and walked on before he could receive a response.

He waited for the elevator, staring at the door's grillwork, thinking of how they had frightened him so deeply and defeated him so easily. And all he could say was "you're sick." He thought of Dietenbacher's icy smile as he had talked. He should have hit him, Cane thought. It wouldn't have been much, but it would have been something. But he thought again of Macy and knew how stupid it would have been.

"Come on, come on," he mumbled and pounded the elevator button with a fury.

The doors slid open, and as Cane started to step in, Ralph Granger stepped out. He carried a giant cup of cola from a nearby convenience store.

"Oh, the famous foreign correspondent is back."

Cane ignored him.

"Hey, I thought your stories weren't bad, but when you get a chance, drop by my desk. I'd like to make a couple of suggestions. There were a couple of things that didn't make sense to me."

The doors shut even as Cane pulled his arm back to hit him. He did not need a condescending preppie from Stanford playing editor. Not now. Someday Granger would push the wrong person the wrong way and get the shit kicked out of him and never know why, Cane thought.

And suddenly he thought of Rolf Makler. He too shared that condescending attitude. He thought Americans were so foolish, and he'd turned out to be the biggest fool of all. It gave Cane a slight sense of solace to know that Rolf had been used. "Jurgen," his own personal informant deep in the U.S. military, had been a setup. Cane was tempted to call, or better yet write him a letter and tell him he'd been used. He'd love to be there when he read it.

But the idea gave him no real joy. It would be a lousy thing to do, he knew. But Cane wanted to strike back, to hurt someone, anyone, and he could think of no one. He thought again of how devastated Rolf would be. No, he wouldn't do it. It would be cruel.

Cane stepped out of the elevator and walked through the revolving door into the heat and smog of the early afternoon. Even the air around him was foul.

Then, suddenly, he smiled. He clapped his hands and thrust a fist in the air. He wanted to dance.

Rolf. God, the answer was that simple.

He pushed back through the revolving door and rode the elevator to the top floor. What the hell, I might as well do it right, he thought and walked into Josh Lobo's outer office.

"Mr. Cane?" The owner's secretary seemed shocked to see him again.

"Mr. Lobo said I could use his typewriter for a few minutes." He had closed the door to the inner office behind him and locked it before she could get around the desk. Lobo, who had once spent a summer as a cub reporter, prided himself on pecking out his own editorials on his old Royal, which sat on a stand in the corner.

Cane wheeled it to the desk, and rolled a fresh sheet of paper into the typewriter and began:

Dear Rolf,

I have been transferred to the United States and thus this must be my last communication with you. I am sorry I cannot call, but there is too much to say in a brief conversation. I know you as a courageous and fair journalist and I think you should know the truth about the terrorist attack in Ochsenburg. . . .

Cane wrote steadily, reproducing much of what he had written on the computer only an hour before. Finally, he was finished and signed it simply, "Jurgen."

Cane knew Rolf would make no attempts to check the information. It had Jurgen's name on it. That would be enough. And by now, thanks to the other help "Jurgen" had given him, Rolf had a growing national reputation. It would be enough to ensure a full-scale investigation by the German authorities. If they tried to extradite him, Cane could tell everything he knew, including tales of a black Opel that ran him off the road and a visit by a man named Dietenbacher. No, once the story was printed in the *Tagesblatt* the neo-Nazis would be too busy covering their asses to worry about Jonathan Cane. Extraditing him would just cause them more grief.

Cane found two envelopes and typed Rolf's name and address, care of the paper, on the first. The second he addressed to Barbara Darling. He put Rolf's letter in its envelope, folded it and put it in the envelope addressed to Barbara Darling. He scrawled a note—"This must have a German postmark. Please mail ASAP. Thanks, Cane"—and added it to the envelope to Barbara and walked out of the office.

The secretary gave him a withering look, but he only smiled. In the hallway, he tapped the elevator button lightly. As he waited he thought of the letter he was about to mail.

There would be no Pulitzer prize. No one would understand what he had done. There would be no recognition. No one would know who Jonathan Cane, the journalist, was. He might even face trouble with the German authorities.

But it didn't matter. It really didn't matter. Because Cane understood. He had learned. Everything is choice. And he had chosen to fight instead of giving up. And because he chose, he won.

The elevator doors swept open and he stepped in. As they closed behind him, Cane smiled and began singing softly to himself, "Jesus loves me, this I know, for the Bible tells me so. . . ."

THE DEER KILLERS, *by Gunnard Landers.* In the mid-1970s the U.S. Fish and Wildlife Service formed a Special Operations branch to run long-term undercover operations to stop willful devastation of the environment. Special Agent Reed Erickson must infiltrate an isolated community of close-knit "jacklighters," or deer poachers, in Louisiana to put a stop to the wanton destruction. But these men will kill a game warden faster than they would a mosquito. A gripping ecological thriller featuring a new kind of hero.

"A moody low-key thriller. . . . Some good hunting scenes. . . . A stately bittersweet tour of the bayous and their divided heroes reminiscent of James Lee Burke's stories." —*Kirkus Reviews*

"A fine novel centered on an intelligent, introspective, and tough-enough hero." —*Booklist*

CABOT STATION, by William S. Schall. In the tradition of *The Hunt for Red October* and *The Cruel Sea*, a vigorously authentic high-tech naval thriller. Cabot Station lies 3,000 feet below the ocean's surface—an undersea listening station and solitary, neglected outpost against crew and captain find themselves called upon to investigate a mystery submarine that is quickly guarded from prying U.S. eyes by two Soviet killer subs. Where has it come from? And how did it get past the navy's underwater detection network?

"A good plot, a fast pace, fine characters—a red." —Clive Cussler (author of *Raise the Titantic* and *Dragon*)

"*Cabot Station* will please techno-thriller fans." —*Publishers Weekly*

"Bloody exciting. Amazingly realistic." —*Kirkus Reviews*

THE VESPERS TAPES, *by Albert Dibartolomeo.* It all begins when Philadelphia schoolteacher Vincent Vespers gets a late-night phone call from his brother, Frank. Arriving at a local bar, Frank, long connected with local hoods, introduces Vinnie to his Mafia boss. The Don is dying, and Frank coerces Vinnie into helping write the Don's memoirs. So Vinnie and the Don make a series of tapes. Vinnie expects a few unhappy people as a result, but he is not prepared for old ghosts that rise up to haunt him and for the imminent danger he faces.

"*The Vespers Tapes* is a powerful and exciting fusion of family saga . . . and well, Family saga. This is the *Godfather* with real people, not caricatures. The people behind the indictments. DiBartolomeo has an accurate eye for gritty city descriptions and a tape-recorder ear for low-life dialogue, but he also has an amazing nose for the unsentimentalized aromas of the Old Neighborhood—the pungencies of ancient friendships forgotten, old loves lost, traditional loyalties betrayed." —David Bradley (PEN-Faulkner Award-winning author of *The Chaneysville Incident* and *South Street*)

"This is a remarkable first novel by a writer who goes from one suspense situation to another with astonishing speed. Although written in the tradition established by Puzo's *The Godfather*, DiBartolomeo has an alluring style all of his own that is refreshingly free of sterotypes." —Jerre Mangione (author of *Mount Allegro* and *A Passion for Sicilians*)

SNAKES IN THE GARDEN, by *L. S. Whiteley.* A sardonic thriller in the *Presumed Innocent* class about a rich, thirty-something Florida real-estate agent accused of murdering his grandfather. But if narrator Tom Clay didn't do it, who, out of his weird family and friends, did?

"Nice brittle characters . . . perceptive asides . . . more than a touch of acid in the clinches . . . and a plot that works. Who could ask for more?" —Robert Campbell (author of the Lala Land series and *The Junk Yard Dog*)

"Here's a tangy cocktail of a novel, it generates a pleasant high and leaves a satisfying aftertaste. . . . A murder mystery reminiscent of Erskine Caldwell. . . . In short, this author has written an amusing, unusual and absorbing novel. I enjoyed it." —Joseph Hayes (author of *The Desperate Hours* and *Act of Rage*)

THE GREY PILGRIM, by *J. M. Hayes.* A striking and original thriller (based on a true incident) set in Arizona on the eve of World War II about the last armed Indian protesting conscription registration. In 1940, a half-American half-Japanese *agent provocateur* is sent secretly to the U.S. by the Kempetai to exacerbate the insurrection. Spanish Civil War veteran, now Deputy U.S. Marshall, J. D. Fitzpatrick must deal swiftly with the consequences before someone gets killed.

"Wow! Here's one you shouldn't miss. J. M. Hayes in my kind of writer. *The Grey Pilgrim* is a clever plot, peopled with great characters." —Edgar Award-winning author Tony Hillerman (*Talking God* and *A Thief of Time*)

"This well-written novel . . . [is] filled with bits of Indian lore, peopled with memorable characters and written with a deft humorous touch." —*Publishers Weekly*

SPRING THAW, *by S. L. Stebel* (with an afterword by Ray Bradbury).
A troubled young sea captain, anxious to prove his manhood, takes
command of his father's sealing ship and sails to the far north, where
he is forced to confront his own ghosts and sins and those of his
father, in a novel as refreshing and insightful as any by Camus or
Hesse.

"Magical and mysterious." —Ray Bradury (from his afterword)

"Electrifying adventure-fantasy. . . . Impossible to put down."
—Publishers Weekly

"*Spring Thaw* has a vigorous moral relevance, and its fablelike
tale of love, betrayal, and redemption echoes with conviction."
—Lawrence Thornton (author of *Imagining Argentina*, winner of the
PEN-Faulkner Award)